GRAVES OF GOLD

A Teke Manion Murder Mystery

ROD SANFORD

Printed in the United States of America
First Printing 2020
First Edition 2020

ISBN: 978-1543143201

10 9 8 7 6 5 4 3 2 1

GRAVES OF GOLD

Prologue

From the Research file of Teke Manion – WorldSpan Underwriters International

Jolly Benoit was a former slave turned pirate. Sometime between 1830 and 1840, he returned to his native North Carolina as a free man of color with an Irish immigrant partner named Sam Gilley. Had Sam come to North America as an indentured servant? How he came under the employ of Mr. Benoit is not clear. Moreover, the supply of Spanish gold coins in Mr. Benoit's possession was presumably part of his piracy efforts.

Over the course of that decade, he bought the freedom of his relatives, friends, and a woman who was to become his wife. Then he and Sam Gilley set about building one of the first African-American town settlements in the country.

As the country reached the brink of civil war, Jolly Benoit became the subject of legend. Benoit was everything from a spy for the Union Army to a financier of the national war effort. Sam Gilley eventually was free of his indentured servitude and helped build the white community across the Tar River from Benoitown.

After the war, both became wealthy men for their time. Benoitown and Gilleyville continued to grow taking advantage of natural resources in the area and Reconstruction appropriations from the US government.

The question that remained during their lives, and after their deaths in 1890 is: "Where did they keep the Spanish gold they used to start and sustain their various real estate and commercial enterprises?"

The legend goes on to say that there was a small fortune of gold coins and doubloons buried with both men. Sam Gilley's mausoleum is located in an Irish part of the New York City, moved there by his extended family who subsequently came to America. Jolly Benoit was buried at the Benoitown graveyard used for slaves, former slaves, and the indigent deceased. His grave was unmarked and known only by his surviving wife. They had no children. At her death, the exact location of Jolly's body died with her. There is a Jolly Benoit Memorial Gravesite on the grounds of the county museum.

By the mid-to-late twentieth century, the gold was dismissed as just another legend and that the treasure never really existed. The legend was used as part of the tourism story told to add to the enchantment of the lower river/tide water area.

Then, in 2013, Hurricane Chester flooded both cities. One of the heaviest impacted parts of the town was the historically protected slave graveyards. In poor condition prior to the storm, the graveyard was thrown into total disarray. What bubbled to the surface would eventually involve state and federal government, treasure hunters, local church groups, historians, the government of Spain, and our firm.

Chapter 1

Apartment of Tekelius "Teke" Manion
– Paris, France (5ème Latin Quarter)

I looked at the missed calls on **my** phone. There had been three from Camille, and it was just 9:00 AM. She would be pissed. I thought about those long toned legs, the tight torso, and perfect breasts. I thought about the large coffee brown eyes common to French beauties from the Bordeaux region and the short-cropped Annie Lennox hairdo. I shook **my** head and got out of bed.

Just like the other messages she left yesterday and the day before that, I wasn't answering. Besides, I was late for my workout session with Rudolph Lemieux.

As I dressed in my gi, I stared at my reflection in the mirror and mused over the last month. I looked at the tall, six-foot-three image, dark hair that grew long if I did not cut it regularly. My immersion into the martial arts had improved my core and strengthened my angular swimmer's body. I stared at the serious face looking back at me. I was always accused of being more mysterious than handsome, yet this morning I didn't recognize the reflection I saw. I wasn't losing my mind or so I thought. I just had a distinct feeling of detachment from my own consciousness.

I couldn't stop the dreams. I called them "dreams" because nightmares were what children had. They were all too real snippets of what happened on White Sand Island—the bodies, the betrayals, and the discovery on Plunder Island.

Several months ago, I was sent home to Florida to look into WorldSpan's exposure as a result of wildfires in the Sunshine State. I found myself mired in two murders, old grudges, and missing mob money. I was double-crossed by those I thought were friends, and it ended with me swimming for my life off the Coast of White Sand Island just south of Tampa Bay.

The doctors said the dreams and sense of surrealism were a natural symptom after the trauma and near-death experiences of that last assignment.

Based on the accidental success of that last assignment, the managing partners at WorldSpan decided to create a new position for me—the "Expeditor." As such, I would go into dicey scenarios and once again be the eyes and ears of the partners at the "point of attack." It meant more money—a lot more. I would be promoted to a rank equal to my boss and sometimes lover, Camille DeSoronne.

What could I do? Turn it down and be stuck at the level where I was? I could quit and go back home to White Sand Island, Florida. That would mean going back to where I recently almost died. The old adage was true: You can't go home again, especially in this case.

I felt like a man with no home. I had been in Paris for over five years, but I always thought it was temporary. Now I felt more familiar here than in the States. So I accepted the partners' offer, and I was already dreading it.

I had hoped Camille would have talked some sense into me, or at least played the devil's advocate, but she was a company woman first.

Smart, tall, sexy and very French, she had been a temptation my American temperament could not resist five years ago when I arrived in Paris. She was good for me—a mentor, a teacher, and an amazing lover. The latter never seemed to get in the way of the former.

Our relationship was common knowledge at WorldSpan but as long as it was not talked about in the open, nobody seemed to care. European companies were clearly not the same as American corporations. My phone rang again. I let it go to voicemail and grabbed my keys.

Rudolph Lemieux was a world-class martial artist and recluse. He seldom left his compound on the Marais (3rd) district of Paris. When he did leave, it was almost always for the best food in Paris and live jazz. Not just any jazz.

The night Rudolph and I met at the Bab-Ilo. We were among the last few listening to the last set of a John Coltrane/Miles Davis cover quartet. When I inquired, the bartender told me of the tall quiet man— who did not order a drink but just stared intently at the band as if he were a bandleader or talent scout. The bartender introduced us, and we spoke briefly that night. He wasn't the chatty type.

I asked Camille about him the next morning and learned he was a bit of a local legend. We talked of his past—former Foreign Legion, five years on a mountain in Tibet, and his subsequent return to dedicate himself to a life of altruism and the martial arts.

When I returned to Paris after my near-death experiences in Florida, I sought out Lemieux. He remembered me from the night at the club. I begged the man to take me on as a what—student? Apprentice? I didn't know exactly what I wanted from him, but I knew I needed to be better.

The expeditor job would be mostly number crunching, analyzing big data, and finding the financial or operational anomalies. This was corporate speak for "rooting out the cheats, the embezzlers, and frauds and finding missed money opportunities."

While there was the promise of "help" to do the dangerous work, I could not be the new expeditor and be so skill-naked to the world. I needed to be better with my hands, with my mind, with weapons.

Surprisingly, Rudolph took me on right away.

This morning was our twentieth session. Most of them were mental exercises, sitting quiet and still for hours at a time or holding poses until I sweated and shook like an old washing machine. Lately things had gotten interesting. I was beginning to learn some basics of jujitsu, judo, and karate. We also worked on a form of French kickboxing called Savate.

Rudolph's gymnasium was on the top floor of a seventeenth-century mansion. There were weight machines and free weights in one corner. There were parallel bars and chin-up apparatuses that allowed me to use my own weight to get in shape. There were also some Old World machines from the 1950s that he used himself. The rest of the floor was matted and used for hand-to-hand combat practice.

"Where is your head at Manion?" Rudolph said about 30 minutes into the drills. He walked away to fill two water glasses. Even with his back to me, Rudolph was still intimidating. I knew better than to play the *"what do you mean game?"*

"It's work. I may have to go out of town again. Another assignment in the States."

"You worry you may face danger again and not be ready," Rudolph said, more than asked. I just nodded. Rudolph was standing over me now, his hulking lean mass still dwarfing my six-foot-plus frame. We drank water and sat in silence for several minutes.

"You need to go," Rudolph said as if finally making his mind up about something. He turned to set up the next set of exercises. He was all business and, per our agreement, I never asked why. Until now.

"Why?"

He seemed to think for a moment, holding a square floor mat under his arm.

"At some point you are going to have to test yourself against the world. Even if you worked with me for a year, your first assignment would be a scary one."

"I'm not scared," I shot back. Rudolph just stared at me from between two pieces of equipment.

"After everything that happened to you, to not be scared would make you a fool, and you are no fool," he said. I nodded.

"You keep comparing yourself to the man who went to Florida and almost lost his life, but you are far from him. The experiences you had in Florida, the time we have spent together, the time you have spent in your head. You are ready for the next test."

Chapter 2
Benoitown, NC

Sheriff Mike Cormac, fifty-five, was the law for Benoitown and its sister city Gilleyville. Both towns sat at the final turn of the Tar River just before it flowed into the tidewaters. Separated by the Emancipation Bridge, both towns held about 15,000 residents and depended on local agriculture and tourism for their income. The main difference was their racial demographic.

Benoitown was founded by ex-slave, ex-pirate Jolly Benoit. His partner, Sam Gilley—an Irish indentured servant—founded Gilleyville. True to their founders, Benoitown was still 75 percent African-American, the rest a mix of Caucasian, Latino, and Asian. Gilleyville was still 65 percent Caucasian, the rest a mix of African-American, Latino, and Asian. Sheriff Cormac had jurisdiction over both of them and the surrounding unincorporated county.

Typically, this was the best law enforcement job a man could have, much better than the central district of Baltimore where he was shift captain for fifteen years. That job had taken years off his life. This job had put them back.

Until now.

Looking out the second-story window of the Government Works Building, where he and his deputies had permanent offices, he wondered about the original plans to construct and populate the building by those who had come before him. Did they put the police force on the second floor because of flood or was it just a happy coincidence? Cormac was grateful for it either way.

Remnant floodwater from Hurricane Chester was still running through downtown. When the storm followed the Tar River from southeast to northwest at every mile and curve, it pushed brackish water over the banks and earthen dams to flood every community along the way. Most of the areas had sparse populations and open fields that drained quickly. Benoitown and Gilleyville were not so lucky.

The buildings and roads of the two towns slowed the retreat of water, turning the main streets into streams of alluvial destruction. Cormac had used several borrowed johnboats to travel from home to home, the same boats he used to save his deputies from the roof of the Benoitown substation, which was totally submerged.

Today the water still stood on the first two streets up from the river in both towns. For Gilleyville it meant clearing the contents of several warehouses, businesses and bars, and moving charter and private pleasure vessels further up or down the river. Benoitown, however, sat on the lower south side of the river. More of their essential services were on the first streets of the town, all of which had to be moved. What could not be moved were the graves.

Part of downtown Benoitown had always been devoted to the Riverside Graveyard. One of the oldest grave sites in the state, it was the burial place of slaves and former slaves from the surrounding plantations in the eighteenth and nineteenth centuries. At one time, it was also the final resting place of the infamous Jolly Benoit.

The graves had been inundated by floodwater, the sacred aged remains floated to the surface, 150-year-old crypts flooded and were compromised. This had been more work than anyone ever imagined. The National Guard had been dispatched, specifically the unit that dealt with the remains of fallen heroes in combat. The other unit, to stand guard over the graveyard, was requested by Mayor Moten.

Benoitown Mayor His Honor Reverend Curtyse M. Moten and his newly formed Citizens for Ethical Treatment of the Ancestry (CETA) had been in Cormac's office every day since the flood, filing complaints about poor treatment of the ruined graves. There had been "raids" for lack of a better word. Cormac wondered who would bother with century old graves.

Cormac thought that was pretty low even for modern-day bigoted rednecks. That was when Mayor Moten reminded him of the legend of Jolly Benoit. Years ago, Cormac was told the story of the ex-slave-turned-pirate, but filed it away as one of many tales that southerners loved to share to charm and scare Yankees out of their tourism dollars.

According to legend, at the end of the amazingly resilient Mr. Benoit's life, questions arose about the gold that he and co-conspirator and friend Sam Gilley brought with them to start these fledging towns in the 1800s. Was there any left? What happened to it when he died?

The predominant thought was that the gold might have been buried with him and with the remains of the slaves in Riverside Graveyard. This is what set off the raids on the hallowed remains. Recent reality shows on cable television depicting quirky, socially unique misanthropes pulling gold from land and sea had everyone talking about the dust from which dreams are made.

This coupled with the explosion of gold prices in the commodities market of that time, and there was a silent gold rush going on all over the country.

Back in Baltimore, his ex-partners on the force told stories of folks pulling gold out of their own fillings to sell to the Cash for Gold brokers. As a result of the flood and now the raids, a parade of outsiders poured into Benoitown, the National Guard, insurance adjusters, Homeland

Security, civil rights activists, rogue gold hunters, treasure seekers, and of course the media.

There was a knock at the door.

"Come on!" Cormac called out as he turned from the window. Mimi Boulage, the dispatcher and secretary, opened the door.

"Curtyse is here to see you," she said.

"Mimi, I believe he prefers His Honor or Reverend."

"Well, I don't live in Benoitown so he's not my mayor, and I don't attend his church so he's not my reverend," Mimi said in her usual clipped efficient tone. "To me he's just Maisie Moten's little brother that talked too much as a kid and followed Maisie, Sis, and me everywhere we went."

"Just show him in," Cormac said with a sigh.

There was nothing little about Curtyse Moten—six-foot four inches, all legs with a broad chest. He had medium brown skin and brooding eyes under heavy eyebrows in a perpetual frown. He had been loud his whole life: on the playground, classroom, football field, and finally on the campaign trail and pulpit. As a college student, he marched with Kweisi Mfume and Bishop Desmond Tutu against South African Apartheid. He was on the organizing committee for the Million Man March, and he was on the guest list for the private wake of Maya Angelou.

His Honor Reverend Curtyse Moten was connected, and he made no bones about the fact that he was willing to use all of his connections to make sure the residents of Benoitown got a fair shake. Sheriff Cormac didn't doubt the man's sincere motives. He had plenty of experience with public figures of all races and styles from his time with the force in Maryland. As the reverend walked into the office, Sheriff Cormac thought the same thing about Reverend Moten as his counterparts up north. The man does seem to be enjoying the attention.

"What's going on, Sheriff? No one is retuning my calls."

"Good morning, Your Honor, please have a seat."

"I don't want a seat," Reverend Moten said in a volume slightly above conversational. His feet were shoulder width apart, and he stood right up against the sheriff's desk. His thumbs were hooked into the pockets of a black shiny vest that girded his broad middle. His jacket to his champagne-colored suit coat was cut long, so it resembled more of a cape when he stood like this.

"I want to know about this secret meeting scheduled for today."

"It isn't a secret…."

"I didn't know about it," Reverend Moten said, getting agitated. "The CETA did not get an invitation. I have friends with the media. They told me."

"Reverend, I assure you there is no subterfuge. I was going to call you."

"But you didn't."

"Because you called me instead at 6:30 AM. Remember?"

It was true. One of the news trucks was always parked outside the reverend's home. He had gotten into the habit of chatting up the occupants while stepping out to pick up his copy of the Edgewood County Times. One of the out-of-town reporters, a young African-American man named Al Harrison, was very talkative with the reverend. Al was twenty-two years old, just out of journalism school. This was the best assignment a young reporter could ask for. In addition to his daily copy for the *Atlanta Informer*, he had already started his blog and Instagram pages listed under a fictitious name.

Al's father, a retired auto factory man from Illinois, explained to the young reporter about the reverend's importance to history. From that day, Al made sure to stick to Curtyse Moten like glue.

That morning, Al mentioned to Reverend Moten that a source told the reporters about a secret meeting on the graves. The meeting involved local law enforcement, national law enforcement, the historical preservation folks, and the CETA. Al mentioned it in an attempt to gain an inside story from the reverend. For Reverend Moten's part, he did his best to hide his ignorance of the meeting.

His first priority would be to make sure the people of color alive or dead would not be thrown aside like trash debris blown up on the shore. It was a tricky thing, defending the remains of slaves with the same fervor as a living group of oppressed citizens. Reverend Moten knew he was up to that task. So every day he was rallying support in the state and calling in political media favors in key cities like Washington, DC, Atlanta, Birmingham, and Philadelphia.

He knew it would be a matter of time before the political machine, through carelessness, lack of a resource, or malice, would try to slip something by him. He figured today was the day. With a growing anger and feeling of betrayal, he went inside after talking to Al on his front lawn and immediately called Sheriff Cormac at home, catching him in mid dress.

"Well," Reverend Moten continued, not willing to have his head of steam diffused by logic or an explanation no matter how true. "What is this meeting?

When is this meeting?"

"It's in an hour, right down the hall," Cormac said, pointing lazily towards the door, trying to show the big bad reverend he was not fazed by the loud talk or the stance.

"What it is? I honestly don't know, Reverend. The only thing I was told is that a discovery was made."

"What kind of discovery?" Reverend Moten asked now more interested than irate.

"That is what we will find out soon," Cormac said and gestured to a seat. The reverend shot the cuffs of his starched white dress shirt and gracefully sat; his brooding eyes focused on nothing in particular.

That afternoon, I felt a sense of déjà vu sitting around the table with WorldSpan leaders looking at flat screen monitors. It was a similar setup when I got 'assigned' to return home for my last assignment. Even though this was voluntary, my right eye twitched involuntarily. I tried to keep the words of Rudolph Lemieux in my head.

That was when it hit me. I was not sure what my assignment was this time. That's what I got for not answering Camille's calls all day. Speaking of the devil, she was there in full corporate mode—cool, efficient, bulletproof, and sexy as hell. It was times like this, I still found it amazing that a woman like this slept with me three or four nights a week.

"We have a closed circuit satellite link with Benoitown officials. We should be connected soon," Camille said in her elegant French.

Marcel LaRoche, the branch leader, asked that she take the lead as one of the few bilingual executives. Camille actually spoke six languages. I could follow along in French but not speak it that well. Camille gestured for me to sit at that point, giving me the iciest of stares. I guess there would be no sendoff sex tonight. Just then, the screens came to life.

It was 9:00 AM in the States. There were a group of four men and two women sitting at a round table looking very serious still sipping morning coffee. One was obviously the sheriff by his uniform. There was a tall, wide, African-American gentleman wearing the biggest cross pendant I had ever seen. I thought he looked familiar.

There were the officials from the National Guard, one was a woman that looked about forty years old with a colonel insignia on her uniform. There was a neatly dressed tall man in a blue suit straight out of Government Issue. I looked at the attendees' list on my info packet. I figured he represented the US State Department.

There was a smaller man with an obsessively neat appearance. He wasn't identified in the dossier. He wore a bright-red sweater vest and a smile as nervous as a beauty pageant finalist. He sat close to the only other woman in the room. She wore bedazzled glasses and a very conservative hairstyle that looked too old for her age. She held a steno pad, so I assumed she was there in an administrative support role.

"Good morning, Benoitown, North Carolina, and greetings from Paris, France," Camille started with a wave. The group waved back tentatively. "Who would like to go first?"

The group seemed more confused by Camille's question. They looked at each other, talking among themselves. Camille looked back at the branch manager and his assistants who had nothing to offer. I let it go on for a few more seconds before I got up from my seat and stepped into the camera shot.

During these video meetings, we spoke through the microphone powered by using a handheld push button control. It kept background noise and unwanted side conversations out of hearing range of enemy ears.

Feeling devilish, I stepped into the camera shot close to Camille. She was surprised but did not step back. I reached into her hand, pushed, and held the talk button on the speaking device.

"Gentlemen, look on your phone console. There is a picture of a face and mouth with curved lines next to it," I said with the biggest, brightest smile. "Push that button to take it off mute."

There was about five more seconds of confusion on the other end complete with pointing and the adjustment of reading glasses. Then the woman in the bejeweled glasses rose from her chair, leaned forward and pushed the button that I described and... viola!

"Um, good morning, Ms. Day-So-Rony," the sheriff started over, pronouncing every syllable, emphasis, and linguistic nuance of Camille's last name.

"We can give you a timeline of events leading up to the discovery."

With her polite smile hiding a cringe, she responded.

"Thank you, Sheriff. And please call me Camille."

There was more rustling of papers and passing of notes on the other end. Sheriff Cormac continued.

* September 20, Hurricane Chester traveled northwest from the TarPamlico River Basin opening and through upper North Carolina. The result was a series of levy breaches along the Tar River.

* September 21, residual water flooded the communities of Benoitown and Gilleyville. The Benoitown riverfront and half of downtown were totally inundated with water depths reaching several feet. The damage in Gilleyville was limited to one foot of water covering the first few streets past the riverbank.

* September 25, slow receding waters began to breach the land, 500 feet inland on either side of the river. This land included the Riverside Graveyard.

* As a result, around 200 identified grave sites have been compromised, resulting in a great deal of concerns. Moreover, these are the remains of African-American slaves and free men and women of color, which also makes the incident a concern of civil rights organizations.

"It's a concern of decent folks all around the country," the large black man said. He was introduced as Reverend Moten, the mayor of Benoitown. I remembered why he was so familiar now. He was one of the faces standing at speaker podiums with Jesse Jackson, Al Sharpton, or as part of speaking panels on cable news shows.

"Of course, Reverend," said the neat one in the sweater vest. He introduced himself as Valentine "Val" Cedars, head of the local historical society. "I believe these—insurance people are interested in what happened next." He was right, although I didn't necessarily care for how he said it. Sheriff Cormac asked the colonel to deliver the next part. She looked down to consult a report in her lap.

"Eighteen hours ago, military forensic specialist Lieutenant Arlene Perales with the 701st Brigade of the US Army Criminal Investigation Command, during the conduct of their duties of securing and preserving the upturned remains as a result of severe flooding, found two items of interest. ."

"They found Spanish gold from Jolly Benoit!" Val Cedars said excitedly, the color of his face getting closer to the shade of his sweater. The military officer sighed and gestured to Cedars to continue.

"Okay, we have in our possession three Spanish gold coins minted in 1805. They were contained inside a tar-covered wooden box used to store items on ships with wet conditions," Cedars said.

Just then, the female note taker in the room placed the items close up in front of the camera. There were three gold coins, mostly round and with a definite patina. They looked more bronze than gold. On one side was a figure of a man with a prominent nose. I later found out that was King Charles IV of Spain. On the other side, there was what looked to be a royal crest showing a castle and a large cross with Latin words surrounding the crest. The box was made of wood about 18 inches by 12 inches and about 10 inches tall with a curved lid. It was partially covered with tar, but I could see the black iron hinges and handles.

I had to admit that I was moved by this piece of history even though I admit to being fairly light in that department. Maybe it was just the early onset of gold fever.

"So do we have a consensus that there is more gold involved in this area?" Camille asked.

"Who knows," Colonel Sanchez said. "We will have to see when we finish with the bodies."

"Well, you know what we want," Camille continued. "We represent bond holders for the Spanish National government. In recent years, the country of Spain has been caught in the grip of economic challenges like many parts of Europe. They have been making a claim for gold lost but reclaimed from sunken Spanish galleons."

"But that was out in international waters," the tall government man said. He introduced himself as Adam Samuelson from the US State Department. "This is different."

"It's different because there are the remains of tortured black souls involved. Me and my people will not let this turn into a grab for gold. This is a restoration of these sacred and historical sites," Reverend Moten said. He was standing now in full oratory.

"Reverend, no one is going to desecrate these graves. That's why we have the National Guard here," Sheriff Cormac explained.

Now that I understood what our position was, I stepped in to speak.

"We understand your concern, Reverend. Our position is one of an interested bystander. We don't plan to get in the way. Where were the artifacts found? Was it from Jolly Benoit's actual grave site?"

"Uh, no," Colonel Sanchez said. "At this point, many of the graves were mixed together in the mudslides. Some of the graves appeared to be mass graves of several bodies. The gold and the box were found among a jumble of mud and skeletal remains."

"Jolly Benoit and Sam Gilley each have vaults on safe ground in their respective cities," Val Cedars jumped back into the conversation.

"But that was just a legend, right?" I asked. "I mean do we really know if he was a pirate?"

"Of course, course he was, Sir," Val Cedars said with righteous indignation. "We have Captain Benoit's journal as well as the journal of Sam Gilley. We have nautical and military documents from the colony of Saint-Domingue also known as Haiti. Captain Benoit received his freedom there as a colonial citizen soldier of France."

"So if we find more gold," Adam Samuelson of the State Department said, "it will be in the custody of the US Federal Government."

"Well, it should be part of the historical collection of Jolly Benoit," Val Cedars said, his voice fluttering with emotion.

"Well, we shall have to explore all claims, including the government of Spain," I said. There was a pregnant silence all around. It was becoming obvious that this forensic recovery operation, this natural disaster story, was now going to be an international event.

The rest of the call was spent exchanging vital information and fielding all the concerns from Reverend Moten about what he would and would not tolerate. Based on what I had seen and heard, I did not think this was just about gold.

So what was this about?

Public relations?

Government relations?

Reading our Memorandum of Understanding, this is what I surmised. The debt holders for the country of Spain caught gold fever. Recently lost treasures pulled from the bottom of the ocean yielded hundreds of millions of euros in recovered gold coins, jewelry, and art. The Spanish mined gold from what is now Central America and Mexico for almost 400 years. That gold was meant to fortify Spain, keep the Moors from reinvading, and to stay in the race with the British and the French for conquering the New World.

No one really knows just how much actually made it across the ocean. Rough estimates by historians put it somewhere between $500 to $600 billion dollars. As for the amounts lost to the sea from storms, military battles, and piracy—no one knows. Fast forward to modern-day Spain. Recession, unemployment, and mounting debt had the country's credit rating falling and treasury agents toiling with the World Bank to keep the debt financed. One way has been to claim their share of these recovered treasures as they are found.

Well, those nameless faceless debt holders, a network of banks, bondholders, fund managers, and individuals so rich they don't register on social media, are interested in getting their return on investment, even if they have to pull it from the graves of dead American slaves. The State Department was here for what—to help Spain? To get their cut? Or could they really be looking out for US citizens?

If the gold was on US soil, wasn't it ours? I was not sure. While I was officially a conduit of the debt holders and by default the government of Spain, I really identified with the locals more than anything. The sanctity of the graves—hadn't these souls suffered enough?

Reverend Moten was a good man who had done a lot of good things. I now connected him from previous political crusades racial and financial in nature, but there is that wild hair when gold is involved. How pure were his motives and the depths of his devotion? Whatever the reverend's plan was, I'm sure the sheriff wished he did it quieter.

Now that I knew why I was here as the eyes and ears of the money people; I did not care for it. This was going to be a headache and maybe a waste   of   time.

Chapter 3

Gerald Phillips was packing angry. He hated packing angry because it meant he was going to forget something. Not small things like deodorant or a toothbrush. Big things like underwear, or the jackets to half his suits. He stayed in his closet hiding from the conflict. It felt stupid, a six-foot three-inch man hiding.

Gerald was able to maintain his slim physique into his early fifties. He even kept his signature low top fade haircut he wore for almost twenty years. He still had enough hair to pull it off. He had the long loping stride of a basketball player, along with a handsome but serious face in medium brown skin. That along with his education and two decades of international law gave him a formidable presence.

There was no getting around this fight. Nadine Charleston-Phillips, his wife of five years, was going to have her say.

"So WorldSpan is bringing you in as their token negro?" she said, leaning against the door opening to their bedroom.

She was in one of his favorite dresses—a pastel coral knee-length number that looked great against her slim waist, round hips, long runner's legs, and copper-brown skin. She had that unblinking brown-eyed stare set in a gorgeous face underneath shoulder-length braids. That stare captivated and scared him in the beginning. Today he refused to be baited. This happened every time he went out of town.

When Gerald and Nadine met, he was logging over 150,000 air miles each year and spending a third of his life in Europe, Africa, and Southeast Asia. Eventually, he had to give that life up to get the love of his life. She still got a little brittle when he left town, especially if it involved his former globetrotting partner, Teke Manion.

"Nadine, this is just up the road in North Carolina. It's not like I'm leaving the country."

"I know that," she answered.

"Then what is it?" he said harsher than he wanted. He did not want her to know she was getting to him. If he spoke in anger, it would be used against him. He busied himself walking over to the closet checking to make sure he did not miss anything.

"I'll tell you," Nadine started. "I have been watching the news. These people are going to raid those graves looking for gold, and you are going to help them."

"The graves are being preserved and reinterred by the National Guard," Gerald said, still searching.

"Oh, and this country has never used the military for commercial gain?" she responded quickly.

"There is no gain for the US government. The State Department is here merely to make sure what you say does not happen. So am I for that matter."

"How you do figure that? You represent needy Spanish. First, they rape the land and steal the gold from the natives, and now they want to do the same thing here."

"Wrong, I will not let them do anything like that. Teke and I would raise the alarm…."

"Teke?" she said her face twisted into a sour lemon frown. "The Mr. Needy number one."

"You just say that because he used to be my partner in Europe," Gerald said.

"True, but isn't he the statistical, numbers wiz WorldSpan sends out to make sure they get every nickel they have coming to them? You said it yourself—Teke is the money; you are the law."

"That's his expertise, Baby. That does not mean he would do anything wrong for money. Just like I would not do anything wrong and hide behind the law."

"Okay, but what about that business in White Sands where they found his ass half dead on a barrier island and dead bodies around every corner?"

"That was different. He didn't kill anyone."

There was a pause in the conversation. Gerald stuck his head out of the closet. He was startled when Nadine appeared just outside the closet door.

"He takes chances. He will put himself in all kinds of danger for WorldSpan. One day, he is not going to be so lucky, and I don't want it to be the day you are with him."

"You don't know what you are talking about," Gerald said. "What we do is not dangerous."

"The world is dangerous now. All the places you and Teke did business have had terrorist events, floods, or disease outbreaks." He just nodded. She was right on that.

"Besides, those are my people you are disrespecting," she said, walking over to the dresser and pulling out a bundle of socks and tossing them into the suitcase.

"You are not from that part of North Carolina," Gerald said, going back into the closet.

"I have people in Benoitown."

"Distant cousins at best," Gerald said. "Never heard you mention them once, even when we went to Raleigh for Christmas two years ago."

Another pause in the conversation. Gerald stuck his head out of the closet again. She was gone.

Oh, hell, he thought. *Now I guess she's really mad.*

Chapter 4

Apartment of Tekelius
"Teke" Manion – Paris, France
(Quartier Latin)

At that same moment, I was finishing the touches on Camille's favorite dish from childhood, Oysters Bordelaise. It is essentially the red wine bordelaise but with white wine and a lighter chicken stock. About a year ago I had been messing around with it in the kitchen on a lazy Sunday thinking she would critique it to death. Instead, she cried with joy as it took her back to some wonderful times growing up in the Garonne River Valley of Southern France.

Like any smart man, I made it whenever I was in trouble. For extra measure, I also had two bottles of Taittinger Champagne chilling for a few hours in an ice bed that I kept replenishing.

She walked in still in corporate mode. She didn't look me in the eye, but read from a sheet of prep notes, quizzing and correcting me on all the things I needed to know for the trip. She wore her hair in a short spike style. It made those big pretty brown eyes seem even larger and brighter. Plus, no one could wear a pencil skirt like that woman.

As she paced back and forth in the living room just off the kitchen, droning on about facts and message points better read on the long plane ride, I could see the muscles in her swimmer's legs flex with each step. Her breasts were on the small side but inviting. She always wore those soft silk blouses that made her look slim but not skinny. I noticed she had the top two buttons of that blouse open to reveal the soft cleavage underneath it. I smiled at that point. She was fucking with me. Literally.

I kept cooking and stayed behind the counter to hide my partial arousal.

She smelled the oysters, saw the champagne, but was going to make me sweat it out just a bit more. Later around 10:00 PM, I put on Wynton Marsalis' Standard Time Volume V: The Midnight Blues, turning the volume down to just past two.

At that rate, you could barely hear the other instruments, but the trumpet still pierced through the night's silence. -Camille lay in bed sipping the last of the second bottle of champagne. The small touch lamp next to the bed cast just enough light on her face, neck, nipples, and the rolls of her tight stomach muscles. Her eyes closed, she swayed her head from side to side with the music. One foot was out from underneath the sheets. Her toes were painted a color between coral and pink and curled and uncurled to the beat. It made my mouth water.

There was nothing about this woman I did not think was cool. I even missed the smoke that used to curl from her last cigarette of the night. She had recently quit after twenty years. Just quit—no patch, pills, acupuncture, nor weight gain. I climbed back into bed. She took a sip of champagne, then rolled over to straddle me. She kissed me and deposited the drink from her mouth into my mouth. You would have thought it was my first drink in months. I ran my hands up her long thighs to her soft hips. She giggled and pushed back, then lay flat with her head on my chest. I watched the long tall expanse of her, marveling way more than I should after all this time but not being able to help myself. During the day in the office, she had a formidable presence, but here in my bed she was like a carefree college girl. I sometimes found it difficult to reconcile the two. That was when I scolded myself for thinking too much.

"You know I should still be mad at you," she started and pinched my side. "I could not find you anywhere, and then you come walking into the meeting as if you had done nothing."

"I just had some things to work out, and I had to see Lemieux," I said.

"I know. I spoke with him when I couldn't find you. I guess I have been mad at myself as well."

"Why?"

"It was me who orchestrated you going back home to the White Sands. I thought it would do you some good to get home, but I almost sent you to your death."

"You didn't know, Mila, and it was good. I got to see my brother, and I did get rid of any longing or wondering for home. As for my old friends, well, I guess I'm not my brother's keeper."

"And now the managing directors have given you this crazy new job. Why didn't you turn it down?"

"Because it's different. I go into these assignments expecting danger. No surprises. Who would have thought going home would be so dangerous?

This time I'll be prepared."

"You know, Teke, we have never asked for promises or assurances in this thing between you and I," she said, propping herself up to look into my eyes. Even in this low light, hers shown like they were electric. It was a little spooky.

"Right," I said trying to maintain my cool pose, wondering where this was going.

"I never even ask you to remain faithful while you are away."

"Nor I, you," I responded.

"Well, I want you to promise me this," she said and crawled up to kiss me, "that you just make it back to me. You said after your last trip that Paris ... that this was your home now."

"It is."

"Then no matter what happens— WorldSpan wins, WorldSpan loses— promise that you make it home."

So of course I promised. That got me extra innings and through the last of the champagne, warm but just as good.

Like most mornings after a champagne night with Camille, I woke to the same Wynton Marsalis trumpet that sent me to sleep, feeling like Paul Newman in that jazz movie he did with Sidney Poitier. She was long gone. I came out to the kitchen. There was coffee, a crepe pastry, and my briefing notes sitting on the counter. I lifted the stack and placed them to my nose. They smelled like her perfume, Arpege' by Lanvin.

There was a small note clipped to the front of the stack which read: JE SUIS TOUJOURS EN COLÈRE CONTRE VOUS! (I AM STILL ANGRY   WITH   YOU!)

Chapter 5
Wheels Down
- Atlanta, Georgia

Three days later in Atlanta, I met up with my old travel buddy and business partner, Gerald Phillips. He was older than me by several years, but we made a good team and were real friends, not just business "friends." He was in his typical travel dress, black slacks, starch white long-sleeved business shirt and light wool beige Ralph Lauren sports coat. I was in WorldSpan colors, navy blue slacks and a gold polo shirt. When we first met we were both looking for the same thing, trying to make our mark on the huge playing field of international business, he in law, and me in finance.

I always admired how he never seemed to lose composure. He had the grace under pressure that really great athletes or actors seem to have. He had a fluidity to his motions and his voice that I sometimes wished I had. Whenever I tried to imitate him, I just came off like a creature from a Boris Karloff movie.

Several years ago near the Jurong Port of Singapore, he and I were working to expedite 65 tons of lumber, copper, and other building materials through a morass of legal issues brought on by some financial shortfalls and tariff disputes. In other words, until the right people got paid, the legal customs chains on the cargo would remain in place.

Gerald was at an impasse from a legal standpoint. Besides making all the proper filings in a foreign court and sidestepping all the obvious racial and cultural obstacles surrounding his American brown skin, he had failed to get the cargo released and on its way to the Middle East. Enter his new friend. Me.

Through some five-way transactions via limited partnerships across five countries and three languages, I was able to find the financing and get things going. Later that night on the flight to Dubai to oversee the next shipment stuck in transit, we joked like business people who were more drunk from success than from the shots of scotch we ordered.

"Listen, man, from this point on, stop trying to copy me," Gerald explained to me that night. "I owe you, so you do you, and that seems to be just fine."

I never forgot the day he said that. It was like a light switch went on in my head. It was coming from a guy whom I know wouldn't say it, unless he meant it. That gave me the final confidence I needed to make it in this business.

"It's been too long, Whelp," he said, hugging me with one arm while shaking my hand on the other side. I never looked up the nickname, but I think it meant young forest animal. He used it for all the younger international business professionals he worked with. It was a compliment and a jest. We were young and wet behind the ears, but we were tough and eager to conquer the world.

"How you doing, old married man?" I asked. "Last time I saw you, we were commandeering a WorldSpan corporate jet at Christmas time to fly a special lady out to Paris."

"And as you can see, it worked," Gerald said, holding up his left fist to show the wedding ring.

"Sorry I couldn't make it to the wedding," I said.

"Man, please! You gave us the best present of all. You helped get her to Paris, so I could propose in the first place."

That was a true Christmas miracle. After about a decade of international bachelorhood, Gerald decided to take the plunge a second time and marry Nadine, a caterer from Jacksonville. I couldn't believe it myself, but he was determined to propose to this woman on the tiny Alexandre III Bridge in Paris during one of the snowiest Christmases in European recorded history. Through some interesting moves with the WorldSpan jet, we pulled it off.

"And how are things at home?" I asked as we walked through the concourse.

"Okay. She always gets a little crazy in the head when I travel," he said with a stern face. "Especially if I'm seeing the usual suspects."

"You mean me?" I asked. He just looked at me and raised his eyebrows.

We were in Atlanta for an extra day to pick up some supplies and equipment needed to conduct business such as copiers, fax machines, secure document storage, and shipping supplies. Then we were to fly into the affected area.

On the day we returned to the airport, I noticed we turned to head towards the international and commercial freight concourse.

"Hey, man, our flight is this way," I said, slowing to go in the opposite direction. Gerald kept on walking but looked over his shoulder.

"No, our supplies are being delivered this way. Come on. We're getting a private ride," he said.

"WorldSpan is sending a jet?" I asked.

"Not exactly," Gerald said, slowing down at one of the private level gates and pulling identification from his jacket pocket. I did the same, showing it to a tall slim airport official wearing an ascot tie. He bowed perfunctorily and pointed with his open palm towards the doors leading to the tarmac.

Halfway to the plane, I saw a pallet with our supplies on a wagon being pulled by a man in one of the golf cart-type luggage vehicles. The side of the aircraft held the typical identification numbers and the red and yellow flag of Spain.

"It's a goodwill gesture from our client that we go together," Gerald said.

"But Spain is not our client. We work for the private debt holders of Spain's debt," I said, but it even sounded like splitting hairs to me. "So much for keeping a low profile."

A man stepped out of the private aircraft and stood on the top of the moving ramp steps. He was dressed like someone about to take the stage in Vegas or Macau. He was about five and a half feet, but wore leather boots with an obvious elevated heel.

His suit was the color of ox blood, sharkskin with tapered pants legs, and a single breast jacket. It was a slim cut that further revealed his diminutive frame. He wore a white shirt and black tie, but his tie clip looked as big as a police officer's badge.

As a matter of fact, it looked like a badge. His hair, which started just in front of the crown of his head, was dyed black and slicked back into a one-inch ponytail. His mustache was the same shade of shiny black and told a different story than the perfect toothy smile sitting beneath it. His light-brown eyes smiled as well, but it was a predator's smile. It was the same smile on the faces of men who sell defective cars and women who talk men into spending the rent money for one night of unforgettable fun.

"Good morning, Señor Manion, Señor Phillips, I am Fedelito Gaspare," he said and bowed slightly. "I am a part of the team to recover the glory of Spain!" He said. I hated to admit it, but he did this last part with the flourish of a bullfighter.

"Um, I don't understand," I started. "We are just going to observe. We don't know what we are going to find here."

"Plus anything recovered has a number of legal claims on it, including the US government," Gerald Phillips said.

"Nonsense," Fedelito said, performing a perfect spin over the edge of the stairway. "This gold shall belong to the rightful original owners."

"You mean the Mayan civilizations it was stolen from?" Gerald said, sharing my mistrust of the little man and letting him know it.

There was a brief silence as the two men stared at each other.

"Listen, Fedelito, we were caught off guard about your presence. No one told us, so we're going to have to check this out. You say you represent the Spanish government?" I asked with my best calm voice.

The predator smile came back as instantly as it left. "But of course. Where are my manners? Please come in, sit, and we will get everything straightened out."

As I entered the plane, Fedelito reached up and wrapped his arm around my shoulders like we were old friends. I could hear Gerald mumble something under his breath. Once inside I asked Gerald to call WorldSpan and get some clarity. It was probably not smart leaving him with the overbearing Mr. Gaspare.

"Technically, I am with the Spanish embassy out of Washington, DC," he started.

We were sitting in facing leather seats with a small table between us. The G4 jet was all lacquered wood and leather. There were multiple seating areas.

Four light beige, almost white seats faced each other from opposite sides of the plane, each with a severely large table attached to it. Behind them was an open space with padded bench seating around the perimeter. The walls and floors were awash in more lacquered wood and carpet so plush you longed to remove your shoes.

A flight attendant came by with a tray of drinks. It was Prosecco. I requested mineral water with lemon.

"First, I want to apologize if I was rude before, but I am what is known as a devout nationalist. Ever since I was a little boy in Pinto, Madrid, I have dreamed to be of service to my country."

I nodded, content to let the flashy little man talk.

"Señor, you know what the economic situation is all over Europe. Spain is a proud country, and we don't like going to the World Bank and private debt holders to maintain our way of life. You can understand that, can't you?" I nodded as the mineral water was set in front of me.

"So we have found a way to reclaim not only a financial foothold but part of our national heritage. I know the stories told on this side of the ocean about the mistreatment at the hands of my ancestors, but it is still part of our history. Like your Confederate South, celebrated though it may have protected some mistreatment as seen through modern eyes."

"Fedelito, I get it," I said wishing he would learn when to shut up— that less is more. I did not want him stumbling around Civil War analogies in front of Gerald or the fine folks of Eastern Carolina.

"What exactly does the country of Spain expect you to do?"

"Well, I … um … observe … and I consult … and um … I report out," he answered, this time his smile more tentative, more honest.

"That's about right," the voice said from behind us. It was Gerald, fresh off the phone from headquarters. "Mr. Gaspare is the eyes and ears of Mother Spain. He is here to make sure that Spain's interests are protected. We are to work together."

"Please, Señor Phillips, accept my apologies for earlier. I guess I am just a bit too patriotic. I forget my manners."

The two shook hands, and Gerald even accepted Prosecco.

Soon we were racing through partly cloudy skies towards North Carolina. On the way we tried to explain the delicacies of the operation to Fedelito, who cut us off with assurances that he understood perfectly, that he had briefings at the consulate in Washington, and that he would be practically invisible in the process. Oh, brother!

We landed on a private airfield just north of Washington, North Carolina. It is the city where the Tar River dumps into the larger Pamlico River and Pamlico Sound. We took a private car into Washington, North Carolina, a small quaint tourist town by the water. There were buildings along the river dating back over 150 years. Most of them housed shops, restaurants, and other businesses associated with tourism. The wide expanse of the river provided for busy boat traffic.

I didn't see much of any hurricane damage here.

From there we were to hop on a vessel about the size of a large charter fishing boat similar to the ones I grew up around. The name Sweet Heat was on the transom. Gerald spoke up at the dock.

"Why are we taking this? I thought we were driving from here," Gerald asked.

"Our vehicles are waiting for us in Benoitown," Fedelito explained. "This way, we can go the way the infamous Jolly Benoit went and see the lay of the land as you Americans say."

"Hey, Gaspare, this is not a field trip. This is business. Now you don't go changing plans without telling us."

"Gerald, it's no big deal. This will probably get us there faster," I said, trying to keep things moving. Gerald motioned me over to him.

"Man, I get seasick on these things. I need to take something before I get on a boat," he said.

"Really, I never knew this. We've been on plenty of boats together."

"Yes, and we knew we were going on them so I took something ahead of time. I got to find a drugstore."

We found a small store a few blocks from a scenic waterfront park of Washington. Gerald dry-swallowed a couple of the pills, and we walked back to where the vessel was waiting. Fedelito stood on the transom still wearing his jacket and tie. The predator smile was back.

"Señors, we want to shove off. It is getting late," he said as if he were the captain of all things. "Meet our pilot."

A woman stepped out from the steering house. She was in her late twenties, maybe thirty, reddish brown hair, light gray eyes set in a cute tan freckled face lifted from every tourism beach advertisement. She wore a pink bandana on her head, a red snug fitting tank top and roomy, mid-thigh black shorts typically used by boaters and black topsiders with glittery sides. Her legs were more naturally slim but not as muscular as Camille's. They were natural like everything else about her.

"Hi!" she said, full of confidence. "Angela Babineaux."

"Teke Manion and Gerald Phillips," I said, shaking her hand and pointing over my shoulder at Gerald. Her hand was surprisingly soft. I also got the distinct scent of jasmine and maybe peach.

"Teke, like the wood?" she asked. I gave her my full name, and she gave a polite smile.

"We should make good time. Angela is the best pilot on this part of the river," Fedelito said.

"You two know each other?" I asked.

"No," Angela said emphatically as she turned her attention to steering the boat away from the dock. "I just told him that before you two came back from the store."

I looked at Fedelito and shook my head. I joined Gerald against the port side railing.

Angela really did have nice legs. They reminded me of the spring break girls who came down to White Sands when I was a teenager. Legs that looked good without even trying.

"So, are you any kin to that Nadine Phillips?" Angela shouted out from the wheelhouse, addressing Gerald.

"What?"

"Nadine, she some kin?"

"Yes, it's why we are in a hurry so we can get to Mr. Phillips' special package, eh Señor?"

"Shut up, Gaspare!" Gerald said, looking confused and turning a pale shade of brown around the cheeks and ears.

"Yeah, she's my wife. How do you know her?"

"Well, she's making waves in Benoitown today," she said.

"Show them the video stream I showed you earlier, Fedelito."

Fedelito held up a small tablet computer. He tapped a few commands on the screen, smiled, and turned the screen to us. It was a video stream from downtown Benoitown. There holding half of a 20-foot sign with the message— DEFENDER OF THE ANCESTRY! —was Nadine Charleston-Phillips, chanting along with about two hundred others.

"They interviewed her earlier," Fedelito said. "Would you like to see it?"

"How did this happen? When did this happen?" Gerald asked, not believing his ears.

"You mean you did not know, Señor Phillips?" Fedelito asked as if he had just stumbled on tomorrow's winning lottery numbers. He was in full predator mode. "You did not know your own wife was coming to town to join the protesters under Reverend Moten?"

"Babineaux, don't spare the fuel. We need to hurry," I said. Then I pulled Gerald out of earshot. "How could she have gotten there so fast?" I asked.

"I don't know, but I guess it's possible," he said, thinking it through in his mind. "I didn't see her the morning I left. That two days ago. I've been in Atlanta waiting on you. While we were waiting on supplies in Atlanta, she could have taken a direct flight on a different airline to Raleigh with a connection to Greenville. Then she would have driven over from there."

"She moves fast for what? Three days?" I asked. As we moved up river, I started to get that feeling I had come to hate—the feeling you get when nothing is as it seems or is expected to be.

After about 30 minutes, the stream became narrower and shallower. Between the time of day and the tree cover on either side of the Tar River, the passage was darker. I felt sorry for Gerald. He looked miserable. I decided to leave him alone in his thoughts. I staggered to the front of the boat and stood next to Angela. More jasmine and the small hint of seawater filled my nose. The vessel rocked starboard and I bumped into her. She seemed to be used to transporting landlubbers because she wrapped her left arm around my waist, halting my lurch.

"Whoa, thanks!" I said, getting my balance.

"Like a good neighbor, Insurance Man," Angela said jokingly, never taking her right hand off the wheel or her eyes off the river.

"Different company," I said flatly.

"Oh, sorry, what's your company slogan?"

"Nowhere near as catchy," I said. "The river seems to be getting narrower."

"It is," she said. "And shallower, but I won't let us bottom out. We can have Baliles come for you in the johnboat if it gets too low."

"Who is Baliles?"

"Well, it's kind of hard to describe Baliles. He's kind of a local hero, historian, tourist attraction, and teller of tales."

"Sounds interesting."

"Uh-huh. He used to be married to my auntie so I guess we were kin at one time. You can find him out in front of the Benoit's Bar."

"Then I'll find him, because I'm gonna need a drink before we're done."

"Oh, yeah, you guys are probably hungry," she said. We looked back at Gerald who was looking more sleepy than sick. "Well, *you* may be *hungry*. Benoit's has the best shrimp and oyster po' boys, barbeque pork, and she-crab soup. Plus, a full bar."

"It's open?"

"Yeah, it's several blocks up from the river. The water stopped right at the door. Locals say Baliles had something to do with that."

"So he's a witch doctor, a voodoo priest, a shaman?" Fedelito asked from behind us.

Angela rolled her eyes and continued to look upriver. There was a light off in the distance. It was bouncing vertically and from side to side. In a few seconds it was twice as big.

"Somebody's coming our way, fast," Angela said.

"Any ideas? Friend or foe?" I asked, already thinking about what weapons I had in my bag.

"Not sure," she said and throttled down to a slow pace. It was just shy of full darkness. Soon I could hear the high-speed motor.

We heard them before we could see them.

"This is the Edgewood County River Patrol!" came a voice over a loudspeaker. "Please halt your vessel. You are entering water too shallow for your draft."

"Shit!" Angela said and cut her engine. "Looks like this is as far as I can take you."

The two speed skimmers came into within thirty feet of Bab's forward bow. They wore military green with large swivel-mounted searchlights at the front of each boat. It kept me from seeing their faces.

"Dang, Quinten, is that you? Point those dang lights down!" Angela said. They complied. A large man with huge jawline and rugged looks came forward. He was wearing the uniform for the water patrol and a hard hat from Army surplus. There was a much smaller man in glasses and the same uniform that remained in the skimmer craft. The other boat held one additional patrol person. I couldn't make them out.

"Angela, is that you, baby girl?" the large patrolman asked, standing proud at the front of the skimmer that was now so close that his foot propped on the bow rail of Angela's boat.

"Yeah, it's me. I'm being paid good money to take these insurance guys up to Benoitown."

"Not tonight you ain't, and not in that boat," Quinten said.

"Why not? Quinten, you got no cause to stop me, shoot!"

"I do, too. Now, Angela, the river is low. They diverting it to do some drainage work, and making sure they got all those bodies. Only watercraft going that far upriver tonight is these official speed skiffs."

"Well, hell," Angela said, slapping the wall of the wheelhouse.

"Angela, we can take your passenger the rest of the way. Sheriff Cormac gave us instructions," the little patrolman said. Quinten jabbed him in the side, almost knocking him down. The little guy shrugged and adjusted his hard hat.

"Well, that's better than nothing," Angela said sadly. "Quinten Clark, you could have told me that at first."

"I would but you started yelling at me and disrespecting my public office…."

"Yeah, that's what you said she was gonna do when you begged the Sheriff for this detail," the small guy said, chuckling and speaking out of turn. "Thor, shut your mouth!" Quinten shouted, shoving the little guy.

"Don't you shove him, butthead," Angela started in on Quinten, kicking his foot off the front bow of her vessel.

"Excuse me, Officer," Gerald interrupted, stepping forward taking control of the melee. "Can you have your partner help us with luggage so we can make Benoitown before we die of old age?"

"Uh, yes, sir," Quinten said, temporarily thrown off his tête-à-tête with Angela. The little guy eased the speedboat next to the Sweet Heat. He and Quinten stepped forward to take bags from Gerald. I went to grab my luggage and did the same. I noticed that at the rear of the boat, Fedelito and Angela were having a quiet discussion that did not seem friendly.

Once we were transferred to the patrol vessels, I jumped back on the Sweet Heat.

"Angela, thanks for everything," I said up close, because I have manners and I wanted to smell that scent again.

"Well, sorry I couldn't take you all the way, but Quinten, Lincoln, and Thor are good guys. They will take good care of you."

"The little guy's name is Thor?" I whispered, letting a snicker escaped.

Then she started and before long it was an all-out laugh. The mood lightened. "So what was that with Fedelito a minute ago?"

"Nothing," she said quickly. She started to speak and just waved her hand. "Have a safe trip, Teke-Wood."

She retreated into the wheelhouse and throttled the engine. I stood there another moment taking in the scent, then jumped onto the patrol boat. Quinten shouted something unintelligible, and they turned and headed up the river. I turned back. I could see Angela reversing the Sweet Heat back down river.

Chapter 6

In about 15 minutes, we came roaring under the bridge separating Benoitown and Gilleyville. According to my notes, the Tar River shows a slow-moving current during most of the year. As a result of the hurricane, that same current reached just 10 feet below the bottom of the bridge. It was much lower now. Steel steps attached to each end of the bridge extended down past the waterline.

"Watch your step, gentlemen," a patrolman said as the boats coasted next to the steps. "We will handle your luggage."

Gerald, Fedelito, and I climbed to the first street of Benoitown that ran parallel to the river. Things were still wet but getting better. A black snake crossed our path, slithering casually down the middle of the street as if it were out for the evening air. Fedelito jumped back, speaking rapidly in Spanish and crossing himself. Once getting control of himself, he directed us to the City Works Building two blocks up Main Street leading away from the river. There, we found our assigned cars that should have been waiting for us earlier in our trip.

"Look, can you handle the local bureaucrats?" Gerald said, looking like his old self. "I need to find my wife and find out what the is going on."

We shook hands and he walked purposefully to a white Subaru Outback, opened the rear door, and threw his luggage into the back. Seconds later, he rolled into traffic heading out of downtown. I wondered briefly how he knew where to look for her.

"All right, Fedelito, let's go find the law around here."

Sheriff Cormac was friendly enough. He invited Fedelito and me into a back-conference room. I recognized it as the one from the conference call several days ago. He introduced me to Mimi Boulage, his secretary and police dispatcher; Val Cedars, the nattily-dressed man in the sweater vest, and Adam Samuelson from the US State Department. We sat down and Mimi offered us Coke, coffee, and cigarettes.

At that moment, another woman walked in from the side entrance of the conference room. She was in a US Army uniform. She was carrying a small box about two-foot square.

"Gentlemen, this is Colonel Aurelia Sanchez. She runs the forensic detail," Cormac explained.

"In other words, you will separate the remains and re-inter them," I said. Colonel Sanchez flushed. I wasn't sure if she was impressed with my quick show of understanding or insulted for the same reason.

"Well, in a nutshell, but it's not as easy as it sounds. There is a lot of accelerated decomposition from the floodwater and exposure to sunlight and open air."

She was tall, just under six feet. Despite her army fatigues and pose, she was beauty-pageant gorgeous. Her serious dark eyes that said she was in charge were set in a face with a perfect nose, mouth, and cheekbones. I am sure she did not make rank in this field without some bare-knuckle brawls with her fellow enlisted. There was nothing shy or awkward. Her gaze never left my face.

"I have watched the news," I started. "I want to assure you all that we have no intention of disrespecting or disturbing remains. WorldSpan is here as an observer and nothing more."

"That's good to hear," Cormac said, his Baltimore accent slight but evident.

"We got a big enough circus. You don't sound French?"

"No—Paris by way of Florida," I said with a slight smile.

"Well, that's good! Another American on this is great," the State Department rep said with a relaxed smile.

"Uh, not so fast," Fedelito said, stepping forward holding up one finger like a stage actor. "Mr. Manion is an adjunct agent of the Spanish government."

"Adjunct agent? What the does that mean?" Cormac asked, looking at me and Adam Samuelson the State Department representative.

I shook my head. "I work for WorldSpan who works for the people financing the Spanish debt. I represent the financiers of that debt."

"Oh, so you and Mr. Spain are here to scrape the bones of these poor tortured souls," Val Cedars said with righteous indignation.

"Uh, I believe you have us confused with your ancestors," Fedelito said with equal venom.

The two little men moved towards each other with surprising speed, but Cormac was faster.

"Gentlemen, I know you two weren't going to do anything illegal in the middle of this office, in front of the sheriff and his deputies?" the sheriff asked.

The two stopped and stared at each other with no love lost. Val Cedars wasn't fat as much as soft all over. Plus, he wore his sweater vest at least one size too small. If fabric could talk, that vest would have been screaming. Fedelito tugged at the hem of his shiny jacket and pushed his chin up and out.

"I assure everyone here that we are all on the same side. WorldSpan and the financiers want nothing to do with any mortal remains. We want the military forensics to handle that. We are only interested that if any property is recovered, it is ultimately returned to the country of Spain."

"Well that's fine, Manion," Val Cedars said, still agitated. "But that property has been sitting on American soil for almost 200 years. I believe that gives us some rights of ownership as well."

He was pointing at Adam Samuelson now.

"Well, I would think we would want to explore that.... I mean there are some rules of maritime law that may have precedence.... "

The representative from the State Department would have gone on like that for some time, but saved himself.

"Colonel, can we see the artifacts?" I asked. She reacted as if in a daydream.

"Uh, um, yes," she said, looking at the sheriff as if for assurance.

She laid the box on the long conference room table. She reached into her right front jacket pocket and pulled out latex gloves. After placing them on her hands, she opened the box flaps and gingerly pulled out the tar-stained half-deteriorated wooden box. I could smell the slight scent of floodwater, old wood, and death.

The wood around the hinges were gone, so she lifted the top of the antique box to reveal the coins. They were shiny but not clean. Maybe it had to do with Old World gold that was somehow better than recent gold. They were about the size of Kennedy half-dollars but twice as thick. They were misshaped by modern coin standards and clearly marked with Spanish inscriptions.

"That gold was pulled from the earth and minted with men, machines, and resources from Spain for Spain," Fedelito said, looking off to my left side standing uncomfortably close, one of his small bejeweled hands holding my arm.

"And you destroyed an entire civilization to get it," Val said, pointing at the proud Spaniard.

"You are one to talk. You, the descendant of slave rapers," Fedelito shot back. I had to give it to him for guts if nothing else, a foreign national standing in the middle of American authority and "asserting" Spanish claims.

"That's it," Cormac said. "Manion, get your guy out of here."

"Please," Val said, his arms folded.

"You get out, too, Val," Cormac said.

After some sputtering and protestations and a little help from a deputy standing nearby, the room was cleared of everybody except the sheriff and me. Adam Samuelson made an excuse about a call back to Washington, DC. Mimi followed behind Val, making soothing sounds. In the last verbal exchange, Colonel Sanchez silently secured the coins and case in the box. She whispered something to the sheriff before leaving the room.

"You see what I'm up against," Sheriff Cormac said, motioning for me to sit. He took the seat next to me. "Okay, so I understand you are supposed to be some kind of expediter, a guy who keeps things going smooth?"

I nodded, wondering who he had been talking to and not trusting my words.

"Well, you seem like a level-headed guy. I noticed you don't have much of a footprint stateside."

"Yeah, mostly Europe."

"Right, so you said. Anyway, I called the law in White Sands after reading the story about that business with the arson."

"Oh," I said. "I try not to think about that."

"I don't blame you," Cormac said with shake of his head. "But you survived. That took guts and brains."

I just nodded. The conversation was getting one-sided, but the last thing I expected to talk about was White Sands. Sheriff Cormac just sat back like he was thinking something over in his head.

"Look—you need anything from my office, let me or my deputies know," he said, exhaling and leaning forward. "Can you do me one favor?"

"Sure," I said.

"Keep that Fedelito in check."

~ ~ ~

Heyworth McLean and Terry Jackson had been friends so long they still had the collective nickname formed in eighth grade, Mac and Jack. They grew up on the same street in Rome Georgia, graduated from the same high school, and enlisted in the Army together.

After a couple of tours each in Iraq and Afghanistan, they finished out their enlistments in the National Guard.

Mac was a corporal and the adventurer, the dreamer, the one to jump in with both feet. He was five-foot eight with a good physique but not from working out. Mac was all energy all the time. He could eat what he wanted, drink what he wanted, and never gained an ounce or lost a muscle.

Jack was a private and the thinker, the careful cautious one. He was taller, just under six feet two inches. He was big, like his all-American uncles who played at the University of Arkansas-Pine Bluff. However,

Terry got his lack of athletic ability and abundance of intelligence from his mother's side.

Tonight, they were in Benoit's Bar after their fourteenth day of guard duty after Hurricane Chester. Their job was to guard the recovered remains pending forensic processing. They were being held in a nineteenth-century warehouse.

It had been a lot of things but nothing in the past thirty years. Special refrigeration cooling units about the size of restaurant walk-ins were set up and run off generators. The noise was maddening. It slowed the deterioration associated with exposure to the air and water. Mack and Jack both wondered about that, since that was what bodies did in graves.

After what they experienced in Mosel and Kandahar, this duty was fairly tame—until the rats came out. Permanent residents of the warehouse, these rodents assumed the bagged and tagged ghostly skeletal tenants in the coolers were their new amusement or feast.

Jack wanted to set out traps. He thought it was disrespectful of what he called "his" people. He never considered himself a politically charged black man, but this detail to watch over the remains of these slaves brought out a racial pride and responsibility that Mac had never seen him display before now.

Mac didn't worry much about ancestry either. For a time, he fantasized about his people being descendants of the original Highlanders from the motion picture by the same name. Right now, he was more interested in money.

"Dude, every time we are on one of these assignments, I fall further behind in my bills," Mac complained over a couple of beers. The two were sitting in a booth across from the bar in Benoit's.

True to the name, Benoit's was dedicated to the legend of the ex-slave turned-pirate. There was a framed sketch of the man himself behind the bar. That was the only known likeness of Jolly Benoit in the United States. The rest of the walls were festooned posters and pictures of nineteenth century sailing ships, early map drawings of the village of Benoitown. From the front door, there were booths and tables to the left. To the right a long bar ran the length of the building. A raised stage with lightning was in the back.

"I thought your boss kept your job at the lumberyard while you were deployed," Jack said.

"Yeah, but he don't still pay me," Mac said sourly. "Man, I got bills up the ass, truck payments, child support, you name it."

"Nobody told you to buy the most expensive truck on the lot. I told you those payments were gonna be too much."

"I know. I know, but I thought I might go into business with my cousin doing power washing. I needed a truck to hold the tanks and shit."

"You and your cousin? In business?" Jack asked, almost spitting his beer out.

"Your cousin that's on house arrest now for selling weed?"

"Yeah, Jack, but this was before."

Jack just shook his head. They sat in silence watching ESPN on the television over the bar. Tony Kornheiser and Michael Wilbon were going on about something having to do with college football. Benoit's was about half full, the transition period between happy hour and the evening crowd. As one of the few places selling food late into the night, it was doing record-setting business with the army of out-of-town disaster response patrons.

"Hey, Jack?" Mac said.

"Yeah?"

"You think there's any more gold in them graves?"

Jack just shrugged still watching television, his lips moving slightly as he read the closed captioning.

"Man, it could be a fortune lying in that dirt."

Jack turned and looked at his friend now, his attention caught.

"Man, are you crazy? I know you ain't suggesting what I think you suggesting."

"But what if there is?" Mac continued. "Just hear me out, partner? If there's say ten more pieces of gold over in them graves, and we found three of them first. Well...."

"Well what, Mac?" Jack said, getting angry, not believing what he was hearing. He was giving Mac his Samuel L. Jackson stare, the actor everyone said Jack resembled when he was pissed.

"Well, three pieces of them gold coins would set me up. Get me outta the hole I'm in."

"No, Mac!" Jack was shaking his head emphatically. "We ain't messing with them graves. It ain't right. Besides, if we get caught it's a court-martial and jail."

"Shoot, Jack, how we gonna get caught? Them graves already a mess and just sitting there in the dark cold refrigeration units. You scared of them rats?"

"No ... well, maybe a little. But not as much as I'm afraid of them graves and Colonel Sanchez."

"Okay, I will do the digging and sifting. You just keep watch out like you doing."

Jack was quiet; he sipped his beer and watched television for a minute. This was how it started with them even when they were kids. Mac would have the idea. Jack would say no. Then he would just be quiet. Then....

"I promise we ain't gonna get caught if only me and you know about it. I sure as hell ain't telling, and I trust you, Jack. How is the colonel gonna find out?"

"Mac, you believe in God?" Jack asked, turning back to him with a solemn face.

"What?" Mac responded, not expecting the question.

"Look, there are just some things you don't do if you a decent person. I don't want to meet the souls of these poor people and have to explain to them why I disrespected their mortal remains looking for gold."

"Is this because they are black people?" Mac asked, feeling his power of persuasion slipping away.

"So what if it is," Jack snapped back. "I don't see you going around digging in white folks' graveyards looking for gold. The white man who started Gilleyville was with Jolly Benoit. There may be gold buried in the graveyard across the river. Go dig over there."

They sat in silence for a minute or two.

"Even if you did find some gold, how you gonna turn it into cash? You got to eventually sell it to somebody without getting arrested."

"Don't worry," Mac said, a wide smile on his face. "I already took care of that."

"You have?" Jack asked, his voice getting louder and his face full of suspicion. "How long you been working on this? My God, you been in them graves already, ain't you?"

"Sssshhh," Mac said, waving for Jack to lower his voice. "I may have poked around a bit, but nothing major. Truth be told, it's a lot more work than I realized."

"You been digging around in them bodies?" Jack said, sounding more amazed than mad.

"They ain't really bodies no more, Jack, mostly bone and bone pieces, some fragment here and there, and the smell." Jack just shook his head.

"It ain't no worse than what we saw our last two tours huntin' the boogie man in Baghdad."

"You know I don't like to talk about that stuff," Jack said, staring into the remains of his beer.

"I know, partner. I don't either, but me and you have been through some shit, and we come through it because we always stuck together. Mac and Jack." Jack smiled at that. He still liked being part of a dynamic duo. "Listen, Mac," Jack said in thought. "Three days."

"Okay," Mac said, working hard to hide his excitement.

"We search for three days. If we find something, we split it 50-50."

"Of course, partner. Like always."

"And we don't take it all. We leave something to be found."

"Yeah, I swear."

"And I want to meet your buyer. I wanna know who we dealing with here."

Mac nodded and casually averted his eyes across the expanse of the bar. He knew there was no way Jack would meet the buyer, but Mac would cross that bridge when he came to it. He spotted Arlene Perales sitting at the end of the bar almost in the shadows.

Arlene was one of the US Army forensic technicians assigned to this operation. She was beautiful and smart but somewhat quiet and sullen. When she did speak she was blunt and to the point. She was raised by a colonel frustrated that he was not able to make it to the top. Probably because at the wrong times he was blunt and to the point. She was the only woman on the forensic team working on the exposed remains and part of the shift that discovered the coins.

"Come on," Mac said, trying to shift emphasis but keep his momentum.

"Let's go talk to Arlene. She sitting all by herself."

"Nope," Jack said. "I'm good right here. That woman is mean."

"No, she ain't. Besides I heard she kind of likes you," Mac said with a charming smile and a conspiratorial nudge to Jack's side.

"No, she doesn't like me, but she does hate you. You tried to get in her pants the first week we were here," Jack said, laughing so hard he snorted beer from his nose.

"Just come on," Mac said, remembering the embarrassing "tell off" he got in front of his patrol.

Lieutenant Arlene Perales was sitting at the end of the bar trying to be invisible. The days were long and made even longer by the heat and the constant verbal attacks she received from the male forensics technicians. She was used to the latter, but this humidity and heat even at night was a killer.

She had been in the arid climate of Iraq and Afghanistan, but it didn't seem to have that smothering feeling that the American Southeast seemed to have. The important thing was for her to keep being focused on her mission and not the constant sweat running between her breasts and down the crack of her ass causing rashes in both areas.

At least it was quiet in the staging cooler room where the remains were preserved and readied for reinternment. Lieutenant Perales liked working with dead bodies. They were quiet and uncomplicated unlike talking bodies.

Momentarily glancing away from the television behind the bar, she jumped when two soldiers were up in her space grinning like infomercial actors. She remembered one from the first week they were there. He fancied himself a ladies' man in that corny, immature way you see in movies. She thought his buddy was all right, kind of tall, shy, and even cute, but he must not have much going for him because he was always with the jerk.

"Hey, Lieutenant, buy you a drink?" Mac started with too much confidence and volume in his voice.

"No, thanks, got one," she said and turned back to the television.

"So how things going on the dig out?" Mac asked.

"It's not a dig out, Corporal," Arlene said, not looking from the television.

"That's right, Mac. It's a reinternment," Jack corrected him.

"Exactly; your friend here read his briefing notes. And he's quiet," she said, still never turning from the television, hoping they would get the hint.

Mac motioned to Jack to ask the next question.

"Um, so Arlene, that was pretty exciting news about the gold, huh?" Jack said, sliding onto the barstool next to her. "I heard your team found it."

"Yep."

"Not to be morbid, but where exactly was it?" Jack asked carefully.

"And did anyone say how much they were worth?" Mack jumped in, getting impatient with Jack's pace of questions. He always ate when he was nervous. Jack and Arlene looked back at him. His face was full of husks and shells from peanuts, served free on the bar and tables. Jack just turned back to Arlene with an apologetic look on his face. Arlene downed the rest of her beer and stood up.

"Terry, right?" she asked, looking at Jack. He nodded. "Take my advice and find yourself a better set of friends. This one is a wreck waiting to happen." She patted Jack on the shoulder, glared at Mac as she slid past the two of them, and headed out the bar.

"What a bitch," Mac said loud enough for her to hear. Jack shushed him and motioned for him to sit down. "Well, she didn't have no right to talk about me like that, and we were just trying to have conversation."

"Why didn't you let me continue talking?" Jack asked. "You just have to take over everything."

"Well, I was right about one thing. She does kind of like you," Mac said, regaining his Tom Sawyer boyish demeanor. Jack told him to shut up   and   watch   the   game.

Chapter 7

Once I reached the Hillside Plantation Inn, a sprawling antebellum home with two twentieth-century extensions. When the main house was built, it was at the highest point in Benoitown. There is some discrepancy in the legend as to whether it was one of the homes built by the ex-pirate. It was now a boutique hotel run by an older man named Broyles, who had eight children, including two sets of twins. There were no non family employees. I said good-bye to Fedelito. I wanted to get unpacked and find Gerald to bring him up to speed.

In my room, I found two large FedEx boxes from WorldSpan. One box contained office equipment. The other one carried copies of standard agreements WorldSpan had with the financiers of Spain. There were also some identification badges on lanyards stating I was an agent for the Spanish embassy. I found my shredder and fed the badges into it.

There was also an envelope that had an old paperback entitled, *Jolly's Journal – Diary of a Black Pirate*. Published fifteen years ago by Geoffrey Paskiewicz. Inside the front cover was a note from Camille.

"My assistant ran across this in a used bookstore near the office. Hope that it helps. Be safe and save your very best for the one waiting for you at home."

Always Yours, Mila

I started calling her Mila during quiet afternoons lying on the sofa at her place reading and listening to play lists of her favorites and my favorites. She said no one ever called her that before, and she liked the sound of it coming from my mouth. No one else could use it, and I couldn't use it other than when we were alone.

I opened the pirate's biography. The cover had a version of the iconic drawing of Jolly Benoit done during his time as a free man of Haiti as a result of fighting with General Jean-Pierre Boyer, a disciple of Toussaint Louverture.

I thumbed through a few pages. It was written in a more Anglicized version of his actual speech. There was a passage explaining Jolly's original journal was written in Caribbean French patois, a language that was one-third English, one-third French, and one-third a mix of African tribal languages. Americans called it patois, but outside of the Caribbean American communities and some populations of Louisiana, very few in this country understood it. I came across a page that caught my interest.

Date: May 1845

Benoitown, NC

I continue to thank the God above and the spirits of forefathers and foremothers for the good fortune of our land enterprise. We have found fair-minded \ white people willing to do business with a free Negro and a poorly educated Irish person. For others, Sama Gilley and I pose as a white businessman and his manservant. Both of these roles are necessary at times but stretch our very beings.

The land we are purchasing is deemed not fit for crop production or hog raising because it floods so much. We will learn from the landowners in Haiti, Mexico, and the New Orleans along the Mississippi. We will use the earth to protect us from the water's rise and fall with the seasons. We will build our homes on higher material.

This may cost more, but we have time and money on our side.

Date: July 1846 Benoitown, NC Through my careful instruction, Sama Gilley has hired go-betweens to look into purchases of the slave family I lived within the Lankin Plantation before being kidnapped by pirates. We also made inquiries into the whereabouts of my blood family. My mother has been with the lord over five years ago now. My father was killed before I was taken. He escaped and fought with a slave capturer. One of them was going to die. The capturer had the pistol. I also have a younger sister and brother, twins. No one seems to know what happened to them. Our working story is that Sama Gilley, being a member of an Irish family of some means, was sent here to start a new life and business. Some talk has started about the source of the currency we are using. Rumors of gold have a way of bringing out the worst in people. I have seen this all over the world, son turn against father, brother against brother. We will have to be very careful in the future. For starters, we will convert a sizable portion of my gold to a bank in Baltimore in Maryland—a long and dangerous journey by small sailing ship and later by train. The majority of it still sits here close to me. I have volunteered to assist slave gravediggers. In this role, I have found respect from black and white settlers along the Tar River and garnered secret support from the slave population. If I am careful, I can get information from hundreds of miles away in a matter of weeks. In my communing with the slave dead, I have also found a resting place for my golden cargo within the sacred souls of my captured kindred. In my time on the seas, I have laughed and cried with the dead. I have laid among dead and dying men for days to evade my enemies in war on land and sea. I have embraced death as a friend, co-conspirator, and brother in all battles of life, and like a brother in arms, it cloaks my treasure under the murky dread, where no sane man dare trespass.

Chapter 8

How in the world did you get up here that fast?" Gerald Phillips asked his wife. Nadine Charleston-Phillips was breezy as she put her clothes away. She was staying in a spare bedroom at the residence of Reverend Curtyse Moten.

After calling her repeatedly on her cell phone, he had finally gotten a call from Mrs. Carrie Moten, giving him directions and an address. Gerald arrived at the house with a head full of steam. He was not a loud or violent man. As a matter of fact, he had made a reputation of being able to "unplug" his emotions from stressful situations.

Only two situations broke him out of his cool repose: his daughter Katie and his wife Nadine. They knew how to take him from zero to a hundred in seconds. Knowledge of this caused him to pause outside the Moten residence where the press was camped. There was no offstage time in this town. From the grave sites to the local ice cream parlor, everything had a news reporter presence or a social media footprint.

He drove around the corner, quickly walked down the paved alley that ran behind the Motens' home, hopped the fence into the backyard, and ripped the sleeve of his shirt on the top of the pickets. He knocked on the kitchen door feeling thoroughly undignified and out of his element— a leading international trade attorney hopping fences and skulking through alleys?

"Good evening, Counselor Phillips," Mrs. Moten said with a smooth Old World elegance. "Glad you could make it. Nadine will be happy to see you." Gerald mumbled standard polite responses under his breath. He thought he sounded like a shy schoolboy asking for a date. He admired the reverend's wife's ability to appear so cool and elegant with fifty members of the media camped outside her door.

By the time he got up the stairs to the bedroom in which Nadine was staying, he just wanted to take her in his arms, but she was busy unpacking her clothes with her back to him. He said hello, expecting her to come to him.

She simply kept hanging her clothes and said, "Good evening."

That pissed him off all over again. Hence his question about her speed in travel.

"I don't know. I just called the airline direct and got lucky," she explained.

"Oh, you called Tremaine," Gerald said. "He got you on one of his hookup flights." She didn't answer, and he knew he was right.

Tremaine worked at Jacksonville International Airport. No one was sure what he did exactly. Whatever he did allowed him to do favors for friends even in post 9-11 air travel. Tremaine was what was known as a "play" cousin. That meant he was a child of a family friend whose kids played with your kids so much that they became as close as blood relatives. Gerald liked Tremaine but never trusted him and his hookups. Nadine was able to separate the man from what he did; Gerald was not as trusting.

"Doesn't matter. I'm here now," Nadine said while she kept unpacking her clothes.

Gerald noticed her skin seemed extra shiny. He was shiny but from sweat. Nadine seemed shiny but cool. He focused on her skin. She had glitter on her skin. He remembered the shimmering lotion she used when they went out that made her skin even more beautiful than it already was. He was no fool.

He understood at that very moment that she had not only come here, showered and changed, but had also put on one of his favorite dresses, put on her favorite special night-out lotion with no plans to go out. It was for him, and despite the cold shoulder, he could not help but be moved by it.

He knew she was taking him through the paces that women do to men who love them, but he did not care. He sat on the bed and after a few minutes of watching her move from her suitcase to the closet, he lay back on the bed.

"You smell good," he said, watching her.

"You can't smell anything from there," she answered, not stopping her unpacking.

"Woman, I know Dolce and Gabbana when I smell it. That's your scent. Or do I owe my compliment to Mrs. Moten?"

She stopped in mid motion, paused for a minute, then turned and leapt on the bed where he laid. She landed a few feet away, but Gerald didn't care. He grabbed her on her sides, hoisting her off the bed and easing her onto his lap. They kissed as if they had not seen each other in a month. Nadine loved this moment, crediting it to the magic of their relationship. Gerald loved the moment, crediting it to her and the black magic this woman held over him. At that moment as they held each other, they couldn't feel anything but gratitude for the experience of each other.

"I know you're mad at me?" she asked about an hour later as they lay naked and spent on top of the bed and clothes with the light still on in the bedroom. If the Mrs. Reverend Moten had peeked in over the last 60 minutes, it would have been a true test of her Christian sensibilities. Gerald was drowsy but was brought to attention by her question.

"I should be," he said in a post-coitus mellow. "We got to talk. That TV interview? I mean. What is it you're trying to do here?"

"I was thinking about this—this whole situation. For days now," Nadine started, laying on her back staring up at the ceiling fan moving at medium speed. It let out a low motor noise that sounded like the buzz of a bee. "I think more attention needs to be paid to this situation, and despite what you think, I did grow up in this state. These are my people."

"Nadine, you wouldn't even know about this if not for me and Facebook."

"And so ... that's the good thing about social media. Things that need attention can get it."

"Okay, but you gotta know now you have set off a firestorm. You are a media figure. Folks are going to start trying to find out who you are, what you are, everything about you. Are you ready for that?"

"I don't know."

"Well, it's too late now," Gerald said, more stern than he meant to do. "Besides, this is going to mean a certain amount of heat for me as well."

"So because you and WorldSpan are involved, nobody else in the Charleston-Phillips family can have their own opinion?"

"No, and since when did you start hyphenating?"

"Don't get off the subject. The reverend said that was good for television. Charleston is a good place name for the Carolinas."

"Yeah. South Carolina. I noticed you only hyphenate your name when you're pissed at me."

"And so...."

"So, I can't help but wonder if this is about the poor lost souls of the past, or is it about you being pissed at me. Now you got yourself caught up in the thick of things."

"Oh," she said repeatedly, quickly rising from the bed, finding her ivory silk robe, and throwing it on and tying the sash. "Now I am the unsophisticated being used by...."

"That's not what I'm saying," Gerald said, sitting up now, realizing he had gone too far. "Nadine, honey, these media things are tricky. I have been involved with them plenty of times."

"So has the reverend and his staff," she replied quickly, looking off into space, her arms folded.

"I am sure he is, but what about you?"

"All I want to do is keep the remains of these old souls in the minds of Americans so they are preserved and reinterred properly. If the country wants to judge me for that, so be it. That includes you and WorldSpan Secure."

"Listen, I'm not trying to fight with you," he said, sitting up still naked but sensing the lovemaking sequel slipping away. "I'm trying to get you to understand what you have walked into here."

"I'm sure you do," she said, still clearly upset. "But do you fully realize what you have walked into here? I don't think any of us do. There is the government, foreign and domestic, the insurance companies, the fortune hunters, the historians, and lookie-loos. Then there are the people who were here before the hurricane and will be here once the news cameras leave, and the uninterred dead. I want to stand on that side."

"Well," Gerald said, standing up, finding his clothes and starting to dress.

"I have a job to do, and I intend to do it."

"Sorry if my being here makes it harder for you."

"No you're not, but that's okay. I will get done what I need to have done. WorldSpan has no intention of desecrating the graves of dead slaves. I would never be a part of that."

"Like you said, my love, it's hard to understand what we have walked into here. This country has a horrid and shameful history where gold is involved."

"I know my history as well as you do, wife," Gerald said and hurriedly dressed, slipping into his shoes. "At the end of the day, I only want one thing: for you and I to come out of this safe and sound."

He walked over to where she sat in the chair now, leaned down and kissed her at the corner of her mouth. She didn't turn her face to him.

"I love you," he mumbled in her ear.

"Take care of yourself," she answered back, thinking somehow that was a more genuine thing to say at that time.

Gerald straightened and walked out of the bedroom.

Chapter 9

Later that night, Lieutenant Arlene J. Perales lay in bed in a foul mood. She had to admit it wasn't just the heat or the two clowns that disturbed her at the bar. She finally climbed out and quickly dressed in the hotel mirror. She pulled her curly brown hair away from her small beautiful face. She would have bags under eyes by morning, but she would get no sleep tonight.

Walking down the dark streets of Benoitown—rendered deserted by curfew—she was barely aware of the surroundings. There were a few of the gas lanterns working showing the quaint southern downtown of a historic village. The ancient oak trees heavy with moss cast long shadows in the flickering light. The brick-front southern river city architecture loomed on either side. All of them were dark save for the few bars and restaurants whose owners were brave and resourceful enough to reopen so soon after the storm. There was no other darkness than that in the wake of nature's wrath. The air smelled of jasmine and sour water. Voices and footsteps in the distance echoed off the walls of the narrow streets.

Arlene was bothered by the gold. As a US Army brat, she spent time all over the world, including the desert southwest. US. Military kids, it seemed, were kept busy by either sports or educational events.

"Nothing good comes from kids sitting around doing nothing," her mother would say. Her father was the military man, but her mother had adopted all the working rules of an infantry squad leader into her home.

Therefore, as a kid she spent her fair share of time in museums, old ruins, and exhibitions. She had visited the dusty defunct gold mines in Arizona and Nevada where all the prospectors for the year only extracted about eight ounces of gold, not even enough to keep the tourist trap open to the public without a yearly grant from the US Department of Parks and Recreation. It had been exciting as a kid working all afternoon in makeshift sloughs to find two-tenths of an ounce of real gold dust. Not worth much in dollars and sense, but priceless to a young female prospector. The memory of those experiences made her laugh, made her think.

She was no expert, but there was something about this gold that didn't seem right to her. It was tested for authenticity. Historians had even given their stamp of approval, but historians had been fooled before. She couldn't put her hand on the specific thing but something in her gut said this was off, and long ago she had learned to trust her gut before evidence proved her right.

It was a game people played with themselves. They do things but won't admit it to themselves. For instance, they will say they are taking a walk in the night to clear their head when they know they are inside the cold storage room of ghostly remains to seek answers that eluded them at daytime. Entering the warehouse, she used her pin light. There was supposed to be a sentry here around the clock.

She would speak to someone about this in the morning. Of course, absence of a guard alleviated her need to come up with an excuse for returning to the cold storage. She stood in the middle of the room, the pin light pointed to the floor, listening for any sounds. She heard none save for the ticks, tocks, creaks, and taps that old buildings make as they defy time with their very existence. And of course there was the sound of the rats.

After a few more seconds, she moved to the staging hold. It was cold; refrigeration kept the remains between 39 and 43 degrees. She turned on the directional mercury vapor light that couldn't be seen from outside. There were twenty stainless steel tables similar to those found in a coroner's examination lab. On each table were mounds of earth held together by the jagged remains of the dead.

When the floodwater uprooted the graves, they were mixed together, some washed out with the floodwaters as they receded down the Tar River back into the ocean. Arlene was a woman of science. She knew, from science, that those bones would quickly disintegrate in the brackish tidewater of the Carolina coast. She was also a product of a staunchly Catholic grandmother. She could hear her abuela Natalia in her head saying that the storm had come to return those remains, souls and all, back to Africa. Back home where they belonged.

Funny how she spent hours with hundreds of deadly remains but very seldom, like on this assignment, did she wonder about such spiritual things. Forensic science work forced her to face the history and the brutality of slave life in early America. She found multiple remains, seemingly thrown together by floodwater. Later, it was determined to be whole families buried together in one grave. What could have happened to kill an entire family—mother, father, and children—at one time?

There were mothers buried holding infant children. Arlene assumed both died in childbirth. There was an alarming number of children of all ages. There was an even larger number of remains with evidence of chronic deformities. There were poorly healed broken bones, deteriorated joints on relatively young bodies at the time of death, evidence of polio, spinal scoliosis, and the ravages of untreated venereal disease on people no more than twenty-five at the time of death. For every stereotype of the strong black slave able to withstand oppression of hundreds of years, there seemed to be at least a hundred of poor unfortunate souls who suffered shockingly short lives racked with what must have been mind-numbing pain. Who was the stronger? Arlene was no longer sure.

She also wasn't sure what she was looking for here. The day the gold and the cabinet were found, the forensic team was combing through a particular massive mound of remains. The bone fragments, feathery and thin, dated more than 200 years old. It was impossible to tell what or who was what. There were fragments from handmade crude caskets. Then in the middle of this mound of soil, rock, bone, and wood lay three glittery coins lying next to a broken wooden box. It was found by the group at the same time. On some level, this did not make sense.

There was a small digital video camera on a tripod pointed towards the 8'×8'×3' mound of remains. All excavations were videotaped. As with all her investigations, Arlene pulled her digital recorder from her pocket and hung it around her neck using a US Army green lanyard. Repeating her morning ritual now in the middle of the night, she took a deep breath, pressed the record button and stated to talk. Initially she identified herself and the date and time of the recording. She placed latex gloves on her hands and picked up the stainless steel instruments. They resembled small gardening tools but were more refined. They were usually tools for crime scene investigations, and they proved useful for delicately working through the soil. Arlene continued her narrative as she worked.

"Objects like the coins in question were usually found by one person first, not at the same time by an entire team. Secondly, the level of aged soil patina on one coin seems inconsistent with the other. We assume the objects were placed

in the ground at the same time. Thirdly when reviewing the history of the legend......"

She stopped talking suddenly. It was that feeling again that things weren't 'right.' The mound had been disturbed, and she said so.

When forensics finished a sample for the day, it was done in a certain way. You didn't just leave the mounds half dug. You prepared the dig for the next day to preserve evidence and ensure against tampering.

She looked around to see if any of the other mounds had been touched. She began walking around and between the tables, carefully examining the mounds but not touching them too much. Panic set into her. Continuing to move among the tables, she told herself to calm down.

"Be systematic, scientific, observe," her inner scientist urged her against her growing dread.

She took a step, and something crunched under her foot. She stopped instantly, reversed her step, knelt down, picked up the object she felt. Before she could register what it was, her head was pulled back violently, and she was forced forward to the stone floor.

She landed hard on her front, banging her chin and biting her tongue. She tried turning her head but the man behind and above her held her head firm. She could tell it was a man by his weight and smell. She kicked and yelled out twice. Maybe the patrol came back around. Then as she tasted the blood in her mouth, she felt the bag go over her head. A plastic bag. He was going to suffocate her. She panicked, struggling to free her hands, twist her hips, anything to get a purchase and buy her some precious time before she ran out of air.

In her panic, she became aware of minute things, the scratching of her uniform against her skin, and cold of the floor tile against her face. She was sweating, and the plastic bag began to stick to her face. God, she had to focus. Terror gripped her to her core, sending tremors that made her body shake. Her wits were laser sharp. Through the bag, she thought she could make out her reflection in the stainless steel legs of the examination tables, her face small, soft, and warped with panic with the knowledge of her slow but definite suffocation. She did not have much time.

She let her body go limp as if succumbing to asphyxiation, her mind's voice screaming for her to stay calm despite the waves of panic washing through her. She took short staccato breaths like an asthma patient in the throes of an attack. Then she felt him ease up just slightly. His weight was growing lighter against her back, his knee pulling away from between her legs. It was now or never.

She went to a spot deep in her core—focusing because she would only get one chance at this; if it didn't work, she would not have enough air or will to fight any longer. The malaise of losing consciousness crept into her mind telling her to let it wash over her.

Then her mind filled with the words—*Go, go, go! Go!*

She pivoted and rolled her hips and torso from her right to her left with all her might. Her arms still pinned kept her from moving much, but she did not need much. He grunted from surprise, realizing she had been playing possum, but before he could regain full purchase over her body, she had enough room now to spread her legs further apart. Her head swooned, and her vision was blurred. She felt blood in her hair and on her face mixing with her sweat inside the bag. She was going out.

She propped her right foot against one of the lower legs of one of the tables nearby. She pushed off from the leg, and she rolled back until she was on top of him. His hands popped free of their grip on her arms.

Instinctively she pushed herself up to a crouch and began tearing at the bag over her face. The stale cold air felt like being born. Still not able to see clearly and coughing violently, she heard the man scrambling to his feet somewhere behind her. She turned and stepped into a strong front kick in his direction. She felt her foot contact his ribs and heard the air come out of him like a Whoosh. Breathing hard and still half blind with sweat, blood, relief, and fatigue, she moved around the lab. She darted in around the tables, bumping and banging on edges. She had to keep moving until her sight cleared.

He can't hold you if you keep moving, she thought through her frantic mental state.

After a few more seconds, she realized that she had some sight. She stopped, blinked, and looked around. No one was there. She staggered to the cold storage lab door and opened it. There was an alarm button at the opening that would silently alarm the MPs on sentry. She slammed her fist against the large red button.

She tried to scream for help now that she was where someone could hear her. She opened her mouth and coughed convulsively. She took in a deep breath and coughed some more. As she bent over to compose herself, she felt a searing pain in her back and blinding pain shoot throughout her body. She turned around to see who or what it was. A man or so she thought. Running away. Back into the lab. He can't get away, but she felt her arms and legs go limp. She fell to her knees and arched her back against the wall. Whatever he used was still in her back. She rubbed her back against the wall feebly trying to bang the knife free. The pain made her cry out and cough up bubbles of blood.

Chapter 10

I was still on Paris time so I woke up at 4:00 AM wide awake. By 6:00 AM I was stretched, exercised, dressed, and debriefed by two of Camille's minions via video conference.

As I came downstairs for coffee, it seemed a lot of activity for this time of morning even for free food. My phone buzzed telling me I had a text. It was from the sheriff.

"Please come to the Tar River Sugar House ASAP with your business partners. There has been an incident that requires discretion but is important to our business."

"You got the same text I did," Gerald Phillips said. He had come up behind me holding his phone screen up showing the message.

"Let's get Gaspare and head over," I said, feeling a dread deep in my stomach.

"He's not answering," Gerald said. "I called him and knocked on his door."

"Where the hell is he?" I asked to no one in particular. I tried his cell phone one more time. I even had the front desk call his room. No answer.

We struck out for the Tar River Sugar House. The street wasn't filled, but the few people on the street seemed to pay a lot of attention to Gerald and me as we moved down the street.

We met Val Cedars and his small posse of historical geeks starchily pressed and looking grim. They gave a nod but did not speak. Tar River Sugar House was the ancient building where the disturbed remains were stored against further decay and preparation for reburial.

The old warehouse was dark and smelled of soil and death. It felt ten degrees colder than outside. Now there were Guardsmen standing around the perimeter of the room watching everyone going in and out.

"Manion—over here!" Sheriff Cormac called from the back of the structure. "Let 'em in, Corporal!"

A large well-armed soldier about my height and a serious face of stone waved us in and pointed to the back of the room. At the rear was an apportioned room built within the structure. We soon learned it was the cooler area where the remains were preserved. Cormac, Adam Samuelson, and Colonel Sanchez were in the room. There were mounds of remains mixed with earth sitting on massive tables eight feet by eight feet. On the floor inside one of the coolers leaning against the wall near the door was a body—a woman in fatigues but wearing a white exam coat and latex gloves.

I looked closer and realized it was the quiet, bookishly beautiful Lieutenant Perales. She was still very fit, very attractive, but very dead. She had the remains of a plastic bag around her neck and a large military knife in her back, only the handle showing from between her shoulder blades. It was the third dead body I had ever seen and the second murdered young beautiful woman I had seen in the last year. Flashbacks of a bloody freezer on White Sand Island, Florida, began to crowd my mind, but I forced it down. The dead soldier's back, legs, and the floor all around her were covered with dried blood.

"I can give some preliminary report outs—Sheriff?" a short round man said. He was in a full hazmat suit and latex shoe covers. He worked a digital camera around his neck. He was about 5'6" with a Danny DeVito body, but he had striking good looks and perfect coiffed white hair. He had alert blue eyes and skin that obviously received ample dermabrasions and pampering. His accent was classic North Carolina.

"This is Dr. Butto. He's the county coroner and criminal forensic specialist for the area," Sheriff Cormac explained. We made quick introductions. "Go ahead, Brady. We're all listening."

"Well, seems to have been dead about eight hours, putting her here at about midnight."

"I don't understand, Colonel" Sheriff Cormac started. "You all don't go into the night like that, do you?"

Colonel Sanchez shook her head. Butto continued.

"There was obviously a scuffle—tables in disarray, one knocked over. There's a broken tripod as well. We did a preliminary search of her body. We found her identification, a small amount of cash, credit cards, and couple of receipts, one from the local souvenir gift shop and one from Benoit's timestamped about 10:40 PM. We also found peanut shells." "In her pockets?" I asked.

"No—stuck on the bottom of her shoes and in a few places on the floor.

They serve free peanuts at Benoit's," Butto explained.

"Perales would not have brought food into the exam room," Colonel Sanchez said emphatically.

"Somebody did, and that person must have been at Benoit's," I said. "I see

Guards all around; any around last night?"

"Should have been," Colonel Sanchez said. "The MP captain is working on that now."

"The knife what killed her, Brady?" Sheriff Cormac asked.

"Probably by the amount of blood. Knife is Italian military—Fox C70 Carbon steel blade, but there's plenty of military surplus stores carrying similar knives as this. Somebody also tried to suffocate this poor girl. She has some evidence of asphyxia around the eyes and lips."

"What about DNA from her attacker?" Sheriff Cormac asked.

"Maybe some, but too soon to tell. She had gloves on, so not much under her nails."

"How can you rule out DNA from all the dead bodies in here?" I asked hopefully.

"Based on the source of the DNA sample, blood, hair, skin, etc., we can differentiate crime-sensitive DNA from that of the unearthed remains."

"We'll know for sure once we get her back to my lab?"

"Wait a minute," Colonel Sanchez said. "I can't let you take custody. This is a military officer."

"You don't have a choice, Colonel," Brady Butto said, showing the first cracks in his Southern charisma. "You don't have any place to hold her or conduct a proper criminal autopsy. Also, this is not a time of war—which puts this body in my jurisdiction."

"Perhaps, Colonel, we can send one of your assistants with Dr. Butto?" I jumped in, sensing this was going nowhere. There was nothing to be done about poor Arlene Perales, but I didn't want her to be treated with the further indignity of a jurisdictional debate. "I'm sure Dr. Butto wouldn't mind one of the Guards accompanying the body."

Dr. Butto started to protest, but the sheriff raised a hand. "Manion, I think that's a good idea. Brady, can we get this poor soul out of here?"

"Of course, we can," the coroner replied recovering his antebellum calm.

"Colonel?"

Colonel Sanchez nodded. She signaled to a couple of her forensic technicians. Butto did the same to members of his staff. They surrounded the body of Lieutenant Arlene Perales. I heard the strangest sound, like a large boot being pulled from this mud, a kind of sucking and then a pop. One of the techs carried the knife that was in her back over to a plastic evidence bag on a nearby table. That same technician retrieved the black military body bag and brought it over to the other techs. They had Perales lying flat on her back. I saw Colonel Sanchez cross herself while her facial expression stayed resolute stone.

She looked peaceful. When they zipped the black bag on her face, I thought it was strange that I felt an emptiness inside that said it was the last time I would see her. I tried to remember her voice. I didn't know the lieutenant, only met her once. Then she was on a gurney and gone.

"I have an update," a soldier said, walking up to our circle. It was the same soldier who let Gerald and me into the building. He introduced himself as the patrol leader of the night guard.

"The night sentry consisted of one Guard. At approximately 10:00 PM, he was approached by one of the day guards, who engaged him in conversation. They were at the back of the building and coming around to the front. He offered him a cigarette, and he accepted. Things were slow, so there would be no harm. He wasn't worried too much because the front door was locked. A few minutes after the guy left, the Guard got drowsy, light-headed. He must have gone out for some time. It must have been something in the cigarettes." "Who was this soldier?" Sheriff Cormac asked.

"The Guard wasn't sure but we can find out soon enough," the Captain of the Guard said.

"Good; we all need to talk to this friendly soldier with the funny cigarettes," Sheriff Cormac said.

"Wait a minute," I asked, moving back to the rest of the scene. "You said there was a tripod. Is there a camera?"

"Yes," Colonel Sanchez replied. "The forensic work is recorded. The camera is focused at the point of the dig, not the technician. The video is recorded on the camera and simultaneously to a cloud account. We will retrieve it and see if we can find anything. There should have been a digital voice recorder, but I guess it was taken with the camera."

"Is the audio on that video feed to the cloud?" I asked hopefully. Sanchez shook her head no.

"What about those receipts?" Cormac started. "She was at Benoit's last night. Maybe someone saw something. I'll start there while we wait to hear about this mystery soldier and the video feed."

"I will go with you," I said to Cormac. "Gerald, why don't you go with

Colonel Sanchez and the deputies to view the video and see what we can find?" "Right," my partner said, all business now.

"I guess it's okay at this point," Sheriff Cormac said. "However, this is a police investigation, so at some point I may need to shut you out." "We appreciate the trust," I said.

"I don't trust anyone like that, Manion," Sheriff Cormac said with a scoff. "I confirmed your whereabouts during the time of the murders through independent sources. Yours too, Mr. Phillips."

"Oh, the hotel staff," I said sheepishly.

"Couldn't say the same for your Spanish embassy friend, which is why he is waiting outside with Val Cedars and his sweater vest posse."

"I see," I said, wondering about Gaspare's whereabouts myself.

"Besides, I think it makes sense to give you all something to do while attaching one of my deputies to you, so I can keep my eye on you."

"But you only have a few deputies," Gerald said. "They can't watch everybody."

"Don't need to watch everybody. I only started getting dead bodies when you three showed up."

The air felt sweet as we stepped out onto the public street. Val Cedars and his historians and Fedelito Gaspare walked up purposely stopping the sheriff, Coroner Butto, Colonel Sanchez, Gerald, and me as we crossed to the street. "Is it true, Sheriff?" Val asked. "One of the soldiers?"

"There was a death, Val. We will make a statement later," the sheriff said as he kept walking.

"But why were we kept from the scene?" Gaspare asked. "There may have been something of importance to the claim of the Country of Spain."

"If there were, Mr. Manion was there to protect your interest."

"Mr. Manion works for me!" Gaspare shouted. "I demand to be included." Sheriff Cormac looked at me. I gave him a look of understanding.

"Fedelito, it's okay. Gerald can use your help," I said.

Gerald patted Fedelito on the shoulder and motioned for him to follow him, Colonel Sanchez, and Adam Samuelson.

"Get you filthy hands off me," Fedelito said, staring at Gerald with deadly venom in his eyes. "I will decide where I go. I will be reporting all this to my superiors in Washington, DC, and Madrid."

"You do that, Señor," Sheriff Cormac said, turning to continue walking.

"Was there any more gold found?" Fedelito Gaspare asked out loud. Those around him looked on with outward shock and disgust, but staying silent.

I thought for sure Gerald, Fedelito, and I would be placed under arrest or run out of town.

"Señor Gaspare, you are treading on thin ice now. Be very careful," Sheriff Cormac said and turned to leave. I followed behind him. Gerald waved me on, as Fedelito Gaspare walked off in the opposite direction.

Chapter 11

Sheriff Cormac drove his unmarked vehicle; I sat in the passenger seat. The Captain of the Guard sat in the back. It was just shy of 10:00 AM. As we arrived at Benoit's Bar, it was still closed. However, I could see people working inside. We parked and walked up the front door. Benoit's sat on the corner of Third and Main Streets.

The local character Baliles was holding court on the side of the building. He was tall, about six and a half feet. His ruddy skin was obscured by matted fuzzy brown hair, and he wore an old brown suit made of a course weave similar to suits of the 19th century. He was talking to a group of locals, making wild hand gestures. His voice came in shouts and long lulls. He seemed excited but not angry. I was still not sure what he was—a street historian, a healer, or an unfortunate homeless man with a challenged mental capacity and a possible drinking problem.

Just then Angela Babineaux opened the door. She had clearly been working. Her Pabst Blue Ribbon t-shirt had streaks of dirt on the front of it. She wore dark blue jeans that started just above her hips and stopped above her ankles. She had a Benoit's apron around her waist. Just like before, she was a bubble of spirit and energy somewhere between a sexy softball shortstop and a girl-nextdoor who hasn't realized the power in her smile or her snug-fitting clothing. "Sheriff and the Insurance Man!" she said, standing in the threshold each foot against the opening. She was wearing deck shoes with "Freak" written on one and "Flag" written on the other. This cannot be good.

"You only one in this morning, Angela?" Sheriff Cormac asked. "Yep."

"We need to talk to you about last night. You here yesterday?"

"Nope, had a singing gig over in Gilleyville."

"Who was working between…," the sheriff paused to look at the receipt in a paper, ventilated bag, "nine o'clock and midnight?"

"Umm, I don't know," Angela said, suddenly much less sure of herself. "I don't do the schedule, man."

"Angela, was it her?" the sheriff asked, getting agitated.

"I said I don't know," Angela answered, more of the girl-next-door now, less of the confident ball player.

Sheriff Cormac cursed under his breath and stepped away from the front door. He pulled his communicator out and appeared to be requesting additional deputy assistance, leaving Angela and me alone.

"By the way, Tekelius, I appreciate you speaking to the Spanish Conquistador about my fee," she said and lightly punched me in the arm. "Gaspare paid you?" She nodded.

"I figured that was the source of the tension on the boat yesterday. You good now?"

She nodded.

"So I don't know what this is about," I started, stepping up to the stoop to be even with her. "We got a dead body down the street. A soldier. She was here last night…."

"She?"

"Yeah, one of the forensics working with the graves. We really need to speak to whoever was working last night."

"We, she…," she started to ask but stopped on the verb trying to negotiate around her shock and fears in mixed company. She had a light sheen of sweat on her skin but smelled of a light perfume, ivory soap and Lysol anti-bacterial cleaner. For the first time I noticed the network of freckles across her face.

"No, she wasn't sexually assaulted as far as I know, but it was bad nevertheless," I explained.

"As opposed to a good death," she said, looking to the floor as if she were deep in thought.

We stood there in silence for another minute or two until Sheriff Cormac walked back from the street.

"My deputy is on his way," Sheriff Cormac said, clearly irritated. "Now where is she?"

Seconds later Angela led us past the bar and around the right side of the stage. Benoit's had that eerie quiet of a place that is usually raucous and loud with televisions going constantly. Angela took the sheriff and me behind the stage in the back. There was a large space used for storage, the rear door to the alley behind the building, a door that read bathrooms and a set of steel open riser stairs leading up to the rear second floor. As we ascended up the narrow case, I could see a set of three doors.

"How long she been here?" Sheriff Cormac asked.

"I don't know, Sheriff," Angela said. "She comes and goes. You know that." "I don't know that, because she doesn't talk to me."

"Who are we talking about here?" I asked, willing to risk being rude at this point.

Angela stopped in front of the last door in the row. She knocked. No answer. She knocked harder. Someone mumbled from behind the door. There was the sound of shuffling and more talk. Just then the door opened, and a small female head peaked out.

"Hey, Frannie, sorry to disturb you, but the sheriff is here," Angela said apologetically.

"Wha ... oh," the girl said. At the sound of the word "Sheriff," she seemed to come out of her stupor.

"Hey," she said and gave a wave at Sheriff Cormac from behind the door. Her hair was all over her head but looked like it had been that way much longer than last night.

"You worked last night?" Sheriff Cormac asked sternly. The girl nodded.

"That rat bastard in there with you?" he asked.

Just then the door was opened quickly by a skinny smelly guy in his midtwenties. His hair was as bad as hers. His clothes were as much dirty as they were old. He didn't appear homeless as much as he seemed just sloppy and nasty. The smell of body odor, cheap marijuana, and sex wafted into the hall surrounding the group.

"No problem here, Sheriff. Just needed a place to crash. I'm gone!" he said and dashed down the narrow hall. Angela pressed herself against the wall to avoid contact with the foul acrid-smelling boy. He took the steps three at a time, never looking back.

We turned back to the small unkempt girl behind the door. I could now see it was a studio apartment. She managed a Benoit's t-shirt over the top of her body, but felt comfortable standing in front of strangers in her underwear. Sheriff Cormac stepped inside the room. Angela and I stepped in behind him. The sheriff and the girl just looked at each other, him very stern and her like an unaware woodland creature. He looked around quickly checking the bathroom, closets, and kitchen cabinets.

"Get dressed. My deputies want to talk to you downstairs," he said and walked out of the room.

"Yes, Dad," the girl said.

~ ~ ~

Angela and I decided to wait downstairs. The sheriff asked her to get the security footage from last night. I noticed there was a second squad car in front of Benoit's. The smelly bedmate was sitting in the backseat, handcuffed and sullen. There was some awkward silence as the sheriff, his deputy, and I stood at the bar waiting.

"That's my middle kid, Francina A. She was the smartest out of all three. Then she went off to college and got lost. I thought bringing her down here would get her away from the bad element," he said with a sigh. "I guess the bad element is in her."

A man like the sheriff didn't want conciliatory words from his friends, less known a stranger. He was a lawman and a man of integrity trying to negotiate an embarrassing tricky situation without losing it. I made a sound like a grunt and mumbled under my breath.

Francina A. Cormac came bounding down the steps like a teenager on a spring Saturday. Before the sheriff saw his daughter, a female deputy stepped forward and gently guided her by her arm to a corner of Benoit's to start the interview.

"I stopped telling her mother how many times I would run into her like this," Sheriff Cormac started again.

"Probably a smart thing to do," I said. He looked at me with an expression I couldn't read, something between surprise and agitation.

Just then Angela emerged from the offices with a laptop. She set it down on the bar. Three of us looked at the screen. The view was separated into four smaller screens.

"This is the footage from last night," Angela said.

"You have it stored digitally?" I asked.

"Yep," she said. "The bar went high tech about five years ago. "
"That date stamp? That get put on by the system?" Sheriff Cormac asked.

"As far as I know," Angela said.

"Let's get to that time of night that Lieutenant Perales was there," Sheriff Cormac asked, all business again.

Angela did a couple of mouse clicks, the footage moved forward and buffered. Sheriff Cormac motioned to the female deputy to bring his daughter over to the bar.

"Frannie was working the bar last night at the time in question," the deputy said. "She remembers the victim from her picture."

"Okay, roll the footage," Sheriff Cormac ordered. Angela made a couple of mouse clicks. All four screens came to life. No sound, but video footage of last night's activity. One screen was of the outside exterior. Two screens were of the seating area in the front and in the rear near the stage. The last screen showed the bar from behind the bartender looking out. Patrons at the front of the bar could be seen clearly. Those on the side rails of the bar were in shadow, but depending on how they moved you could still make them out.

"Okay, tell the Sheriff what you told me, honey," the female deputy said to Francina in a motherly voice.

"I was working the bar last night. The lady was on the left. I think."
"Your left or the patron's left?" Sheriff Cormac asked.

"Huh? What?" Francina answered, showing an old familiar flustering and frustration, borne out of many mismatched conversations between her and her lawman father.

"Just think," the female deputy started to explain using hand gestures. "When you were working and looking out past the bar, was she on your left or right?"

"Oh," Francina said with a confidence that broke through her sleepy, drug induced fog. She looked at the sheriff with relief. "My left."

I looked at the shadowy figures to that part of the bar. In a few seconds she leaned to the right for her glass.

"That's her," I said out loud to no one in particular.

We watched in silence as Lieutenant Perales sat there consuming her drink and looking at no one in particular. I thought that was odd, a woman at the bar by herself, talking to no one, not watching television or working her phone, just sitting and drinking looking straight ahead not left or right.

"Oh, yeah, I remember these two," Francina said pointing to the screen.

Two enlisted men, one black, one white, approached the Lieutenant and seemed to be conversing with her. They seemed to be having a good time, but Lieutenant Perales did not seem to pay much attention to them. After maybe a minute or two of conversation, she got up and left the bar. The two men seemed to have a brief agitated conversation.

"Do you know who those men were?" the deputy asked.

"Duh, they're soldiers? Working here on the flood?" Francina said in a sarcastic tone.

The sheriff made a slight motion towards her and started to speak. The deputy made a halting motion with her hand. Angela made a noticeable flinch.

"Francina, do you know the men's names? Were they regulars?" "Oh, don't know their names, but they come in a lot." "Always together?" Sheriff Cormac asked.

"Uh-huh," Francina said with a nod.

"This is very important. The lady at the bar, the lieutenant—she's dead," Sheriff Cormac explained.

Francina showed the first signs of being truly alert and awake. She stared down at her shoes.

"Did they do it, the guys in the video?" she asked.

"Don't know, but did you get a chance to hear what they were talking about?" Sheriff Cormac asked.

"No," she said, tears filling her eyes.

"Think carefully, Frannie," Angela said, reversing the video. "See here on the video stream, you walk near them several times during the time they were talking. Maybe you heard something."

Francina watched the video and continued to tear up. I wasn't sure if she even heard Angela's question.

"Were you even sober last night?" the Sheriff asked, his voice full of recrimination.

"Yes," Francina said sullenly.

"You didn't seem like it based on how you look now," Sheriff Cormac said.

"I had a little something after work," she said defiantly.

"Well, did you hear anything or not?" Sheriff Cormac prodded.

Francina started rocking slowly while her tear-filled eyes stared ahead.

"I…," she started and stopped. "I think . . ."

Even Cormac kept his impatience at bay, the cop in him knowing its best to keep quiet when someone is struggling with critical information. We waited another almost 30 seconds of stops and starts.

"Yes, so okay, I didn't hear everything, right? But I kind of heard some things," Francina said, holding up one small dirty hand with broken, cracked, half-painted nails. "The black guy was trying to make conver-sation. She, the lady soldier, was ignoring him, giving him one-word answers."

"Okay," the deputy said. "What else?"

"Then the other soldier, the white guy, said something to her, and that was when she left. She just threw down some money and left. I remember that because it was the biggest tip of the night."

"What did the white guy say?" Sheriff Cormac asked.

"I don't know," Francina said with a finality. Everyone looked at her wondering the same thing. Sheriff Cormac asked the question.

"How do you know he talked but not know what he said?"

Francina thought for a few seconds, her bloodshot mascara-stained eyes looking up to the ceiling as if she were trying to gather her words. She looked at Angela and pointed to the computer.

"Rewind it just a bit, just before she got up to leave."

Angela complied and made a few mouse clicks. The video rewound at about two times the speed.

"There! Stop there," Francina said, pointing with the same filthy appendage. "Now run it and I will show you."

We watched the same footage—the men approaching the lieutenant, one leaning over the bar next to her.

"See, that guy was just asking her how she was doing, what she was drinking," Francina said and tried to bite the almost nonexistent nails as the video went.

"There," she said, pointing with that same finger that now had blood on the end of it from the biting. "She gets up and leaves kind of quick like. Then the black guy turns to the white guy and he says, 'What did you say that for?'" "You heard him say that?" Sheriff Cormac asked.

Francina nodded.

"But didn't hear what he said?" he asked.

Francina shook her head.

Then the bar was quiet as everyone thought about what else to ask the drugged-out unfortunate young woman. I felt it was time to speak.

"Angela, the sheriff will of course want a copy of the video, but if we can get a screenshot that shows the two soldiers, we can get that over to the colonel and Captain of the Guard so they can identify them and go after them before they get lost."

Sheriff Cormac nodded in agreement. Angela rotated the laptop to me and handed me the mouse. After a few practice clicks, I figured out the lay of the laptop. After a few more clicks and drags, I had a JPEG image of the two soldiers. I saved it on the desktop. Angela emailed it to the police station and the sheriff, who sent it from his phone email inbox to Colonel Sanchez. It seemed like we were done there, but the presence of Sheriff Cormac's daughter prohibited an official exit. We should be leaving but he couldn't just leave her like this, and the deputy had work to do.

"Go ahead, Sheriff. I know you got work to do. We'll be fine," Angela said and walked around to the front of the bar. She put her hand on the shoulder of Francina, who appeared well on her way to going back to sleep. That was the moment I started to see and feel a warm kind of way towards Angela Babineaux.

Chapter 12

Gerald and Colonel Sanchez were at the command post watching hours of forensic grave examination. The room was cold and void of color. There were monitors covering the left wall. The rear wall had windows. The right wall was covered with file cabinets and tall steel closets.

They sat at a desk and chairs below the monitors. They found the streaming video on the cloud account and were going through it at half speed.

"What do we hope to see here?" Gerald asked.

Colonel Sanchez kept her eyes on the screen and her hand on the mouse.

"Here, we see her hands leave the mound and her tools," she said.

"There—the attack has started!" Gerald almost shouted. "I saw a shadow go by the camera."

They reversed the footage back and forth trying to get a glimpse of … something that might help.

The video was a static shot of a mound of soil and rotted bone matter. Next the shadows all around the room began to move slowly at first—then rapidly as if people were moving about the room. The shadow swings became faster and violently. Colonel Sanchez kept her hand on the mouse, the other clinched in a fist. There were flashes of fabric, and the table was bumped violently and repeatedly. Knowledge of what happened in that room made this muted video almost as terrifying as the actual crime.

Then suddenly the camera footage jerked once, twice, turns on its side, and went black.

"That must have been when he took the camera," Gerald said.

"What makes you say, 'he'?"

"Um, don't know. Just seemed like a guy crime," Gerald said. "I'm no expert, but…."

"No harm, Mr. Phillips; you are probably right. I'm just trying to keep an open mind. I'm no detective of crimes. Just of science."

She had tears in her eyes, but Gerald respected her too much to say anything. He kept his eyes on the screen as she reversed the footage to just before the camera was taken. She began to move through it as frame by frame. Nothing seemed remarkable, until two frames before it went black. The video caught a glimpse of a hand.

"Hey!" they said at once.

"Did you see it?" Gerald asked. Colonel Sanchez nodded as she moved back to the frame that showed it again.

It was actually the side edge of a hand—a man's hand. It was Caucasian, average size, with a silver ring. The ring had a design, but it was blurry.

"Maybe, the police can have someone with video knowledge clean this up?" Gerald said.

"This police force? Not likely," Colonel Sanchez started. "However, the

Army might be able to assist."

This was what they were doing when the Captain of the Guard came into the room showing pictures he had received from Sheriff Cormac.

"We know these men," the Captain said. "Corporal McLean and Private Jackson. They are part of the day sentry for the examination /reinternment building."

~   ~   ~

Fifteen minutes later, a silent fleet of federal and local law enforcement approached the Jackson Garden Inn in Gilleyville. It sat out on State Road 33 across from a TA Truck Stop. The hotel was a rectangular building, six floors. The front faced the state road.

Sheriff Cormac called ahead to the manager, who confirmed through housekeeping that both men were in 214, a room in the middle of the hallway.

The military Captain of the Guard and four MPs parked on one side of the building. Sheriff Cormac, Deputy Laurie, and I took the other side of the building. We did not want to be seen by McLean or Jackson. Gerald was stationed with another deputy posted in the lobby, in case McLean and Jackson came that way.

"We in the cop business now?" Gerald asked me on the way to the hotel. He was sitting in the backseat of Deputy Laurie's vehicle leaning forward to me in the passenger seat. He asked because he thought we were getting a bit too close to the heat on this thing. His question was rhetorical, and he knew it. I was going in as far as the authorities would allow. That meant he had to go as well.

When we got to the second floor, Sheriff Cormac and Deputy Laurie motioned for me to stay at the end of the hall near the stairwell.

"You hear gunfire, you head down those steps, you hear?" Deputy Laurie instructed, pointing her light brown finger in my face. I nodded, slipping back behind the stairwell door. Suddenly my survival instincts were tweaked. This felt like more than an inquiry.

Soon the Captain of the Guard was at the other end of the hall coming from the opposite direction. He gave a head nod to the sheriff and hand signals to the MPs, who stayed a few feet behind him.

"How do you want to place this?" Sheriff Cormac asked the Captain of the Guard.

"Knock on the door. It's your jurisdiction. Let's play it by ear. I will be your backup," the Captain of the Guard said.

The Captain of the Guard and his men leaned against the wall on the other side of the door. After a few seconds, the sheriff knocked on the door. It opened quickly.

"Come on in," the soldier who answered the door said. He opened it and casually turned away. He was shirtless, a towel around his well-developed brown shoulders. He started brushing his teeth. The high-pitched whine of the electric toothbrush filled the room. Sheriff Cormac signaled for his deputy and Captain of the Guard to step inside. Terry Jackson was preoccupied with his dental health and returned to the sink and mirror.

"Just sit the towels on the bed," he said in a garbled voice impeded by brush and paste.

The law enforcement entourage just stood in the doorway waiting for him to notice him. He did a few seconds later, and the toothbrush fell out of his mouth.

"You are Private First Class Terry Jackson?" the Captain of the Guard asked, his voice slightly above conversational in volume. He already knew the men. Asking was matter of protocol and record. Terry "Jack" Jackson nodded. "This is the local sheriff. He has some questions for you and your roommate." Another nod.

"Where is your partner?" Sheriff Cormac asked.

"Uh, yeah, he's in the bathroom," Terry Jackson answered.

"Get him out here," the Captain of the Guard ordered. Terry Jackson nodded, toothpaste froth oozing around his lips. He spat the toothpaste into the sink, the brush still whirring on the floor.

"Mac! Heads up, we got company," he said knocking on the door that led to the toilet and shower, but never taking his eyes off the sheriff, deputy and Captain of the Guard. There was a muffled response from behind the door.

"Private Jackson, can you account for your whereabouts starting at 6:00 PM yesterday?" Sheriff Cormac asked.

"Uh, yeah, me and Mac went to Benoit's last night. We had some beers and watched ESPN."

"And did you speak to anyone?"

"Well, um, yeah we spoke to a lot of people. They can vouch that we were there."

"Did you have a conversation with any one person? Another soldier, maybe?"

"Uh, not really but..... Yes—wait, we did talk to Lieutenant Perales. She's one of the military coroners. Mac and I are part of the guards of the recovered graves."

"What did you all talk about?" Sheriff Cormac asked.

"Uh, nothing much. Uh, just said hello," Jackson explained his clumsy response, downward glance, and lip biting betraying him. "What's this about? Did the lieutenant make a complaint?"

"What would she have to complain about, Private?" Captain of the Guard asked.

"Uh, nothing. I mean, we didn't do anything, but you know sometimes … well, I was just wondering what this was about, that's all."

"What's taking your partner so long?" Deputy Laurie asked, cutting her eyes at the door leading to the toilet and shower.

The Captain of the Guard moved to the door and tried the knob. It was locked. He knocked hard on the thin panel door. The response was a loud but distant metal thud. Everyone in the room looked at each other for half a second.

"He's running!" Deputy Laurie said and bolted out the door leading to the hallway and down the steps. Sheriff Cormac stepped towards the shower door, but the Captain of the Guard beat him to it. He opened the door with one swift kick. He entered the shower room and returned in less than a second.

"He's out the window!" he said and ordered his MPs down the hall to take pursuit.

At that point, everyone turned their attention back to Terry Jackson who was in the bathroom looking out the small window over the tub. Stunned, he watched his partner Mac scurrying across the parking lot, weaving between cars. He was dressed in military boots, a beige military shirt, and his white boxer shorts.

The window was about two feet by two feet with metal edges to them. There was torn white cloth snagged on a jagged part of the frame. Terry Jackson lifted the four-inch bloodstained strip of cloth from an exposed screw in the frame of the window. Looking down at the ground two stories below, he saw an old Buick LeSabre with a badly dented roof.

"Jesus, Mac, what did you do?" he mumbled under his breath.

"Freeze, Private!" Sheriff Cormac shouted, his weapon drawn.

Terry heard the metallic click of the Glock pistol behind him as he looked out the window. He threw his hands up and slowly stepped out of the tub. He lowered to his knees. He was still holding the cloth.

"I am surrendering. I am not resisting. Hands up. Don't shoot," he said, his voice shaking.

In the hallway I also heard the distant metallic thud and the subsequent commotion from room 214. I followed the sound and looked out the window at the end of the corridor. I saw a man half-dressed and running around the side of the hotel toward the front. Instead of running to a car, he crossed the highway towards the mass confusion of the truck stop. Just then Deputy Laurie ran past me and down the steps. I followed her as quickly as possible.

As I reached the parking lot, I passed Gerald who was asking what happened.

"We got a runner," I shouted as I ran towards the truck stop. Waiting for a couple of cars to pass, I could see the MPs had made it across the highway and were actively looking for who I assumed was Corporal McLean. Their pistols were drawn. They were moving between the eighteen-wheeler trucks, looking underneath the cargo boxes and stepping up to see inside every cab.

I ran across the street, thinking what I would do if I found the underwear-clad enlisted man. Gerald was yelling my name from the hotel parking lot. I had to do what I could to keep the man alive to get to the end of what happened to Lieutenant Perales. I came up on the opposite side of the truck stop parking lot, where cars parked and bought gas.

By now the MPs had caused a level of commotion among the patrons. Folks were running and panicking in one part of the store, which led to a domino effect of alarm in other parts of the truck stop. Customers were bumping into each other. Employees were shouting for calm. I saw no signs of the soldier in his underwear. I figured he must have been hiding, waiting for the chance to … what? I thought about him being armed. I didn't see where he could hide it. Nevertheless, I tried to stay close to the MP's.

I headed to the bathrooms and showers in the back of the store, wading through people headed for the doors. I hit every stall and every shower, even in the ladies' room. Nothing.

Coming back out into the store, I met the MPs.

"I checked both bathrooms. He's not there," I said.

"Check again," one MP said to his partner while looking at me with a deadpan expression. One MP went for the restrooms. The other one kept searching the store. I headed out to the parking lot. I found the sheriff and Gerald out there searching. I joined them.

"No sign of him!" I said.

"Oh, he's here. We will find him," Cormac said. "Meanwhile the deputy and Captain of the Guard took Private Jackson into custody.

Sheriff Cormac ran off to continue the search, made more difficult by the confusion of cars moving around the parking lot at one time. Gerald and I stepped onto the front stoop of the truck stop store.

"Let's look this way," I said.

"And what do we do if we find him first? We are not the police, Man," Gerald said, grabbing my arm.

"Try to get him to stop before those MPs or the police put a bullet in him."

"So what?" Gerald asked. "He's acting pretty guilty to me right now. Besides, I'm trying to keep a bullet out of my black ass. I don't want any confusion about who the suspect is here."

"If he did kill her, why? I think it has something to do with our business here."

"The gold?" Gerald asked.

"Lieutenant Perales was part of the team that found the gold and the chest. It was found during the day shift. Jackson and McLean are part of the shift sentry. What other connection would they have?"

"I don't know. It sounds pretty flimsy," Gerald said, rubbing his chin and looking around nervously. The sheriff and the MPs were making a second and third pass over the parking lot. Cars were moving off the lot in a rapid line.

"Hey, Phillips, what's the commotion?" someone yelled from a car, an old black Pontiac Bonneville.

As it pulled to a stop in front of us, we saw it was driven by a young AfricanAmerican man between eighteen and twenty-five. He wore a big smile which was out of character with the commotion occurring at that moment. "What? Do I know you, son?" Gerald asked, clearly agitated.

"Albert Harrison, *Atlanta Informer*. I interviewed your wife."

I saw Gerald's expression change for the worse. He stepped off the front stoop of the truck stop towards young Albert's car. I grabbed his arm for a moment, and he turned to me.

"Remember he's the press," I said. Gerald's expression softened as he pulled his arm free. Just to be safe, we both walked over to Albert's car.

He reintroduced himself, explaining he was just noticing the commotion; he thought it might be a story here.

"No, Albert, there is no story here, Man," Gerald said patiently. "The police are just looking for someone for questioning."

"Who? Does he have something to do with the dead soldier, the coroner?" "How do you know about that?" Gerald asked.

"Those historical society guys are telling everyone who will listen. Plus, your partner is pretty loose with the tongue."

"Who?" I asked.

"Don't know his name, the Spanish guy with all the jewelry and shiny suits," Albert explained with a laugh. "So how about it, Fellas? Can you give a young brother a story? Help me out? I can keep the source confidential."

"Listen, Albert, this is not a game out here. People are killing each other…," Gerald started.

"Oh, so you sayin' that's the killer they lookin' for?" Albert asked, his eyes lighting up.

"No, Albert. We are absolutely not saying that. They just want to talk to the guy. He was one of the last people to be seen with her," I explained.

Albert nodded in thought, taking in what I was saying.

"He's not a suspect?" "Nope," I said. "So you can't tell me his name?" Albert asked.

"No," Gerald and I answered loudly at the same time. Albert literally jumped in his driver's seat.

"Albert, I am sure the sheriff will have a statement later. For now, just get out of here," Gerald answered, using the last bit of patience he had with the young reporter. Albert nodded nervously, slammed the gearshift into drive, and joined the rest of the cars leaving the lot.

Chapter 13

Val Cedars sat in the back of the Kreamy Kow Ice Cream Parlor, where he held court with members of the Benoitown/Gilleyville National Historical Society (BGNHS). The society had no national charter, no state charter, or local authority. That was the name Val Cedars and his wife Pat gave it. He volunteered all his time. He and his team received no salary or financial compensation.

The BGNHS had two purposes.

They preserved the historical integrity of the south-central Tar River Basin. This included the legend of Jolly Benoit. In addition to the Benoit collections at the Edgewood County Museum, he also ran a small museum on the second floor of Cedars Furniture store. The store was a Benoitown landmark started by Joseph Cedars, Val's grandfather. The museum also held small collections of nautical equipment, slave shackles, unreadable parchment papers, and a questionable certification from a dead history professor from a junior college in New Bern.

The second purpose of the society, and the source of its influence, was to uphold the historic integrity of both towns. Val and his rabid group of volunteers rooted out every code violation or attempt to modernize in commercial or personal real estate property. In turn, they complained to the point of distraction.

It was all legitimate. If the authorities in the public works department or the sheriff's office did not want to pursue them, Val and his crew would keep complaining higher and higher until something was done. The Cedars name still held high respect up and down the tidewater from Val's grandfather's day.

As it usually turned out, it was easier for property owners to do what Val wanted than to spend time battling him. Most people had more important things to do. Val did not.

Meanwhile Pat kept the store going. She was older by almost ten years. She was a stunning but shy beauty, a tall willowy blonde, artistic and creative with her hands. She lost her first husband and the love of her life during a fire in his wood workshop. Val was a furniture restorer on the construction/decorating crew provided by the insurance company. He spoke a language that she understood—furniture, fine wood art. Their friendship was her transition from her former life. She always felt she never could have done it on her own. Val made sure she would never have to find out on her own.

The rest of the society included Bo Boulage and the Bandy Twins, Willow and Winona. Bo was the son of Mimi Boulage, the sheriff's secretary and dispatcher. Bo was twenty-three years old, dark brown hair, broad shoulders, narrow waist, and chiseled good looks. Before realizing he had an affinity for woodwork, Bo found his outlet in fighting any and everybody he could. That is until he got into a scrape with a trigger-happy trucker from Kinston who carried a Walther P22 for protection. The bullet went through Bo's right jaw and out the other side, lodging in the 1930s jukebox in Benoit's. He survived with only a small blemish to his handsome face, along with severe jaw pain on rainy days. The Bandy family owned a great deal of real estate up and down the Tar River. The twin's parents were on the school board, board of aldermen, local church usher board, and in the case of the father—the Board of University

Regents for the state of North Carolina. With all that importance to manage, the parents had left the twins to their own devices. Val Cedars liked them because they stayed quiet and did what they were told.

Mimi was probably Val's only consistent friend since high school. At her insistence, Val took Bo on as a type of apprentice to keep him out of trouble. Bo had a natural affinity for working with wood, stone, and glass. However, Bo had a temper. Val found a use for that as well. People who decided to go against Val's suggestion that they comply with county codes or just his idea of civic duty sometimes found their structures destroyed while they were away for the day, or caught on fire in the night. After a few of these successful clandestine ventures, Val and Bo were inseparable.

"I can't believe they kept you out of the crime scene, but let them insurance people in there," Bo said, taking a greedy slurp of his shake. He drank straight from the glass, getting a whipped cream mustache.

"That's okay," Val said, speaking softly like a mortician on the day of the viewing. "I have put some things in motion to get us back in the game."

"You need me to pay some nighttime visits?" Bo said, his eyes lighting with anticipation. The boy truly had a fetish for destruction. "I could take the twins with me."

Val looked at the twins who were sitting there staring at a tablet computer, letting their ice cream melt into the table. They were tall and heavy in unflattering places, their chins, stomachs, and thighs. They wore their dull brown hair in a flat mushroom with severe bangs just above their light brown eyes. However, their Mediterranean ancestry gifted them with creamy perpetually tan skin and sensual lips.

They were actually very intelligent, each graduating at the top of their class in high school and automating Val Cedars business. They were just socially stunted. Moreover, they feared and worshiped Bo Boulage. Hanging out with him gave them a certain amount of street credibility.

"No, my boy," Val said, patting the street pugilist' beefy hands, as if pacifying a growling guard dog. "We shall take the more civilized approach."

"But VC, if they find gold or treasure in those graves, they should be part of our museum, not going to some insurance company or Spain, or…." Bo was getting riled up. Val patted his hand again.

"I agree. I agree," Val said.

"When I see them in their Abercrombie rain gear and Brooks Brothers Chinos, I just want to smash their faces in," Bo said and punched the palm of one hand with the fist of his other. The twins let out a conspiratorial laugh and began eating their ice cream.

"And that guy from Spain, with the fagot jewelry and shin…. *Ow!*" Bo shouted loudly. Val's index finger was dug into the spot on the side of his face where the bullet entered. There was a permanent misalignment of his jaw as a result. The pain was so bad it made Bo's sight go white for a second.

"Mr. Boulage, you know I do not tolerate that homophobic language in my presence," Val said. His finger was deep into Bo's jaw, and he was staring at the twins who were looking terrified and dropped their spoons. Val released his finger and Bo rubbed his jaw in silence, mumbling an apology.

"I understand your passion and your frustration at the situation, but members of the society maintain our dignity and our poise."

"Yes, VC," Bo said and slapped one of the twins on the arm.

"Yes, VC," the twins said in unison.

Chapter 14

It was about three o'clock when we all returned from the truck stop. Sheriff Cormac wanted all of us in his office. Everyone was in a bad mood because Corporal McLean was never captured. Private Jackson sat in a holding cell praying silently to the Almighty.

In the meantime, Sheriff Cormac, Deputy Laurie, the Captain of the Guard, Colonel Sanchez, Adam Samuelson of the State Department, Gerald, and I sat upstairs and planned our next move.

"How the hell can a half-naked soldier disappear in a one-horse town like this?" the Captain of the Guard asked to no one in particular.

"Hey, watch that one-horse town bullshit," Deputy Laurie said sitting on the sofa in the sheriff's office. One of her cowboy boots propped against the small coffee table. The Captain of the Guard held a conciliatory hand up by way of apology.

"Well, I mean, he has to be somewhere. He knows no one. He has no pants. You will find him," Adam Samuelson said, ever the diplomat.

I had some ideas. I stood. Gerald reached out for me, but I slapped his hand away.

"Sheriff, we have his partner. I say we continue to work on Private Jackson.

He obviously knows more than he is telling."

"We'll get more out of him as soon as we get him back to the barracks," Colonel Sanchez said. "We'll be taking custody, Sheriff."

"Like hell you will. He is my prisoner."

"He is a US enlisted and falls under our jurisdiction," the Captain of the Guard said, stepping forward to stand next to the colonel.

"Well, he's in our jail, and we don't hand over suspects in murder cases," Deputy Laurie said, rising from the sofa.

"He's not a suspect," the Captain of the Guard said.

"Oh, so you a lawyer now, MP?" Deputy Laurie responded, throwing out her chest and letting her hands dangle to her side near her holster.

"That's *Captain*," he said, taking a half step forward.

"Well, Captain, he is what we say he is," Deputy Laurie answered, taking a full step forward.

"Wait a minute," I said loudly to catch everyone's attention. All the parties looked at me. Gerald was sitting behind me, and I heard him moan as his shifting body made a sound on the leather settee.

"Colonel, where do you plan to hold Private Jackson if you take him?" I asked.

"Did you hear me, Manion? He's not leaving," Deputy Laurie said.

"Humor me?"

The colonel and the Captain of the Guard exchanged glances and a couple of mumbles.

"Private Jackson would be confined to his barracks under constant guard," she explained. Deputy Laurie mumbled something under her breath about bullshit house arrest.

"I thought so," I responded. "What I propose is we leave Private Jackson here.... "

The Captain of the Guard was shaking his head; I raised a hand for patience.

"Sheriff, in exchange, you allow space for the MPs to watch him here at the facility."

"How many MPs?" Sheriff Cormac asked.

"Captain?"

"Four!" he said emphatically.

"Man, this ain't no military base," Deputy Laurie said. "We don't have that kind of room."

"Then no deal," Colonel Sanchez said haughtily.

"Colonel, we already have a black eye because we let Corporal McLean slip through our fingers," I explained. "We don't know how many others they are working with. Our best chance to get to the bottom of this is to keep him separated from any co-conspirators and under a real jail." The room went silent, but no one budged.

"I propose two MPs remain here at the jail around the clock," I said tentatively.

Sheriff Cormac looked at Deputy Laurie, while Colonel Sanchez silently consulted with the Captain of the Guard.

"Okay, that works for us," Sheriff Cormac said.

"We're good with that," Colonel Sanchez said. "I have to go. We are still sifting through evidence at the scene. I want to analyze that blood on Corporal McLean's torn clothes. Captain, you can handle it from here?"

The Captain of the Guard saluted as she left the room. He followed behind her, and I could hear him giving commands to his MPs waiting in the hall.

Deputy Laurie strolled over to me, her face still stern.

"Lucky you were here, Manion. I wouldn't have given them a damn thing," she said letting her face fade into a grin that made her look like a devilish thirteen-year-old. She followed the Captain of the Guard out into the hallway to show them where they were going to be stationed.

Things were quiet for a moment. Adam Samuelson, Sheriff Cormac, Gerald, and I sat around the room in reflection. Gerald was looking at his watch, clearly wanting to be elsewhere. Sheriff Cormac was sifting through notes on his desk. Adam Samuelson was standing looking down with his arms folded reminiscent of a popular portrait of John F. Kennedy. I was wondering what Private Jackson really had to say, and what would it take to get him to reveal it.

Then in came the reverend.

We heard him before we saw him, pounding footsteps growing louder just outside the office. Then he stepped in with grand flourish, the door nearly banging on its hinges.

"Sheriff, I demand the release of Private Terrance Jackson immediately pending charges and a hearing!" he said in his typical booming voice.

"How do you know we have Jackson in custody? We just returned to the station."

"Does that matter? News travels fast. The man has rights, even a black enlisted man," Reverend Curtyse Moten said. He was dressed in a dark blue double-breasted suit, black shirt, and white tie. It was late afternoon, but he looked television camera-ready.

"Come on, Reverend? This ain't Baltimore or Ferguson, Missouri," Sheriff Cormac said.

"Nevertheless, I am acting as his attorney, and I request to see him and to know what the charges are against him."

"We haven't charged him with anything yet, but we will be holding him for the total number of hours the law of North Carolina says I can hold him. He has information regarding a murder and the fleeing of a person of interest."

"What information is that?" the Reverend asked. "What person of interest?"

"I am not at liberty to say at this time. It's an ongoing investigation."

"Sheriff, you are stepping out there on thin ice."

"Maybe, but I have him in custody, and I'm holding him until he tells me what I need to know or I charge him. Now you can talk to him and maybe he will tell you what's going on, and you can convince him to tell me. Either way, there will be no bail tonight."

Chapter 15

We found Fedelito about an hour later at the hotel. He was in a ballroom he rented. The tables and chairs were removed and replaced with various sporting equipment. Around the room were tumbling mats, punching bags, free-standing bulls eye targets with knives stuck in them, dumb bells, and a chin-up bar.

He was sweating and stripped to the waist. I noticed Fedelito was small but surprisingly muscular. He had the stomach paunch, but his chest, stomach, and lower arms were covered with hair. He was breathing hard as if he were in distress.

"He all right," a voice came from the corner. I looked around to see young man in his early twenties and big as a college linebacker. He was also shirtless, sweating and winded.

"What's going on here?" I asked suspiciously.

"This," Fedelito started, "is Xanadu Waters. We met at the local gym, your Y-M-C-A? Well, I don't like to, as you say, 'work out' in a room full of strangers. Xanadu here has allowed me to hire him to work with me in our little *gymnasio*."

"It's all good, gentlemen," Xanadu Waters was saying now.

He stood and walked over from the corner of the room. He was about six-foot five inches, baldhead, a boxer's nose and jaw, and medium brown skin with muscles everywhere. He reminded me of the actor Terry Crewes, dancing pectoral muscles and all. Gerald and I shook his sweaty hand.

"Hey, you Phillips the lawyer?" he asked. Gerald nodded. "Yeah, I met your wife. She something else, Man."

"Thanks," Gerald mumbled, not sure how to take what appeared to be a sincere compliment.

"So Mr. Gaspare and I just been doing a little sparring. I did some boxing back in the day, not much of that going on around here now."

"Yes, Xanadu packs quite the punch," Fedelito said, smacking his torso, which, at closer examination, was festooned with purple and blue bruises beneath all the hair.

"Sorry about that, Mr. Gaspare, but you got to learn to protect yourself a little better. You said you wanted full contact sparring," Xanadu said apologetically.

"No, no," Fedelito said dismissively. "Don't apologize. It was just what I needed. It is the man who can take a punch and get back up who is the greater champion in life. Remember that!"

He handed Xanadu a roll of cash that clearly was more than what the young man expected. He thanked us all profusely, gathered his shirt and gym bag, and left.

Fedelito was wearing green and black spandex workout leggings with black boots that came up to his knee. He wore a green headband and black gloves with the fingers cut out. Now he was holding what appeared to be two short ceremonial knives.

"Exercise, you see, is a private endeavor," Fedelito said, wagging his finger at us, his mouth turned down as he fought to breathe evenly. "Besides, this is the workout of the European gentlemen."

I had never seen any of this at Rudolph Lemieux's salon or studio or any other place in Europe, but I didn't want to get off topic.

"Listen, Fedelito, we want to bring you up to date on things. Can we talk?" I asked.

"No," he said casually. He turned his attention to a table holding many small knives.

Fedelito gingerly picked up about four additional knives. He stared down a target on an easel about 20 feet away, and, with a cat-like quickness, he threw the knives in rapid succession one at a time. They all landed within inches of each other all near the center of the target. I looked around, and Gerald had stepped a few feet away.

"No?" I asked.

"It is not necessary. I have been 'briefed' on all matters necessary," he said with a dismissive sniff. He picked up several more knives.

"For instance I know that the unfortunate Lieutenant Perales was stabbed; before that she was suffocated."

He threw a knife to center of the target.

"The guards were compromised and did not come to her aid." Another knife throw. Bulls-eye.

"The murderer further compromised the graves, probably taking gold that belongs to the country of Spain!" This he said a lot louder.

He threw the three last knives in quick succession, the third one missing the target and sticking into the drywall post behind it.

"Who briefed you?" I asked sternly.

"It does not matter," he said, stepping close until he was inches from my face. "I should have been briefed by you two. You work for me, for the country of Spain."

"We do not work for you, Gaspare. I told you that before," I responded slow and low. I was getting tired of his macho posing. "We were here to brief you now. We have been busy."

We stood face to face for a few seconds. Then he smiled and turned away, the smell of sweat and clove tobacco in his wake.

"Yes, yes, I know. There was a suspect who is on the run. You and Señor Gerald, the police, and the United States Army lost him. Yes, very impressive." "Who briefed you?" I asked again, my gaze not fading.

I was getting tired of the little Spaniard's act of superiority and puppet mastering. People were dying, and he was role-playing. He finally turned back to me seeing that we were in a go/no-go place. Either he became part of the solution, or I got on the phone to Paris and made some changes.

"Relax, Signor Manion, I spoke with *my* counterpart from the US State Department, Mr. Samuelson. He called me with updates."

"Why would Adam Samuelson give you updates? Why wouldn't he just tell you to contact us?" Gerald asked.

"Because he is bound by law and duty to cooperate with State Department operatives from friendly ally countries and republics. He was doing his job, unlike you two."

"What is that supposed to mean?" Gerald asked.

"I just don't know how hard you two are working at recovering Spanish assets. Maybe you two want to see Spain fall. Many countries have tried in the past."

"I'm outta here," Gerald said, turning to leave. "I will touch base with you later, Manion. I'm going to find my wife."

After Gerald left, I turned back to Fedelito. He was smiling as if he knew all the world's secrets.

"Fedelito, why would we not want to find the gold? Your gold means you can make good on the interest payments on the bonds WorldSpan is holding on Spanish debt."

"Yes, but if we default on the debt, then you would have access to galleries of Spanish art, and Spanish political influence around the world, or maybe France would want to just embarrass the Spanish government. Who knows?"

"Okay, I'm out of here," I said, having already had my fill of this crazy little man. "Be careful out there. I will let you know if we find anything."

"And maybe I will be the one to let *you* know. Do *your* job," he said to my back as I walked out of the ballroom.

He was a delusional fool, but Gerald and I were stuck with him for now. People were dying. Suspects were on the loose, and no one was telling the whole truth. Throw in one fool, and this could be disastrous. I guessed that was why I was sent.

Chapter 16

From the *Journal of Jolly Benoit*:

Date: *January 1859*

Benoitown and Gilleyville

This New Year is a bittersweet one. The city continues to prosper. Benoitown has been able to sustain itself even after bouts with flooding, and the horrible disease brought on by insects afterwards. The medicines and herbs of my people have saved our lives. Sama Gilley has even started a settlement named Gilleyville. It has grown into a real village that will one day eclipse the size of my own. While one is mostly Negro and the other white, there is harmony.

Some mornings Sama and I meet at the river's edge just north of town just before the start of day. We make plans for our growing towns, work out problems, and share secrets. It is also the time when we harvest our treasure from our compatriots below ground. Two days ago we stood in our spot and looked downstream at what we have built and marvel at the fortune of the Great Creator. This life is so different than that life on the sea or our time in Haiti.

As we have grown more prosperous, former slaves and shopkeepers have been able to buy the freedom of their relatives and friends.

Sama has been instrumental in this regard, providing us unfortunate facts about various slave owners. Who is in debt? Who has problems with their farms or businesses? Who has illnesses that put them closer to death than to life? It has made negotiations easier. When we come up with the money, everyone thinks it is from our hardworking commerce and plain living.

We have been able to pass off the discussion of hidden gold as the fables told to children to help them sleep. After all, why would a pirate with a mountain of treasure live like we do among common folk?

Due to the rains and the floods of recent years, Sama and I have had to move satchels of gold from the vault of graves, sometimes in a hurry. At the end of last year, I dedicated a high plot of land as a new grave site, for future slaves and free men of color. It is many a dying slave's wish to be buried on what they call "freeland." I have reinterred my treasure there among them. Sama has done the same in Gilleyville, ensuring the peace on both sides of the river. Sometimes, Sama and I are still not sure if we removed all the gold in the lower original graves. We can never agree on the number of satchels. I worry that one wet summer a few gold coins will wash out on the streets, and man's wide-eyed lust will destroy all that we have built

But clouds of war are on the horizons, the growing national talk about slavery, the John Brown rebellion, and the manipulation of Southern farm prices are making blood boil. We have had ten slave revolts of various sizes in this State alone, and the same sacrificial lynching afterwards. It is the horror that is seen but not discussed in our sleepy little villages. I shudder to think what our world will look like if it comes to war. I have been to war, great and small, on land and at sea. The places where they fight and the people who fight them are forever changed and seldom for the better.

Also, Sama is becoming increasingly fonder of big cities. Our gold has done well in Baltimore, Philadelphia, and New York, growing each year if the bankers paper reports are to be believed. Sama visits there often and stays longer each time, and speaks more and more of making a permanent move, probably to New York. There are

a lot of Irish there, maybe extended family.

If that happens I will be a much sadder being,

but I would never stand in the way of a soul's yearnings

as   I   would   never   have   let   anyone   stop   me.

Chapter 17

Gerald pulled in front of Reverend Moten's home. There was the usual circus of reporters, protesters, and nosy neighbors milling about the front yard and driveway. Ever since he left me and that fool Gaspare, Gerald had been trying to reach his wife Nadine by phone. It went to voice mail the first three times. Later, it didn't even ring, like she had turned the phone off.

They had installed a phone location app on their phones that worked anywhere in the country. He figured it would be a good way to locate her, although he had never thought to use it for that purpose before now. When he opened the app, he realized she had turned her notification off. That was when he took it upon himself to head over to the last place he saw her.

"Gerald, come on in," Mrs. Moten said, opening the door before he could knock.

She led him into the kitchen. There were college-age kids working on some campaign, making phone calls and devising strategy. There was another group doing the same thing out on the patio. Gerald could see them through the sliding glass doors off the back of the kitchen.

"I was looking for Nadine," he said, taking a bottled water from Mrs. Moten.

"I'm sorry, Gerald. She is not here," she answered in wide-eyed surprise as if he should know where his wife is. It irritated Gerald just below his surface.

He didn't like being pandered to even if the pandering was accurate. However, he didn't think it was Mrs. Moten's fault that Nadine was being so elusive.

"Do you know where she went or when she will be back?" Gerald asked, thinking the honest approach was best. "I'm just a little worried. It's been a crazy day, and I haven't talked to her, gotten a text, or anything."

She gave him a momentary pensive look. Then she instructed one of the students at the eat-in dinette to get the reverend. After a few minutes of small talk between them, they were greeted by the reverend who actually had to duck his head to come through the doorway leading from what appeared to be his study.

"Curtyse, Mr. Phillips is looking for his wife," she said by way of setting up the conversation.

"Nadine—I have not seen her all day," the reverend said just a bit too quickly. Gerald may have been upset about his wife, but he was one of the top legal negotiators for international finance. He could read people like second nature.

The reverend was hiding something.

"Did she stay here last night?" he asked. The reverend chuckled.

"Man, you don't know where your wife slept last night?"

"Last I saw her, Man, she was under your roof, so figured I better start here. You say you haven't seen her all day. Then let's take it back to last night? Or breakfast this morning? Exactly what do you mean by *all day*?" Gerald asked, feeling his patience running out.

These people wanted to play political ping-pong around race, gold, and some dead bones the souls of whom had long been gone. All he cared about was finishing this assignment and getting his wife out unharmed. At that moment he really didn't care about whatever the reverend's agenda was.

"She was here this morning," Mrs. Moten interjected, sensing the growing tension. "Then she went out, and I haven't seen her since. She did not say where she was going to me or the reverend."

"That true, Reverend?" Gerald asked. He wanted to hear from the Reverend Moten himself.

"Right," he said, a knowing smile on his face that made Gerald want to punch him. "Phillips, you know your wife is doing good work over here. This is a war, Man. If we let the greedy, the corrupt disrespect our dead like this, what do you think is next?"

"It's a war, but my wife won't be a casualty of it."

"And we don't want her to be. With your help we can end this thing sooner rather than later. If you can just give us some information, we can keep anyone from getting hurt. We are on the same side here."

"What information would I possibly have that you could use?"

"Well, like if they actually find any more gold? That could be helpful. And what are you and your slick little white friend from Paris supposed to do when you do find gold?"

"I thought your concern was the graves?" Gerald asked, confused. "Besides, I thought you had spies all over town."

"People tell me things. Information is power. Power our people need to rise up. How about you laying a little of that information power on us."

"Mrs. Moten, thank you. If Nadine shows up, please let her know that I'm looking for her," Gerald said and turned to leave so he didn't curse the reverend out in his own house.

~ ~ ~

It was about 10:30 PM in Paris. Since I was having a status call at this hour, it meant Camille had a date. Despite the facts that she is my boss and routinely shares my bed, it is also a vague relationship at times in terms of our status. There are corporate and cultural as well as emotional things to consider.

When I saw her on the screen, I missed home immediately. She was still in an evening dress, a dark red off the shoulder number that stopped just above the knee. Camille had shoulders made for off-the-shoulder evening gowns and formal dresses with spaghetti straps. Her legs were long with the right amount of muscle tone at the calf and thigh. I could see they were crossed over each other just at the bottom of the screen. Occasionally she would idly shift her weight and I would get a fuller view. I missed home a lot.

I told her everything I knew about today. When I got to the death of

Lieutenant Perales, she made another drink. She made to reach for her cigarette case, then cursed as she remembered she quit. Her brows furrowed in that freckled pixie face. She typically wore her hair very short and curly, like Annie Lennox. Tonight it was gelled and combed straight back in a utilitarian style.

"First, how are you doing my love?" she asked, her eyes serious and piercing.

"I'm good."

"This is bad, Tekelius. More death, more trouble."

"It's what I signed up for, right—the Expeditor."

"I don't care about your new job. I would fire you and put you back in your old job before I let you get hurt."

"Thank you," I said, blushing. I loved it when she went all mad French woman on me. "I'm fine."

"I would tell you to be careful, but you won't do it. You claim to be scared to death, but still you go forward not backward."

"Well, I'm not being brave this time. Just observe and report, right?"

"It's even worse that the dead person is a woman. You always get so chivalrous, like before with your ex-wife."

"Ex-fiancée," I corrected.

"Same thing," she snapped back, reached for the case and cursed again.

"When there's a woman in trouble, you think you are the Commandment des Operations Speciales. Did you know this woman that was killed?"

"No, just met her once," I said.

"Was she pretty?" Camille asked with a slight pout.

"Mila, please. The woman was murdered."

"That means yes, which means you will stick your skinny heroic American neck out to find her killer. You never stick your neck out for me," she said in a full pout now.

"That's because you never need saving. It's always some wealthy old European bastard of a 4,000-year-old family that discovered a rare vintage of champagne waiting to take you out as soon as I leave the city. What was it tonight? Puccini, Paganini?"

"It was Wagner," Camille said with a slight eye roll. "I love the music, but some of the arias give me a headache after two hours. And my date was not so old this time, an American oilman, about your age."

"Don't tell me," I started. "Afterwards he tried to get a private audience with the principal members of the cast, who refused. Then he complained throughout dinner about everything from the service, the food, the napkins, and the lighting."

Camille started to laugh and nodded. "How did you know?"

"Let me guess! He was from Chicago or Dallas. Am I right?"

"Yes, yes Texas," she laughed lightly, pleased with my insight. I loved that laugh and the look in her eyes when she did it. She continued, "WorldSpan is thinking of getting into some oil leases while the prices are low, and every oilman around the world is looking for capital to stay afloat," she explained.

"I'm glad I'm on this assignment," I said. I had to ask. "He still there with you?"

"God, no!" she said, sipping her drink and making the cutest frown that I had ever seen. "We arranged after-hour escorts for the CEO of Muddy Maverick Oil Ltd."

"Muddy Maverick? How original," I said, and we both laughed.

There was a knock on my door. I excused myself.

It was Baliles, the quirky street personality. He asked to come in, and I stepped aside for him to enter. He was clean; his hair was freshly washed but just as wild. He wore another antique suit. This one was black. However, his crisp, white business shirt was new. I could still see the packaging folds in the fabric and the Ralph Lauren Polo emblem on the pocket.

He saw the video call going on with Camille on the screen. I introduced them.

"This is my boss Camille DeSoronne'. Camille, this is … Baliles of Benoitown."

Before I could say another word, they began to converse in rapid French. It was very casual French with a lot of slang and folk references in it. However, I caught the obvious flirts and compliments. There was a reference as to what she saw in me, a clumsy American, and finally an invitation for Camille to come visit him. This went on long enough for me to make a drink of my own—scotch and soda. Then I returned to the desk where Baliles was leaning back in my chair with his dirty boots on the desk, listening to Camille describe what I think was her outfit for the evening.

"Excuse me, Baliles," I said with a clear of my throat. "You wanted something? To deliver a message?"

"So I did," Baliles said, reaching into his shirt pocket pulling out a small beige envelope similar to the size of an invitation.

I opened it. There was a single sheet of paper with a handwritten note.

Insurance Man,

I'm inviting you to my set tonight at Benoit's. You could probably use a break, and I owe you for keeping Fedelito honest. Set starts at 9:00 PM Don't be late.

– A-Bab!

"What is it?" Camille asked.

"Nothing," I answered. "Just a thank-you card."

"She didn't seem to treat it like a 'thank you' card when she gave it to me," Baliles said in a more robust tone.

"She?" Camille asked, her interest piqued.

"Yes, from one Angela C. Babineaux, local small boat captain, tender of bar, and quite an accomplished vocalist of tavern songs," Baliles was so eager to explain. "I believe she is performing tonight."

"Oh, an invitation from 'Angela,'" Camille said, only half joking. "I knew there was some pretty woman needing your protection."

"Baliles, thank you. You can go now," I said.

"Oh, no," Camille interrupted. "It's late. I should go. Baliles, please keep my friend there out of trouble. He is a nuisance, but he is important to me." With that they blew each other kisses, and Camille broke the connection.

"Dude?!" I started. "Where do you get off coming in here and exposing me like that? That was my boss. I swear I don't get you."

"That makes two of us," he said, rising from the chair and turning to leave.

"You leave a beautiful woman like that in a city like Paris by herself?" I shrugged.

"Then I see you are still reading this tale of lies," he said, leaning down and reaching past me to pick up the published copy of Jolly Benoit's journal from the desk.

"So you don't believe the legend? I thought you told Jolly Benoit stories for tips?"

"Have you ever listened to my oral histories?" he asked, pointing at me with the book.

"No," I answered.

"Well you should. Like I told the unfortunate Lieutenant Perales, you will never find what I say in this fraudulent tome," Baliles said and pushed the book in my chest and turned to leave.

"Wait, you spoke to Perales before she died?" I asked urgently, catching him as he was opening the door to my hotel room.

"Yes, I heard her at the local bookstore. She was asking for a copy of the *Journal of Jolly Benoit*."

"What else did she say? What all did you talk about?" I asked urgently. I didn't realize I was holding his arm until he pulled it from my grip.

"Nothing," Baliles said, his face turning pensive. "I believe she may have been affronted by my manner. I seem to have a proclivity for doing that sometimes."

As he slipped out the door, all the machismo he displayed just seconds ago was gone. I watched him walk down the hall and wondered if he were suffering from a mental challenge or a good actor. I couldn't tell. I also realized that no one had asked or followed up on the receipt in Lieutenant Perales' pocket from the local bookstore. I checked my watch. I had just enough time.

I showered and changed. The Serendipity Bookstore was about to close as I arrived. Benoit's was across the street in the next block. Serendipity was fortunate enough to be above the flood line and spared a lot of the damage.

It was run by Teresa Dorterre', an upbeat chatty woman with a beautiful face and smart dancing brown eyes behind jeweled glasses. Her small hands were extremely soft with rings on every finger. For a book maven, her face was made up like she had a date later that night. She was dressed in a blood red man's oxford shirt that caught the blush in her honey brown skin. I know there are a lot of cool things women can do with make-up, but I swear her face seemed to glow.

She wore black leggings and dreadlock black and grey hair pinned at the back of her head. She had an ample bosom for her height, about five-foot three, and well-proportioned everywhere else it counted. She walked with a confidence that made it hard for me to guess her age. It didn't matter. She looked good no matter what her birth certificate read.

Her store was a combination gift store, souvenir shop, and book provider. There was a small sitting area and a raised podium in the back. She explained she also held concerts, poetry, and book readings from time to time.

"Ms. Dorterre', I'm not the police," I started.

"We know," she said with a chuckle, her eyes never leaving my face and never blinking. "Call me Teresa. And you're part of the I-Spy partners from the insurance company. You want to make sure you get your cut if they find gold left by James Blue."

"Who?"

"Yeah, that was Jolly's name before he became Jolly. The name he was known by as a boy slave here."

"You talk like you knew him," I said, trying to be conversational. She laughed a full but light chuckle, like a child but not immature. Her voice was light, but she spoke with the measured elocution of a storyteller. I found it hard not to watch her mouth when she spoke.

"In a way. My great, great, great grandmother Sarah knew him. They were two of many children on a plantation that was less than 10 miles from here." "Wow," I said.

"When he came back as Jolly Benoit, he made arrangements using Sam Gilley to buy the freedom of my family—Sarah, her husband James, and their three children, James Jr., Thomas, and Teresa, my namesake. He taught all of them how to read and write, and Sarah kept a diary of those times."

"That's amazing," I said, clearly impressed. She nodded as if she had heard this before. She spoke with a spirit and wisdom that was a bit arresting. Her voice had a lilt to it as if she were singing.

"So you really think there is gold in those graves?" Teresa asked.

"I have no idea. Could be? You know what I worry about?" I said.

"Tell me, Handsome?"

"We find a few more coins, and it sparks millions and millions of dollars of searching, heartache, protests, and legal action. Then we don't find any more gold, and it's a losing proposition for everyone."

"Hmmm, that would be awful. So much bad energy in our town," she said to no one in particular.

"Did Mother Sarah's diary mention anything about gold?"

"Noooo, it was about things way more valuable than gold," she said with a knowing look.

"I understand—love and heritage and stuff like that?" I said, smiling.

"Stuff like that," she responded, leaning over the front display case, her men's shirt pulling snug against the counter revealing her full, inviting cleavage. My eyes snapped up quickly feeling like they had lingered there too long. She was staring off in reflection. I started the next conversation.

"You never know. It may be helpful. I could come over some time and read it while we sip tea," I said, surprised at my own flow. Something about this woman made me brave and strangely curious.

"Oh, thank you, Teke," she said and locked eyes with me for a second. "But if someone like you came to sip tea with me, I'm afraid you would get no sleep."

"What?" I asked, pointing to myself in mock shock. She was flirting with me now. I liked the flirt.

"Yes, you," she said and poked me in my chest with a well-manicured middle finger. "Anybody can pick up the scent of sex, determination, and trouble on you. Besides, you didn't come to my shop for that; ask me for what you need?" "Need?" I asked dumbly.

"Yes, what you were seeking?"

"Seeking? Yeah…, I…," I mumbled. I was struggling to make my thoughts match my words. If you had asked me Teresa Dorterre's age when I walked into her shop, I would have said late forties. At the moment she asked me what I needed, I was starting to believe in sorcery.

As she stared unblinkingly at me from across the counter, I pulled out my phone and showed her a picture of the receipt from Lieutenant Perales and her picture. Teresa merely glanced at both.

"Yes, I remember her coming into the store the day after the gold was found.

She bought a copy of Jolly's Journal."

"She say why she wanted it? Souvenir?"

"She didn't say exactly. I didn't think it was a souvenir. She walked in and went straight to it on the rack, returned to the counter to pay for it."

"Did you exchange any words?"

"Sure; I asked if she was working on the graves; she said she was. I tried to gossip about how exciting it was about the gold that was found. She responded

that I shouldn't believe in everything I see and hear."

"What did you think she meant at that point?" I asked.

"Figured she didn't feel like gossiping. Maybe she thought I was not respecting the dead. Not sure but she left right after that."

We talked about a few other things of no consequence, and I realized she was closing soon. Moreover, I had some place to be, and I felt my thirst for tea returning. I glanced out the window. The sun was just setting over the Tar River. Gas lanterns were glowing throughout the neighborhood, adding to the historic feel of the old buildings. I noticed a group of people under one of the lamps. It was Baliles regaling the crowd with a tale of Jolly Benoit and nineteenth century pirate life.

"Hey, Baliles doesn't seem to be a fan of the Jolly Benoit's Journal," I said to Teresa.

"Yeah, he hasn't been the same since it came out," Teresa explained. "It's hard to reconcile yourself to something you take no pride in, no matter the popularity."

"Why would he have pride in the journal?" I asked. Teresa looked at me with an expression somewhere between amusement and sympathy, like I was the object of a joke she heard behind my back.

"Because he wrote it, Handsome. Baliles is Dr. Geoffrey Paskiewicz."

Benoit's Bar 8:00 pm.

I walked into Benoit's, and it was packed. I stood just inside the doorway trying to be unnoticed. By now Gerald, Fedelito, and I were pretty well known. People in the small town were starting to make up their minds about us, most of it probably negative. Despite the sideway glances, everyone seemed to be engrossed in the music.

Angela C. Babineaux was transformed from boat captain to queen of the stage. She was wearing black tight leather pants, with a pink and black t-shirt sporting a pattern of tears to resemble the work of claw marks. She was halfway through a version of No Doubt's "I'm Just a Girl!"

I felt a tap on my shoulder. It was the bouncer who turned out to be one of the boat patrols that brought us into town, the big loud one called Quentin. He pointed over to the bar. The barmaid was waving me over to her. As I weaved through the crowd, I realized the bartender was Sheriff's Cormac's daughter. She looked a lot better than the last time I saw her.

"Hey, you're Manion, right?" she asked. I nodded. "We saved you a seat over there."

She pointed at the end of the U-shaped bar closest to the stage. There was an empty stool.

"Make your way over and I'll get you a drink. Jack Daniels or Jameson?" "Jack Black, straight, with ice and a lime," I answered.

I nodded, wondering how she knew my drink choices. By the time I reached my seat and took my first two sips, Angela, stage name A-Babs, was getting into Pink's "Get the Party Started," and everyone was singing along.

She was good. She did everything I had seen great performers do. By the end of my first drink, even I had loosened up and joined in on the singing. I stayed past last call for the bar and the last set of the band.

My head was still humming with all the things I learned that day. I needed to talk it out with someone. It had to be someone local who knew all the players, but wasn't a beguiling book seller or an angry street performer.

"Thanks again for that deal with Gaspare. I knew he was slick when he hired me, but I never thought he would try to get totally out of paying me," she said as she sat at the bar next to me. She sat straight up, her eyes still wide with energy from performing. She turned down a drink and took a cold bottled water she kept behind the bar.

"No problem. Thanks for the invite. Damn, is there anything you don't do well?" I asked.

"Yeah," she said with that same athletic girl-next-door laugh. "Make enough money in any one thing to keep myself alive."

"What about the singing? You ever thought about a career in that?" I asked.

She shook her head and took a swig of water and continued.

"Naw, I sing for fun. I couldn't see myself on *The Voice* or any of that TV shit. If I could get the charter boat thing going, fishing, sightseeing, private hire, whatever, I would sail by day, sing by night, and leave the bartending to the kids."

"What's stopping you from making a go of it? You seem like you got a good reputation around here. You can handle a vessel?"

"Yeah, the good ol' boy club is alive and well in boating. Most of these guys got their start from my grandfather and uncle who taught me.

Now that I am the only one of my family left, I can get some work after all their boat appointments are full or when they are away on vacation."

"Who's your biggest competition?" I asked.

"Oh, there are a lot of them but the biggest one is Clark Charters. You know, that big-mouth Quinten we ran into the other night? His daddy's vessels."

"Is he a bouncer here?"

"*No!*" she said emphatically. "He just hangs out at the door in black clothes like a bad ass for no reason. Owner lets him do it because he looks like a bouncer and people won't cause trouble."

"He seems like he's into you," I said by way of inquiry. Angela took a long drink of water and looked at me with mischievous eyes.

"Nope, he just hangs out at the door like he is. Stupid. Quinten is part of my history long ago and better left there. Any more questions, Insurance Man?"

"Just curious, and its Teke," I said, giving her mischief right back.

"Well, Teke, let's get out of here. I need to walk some of this energy off. Plus, I know a place you will love, and they will love you."

We were out on the muggy streets. It was about 1:00 AM. She told me about her childhood, the only child of Cecil and Sarah Babineaux who was part of the first fishermen families to do charters in the Tar River-Pamlico Basin. Her mother worked for the City of Washington, NC, a few miles down the river. Her mother never cared much for life on the water, like her husband and his brothers who were Angela's uncles. Angela's father died when she was young.

She said she barely remembered him.

At age eleven, Angela started spending weekends in Gilleyville, and she learned the business by her grandfather's side, and after he passed she continued to learn from her uncles. Her love of charter boating would be a point of separation between her and her mother, but they worked around it, coming to an agreement to disagree.

"Occasionally, I go down to Washington and take her out on the boat just before sundown when it's calm. Mom said she did enjoy that from her childhood."

Eventually we came to the Emancipation Bridge that separated Benoitown and Gilleyville. We began to walk across it. We stopped halfway and looked north up the river. At a point 500 feet upstream, each side of the riverbank was cordoned off with yellow tape. There was temporary lighting set up and a military sentry standing at the top of each steep, muddy riverbank.

"They say Jolly and Sam used to meet right about where those lights are set. They planned the two towns and hid the gold they stole from 100 Spanish ships," she mused.

"Was that in the book or is that a Baliles story?" I asked.

"Both, I think," she said. "It's one of my favorite stories. Two dreamers working through their differences and a world set against them to carve out

their little piece of this world their way." I nodded but said nothing.

"Sounds corny don't it?" she said sheepishly.

"Not at all," I responded.

"You see, Teke, I know your type, Man," she said very looking intently at me, genuine but sounding like a really cool eighties female rocker, her thumbs hitched in the belt loops of the jeans she wore now.

"I read about you: financial deal maker jumping around Europe; read about White Sand Island to; even read about your brother the musical prodigy," she said, doing air quotes around the word "prodigy."

"And you think you know me?" I asked flatly.

"No, not totally, but I know the kind of personality it takes to do what you do—wandering hunger, endless curiosity, restlessness with things too familiar." I smiled despite myself.

"See, I'm right," she said and playfully pulled my ear. "I even saw a picture of that French boss of yours, looks like a fucking model. You live in that world.

But see—I'm like Jolly and Sam. I just want to carve out a small piece of the world my way and be left alone to live it. I can't do that chasing some singing dream, but I can live that dream on my boat."

"But Jolly and Sam had each other; Jolly was married for almost fifty years?" I said before even thinking about it.

"Wow, the insurance man has a domestic streak, wants to marry me off," she said and laughed just a little too loud to be totally genuine. "Who you got in mind?"

"I don't know," I said, stepping closer to her to purposely break the rocker façade she was giving me. To her credit she didn't step back, just glanced up in my face with dancing eyes.

"Wandering hunger has taught me a lot of things," I said. "For one, dreams are more valuable and longer lasting when shared."

She looked very kissable right there on the Emancipation Bridge in her Joan Jett attitude and low-slung jeans. I would like to say I turned away first, but it was her. Since I needed information and not distraction, I turned to finish walking across the bridge with her.

"I am sure there will be someone," she said. "But that someone will love my dream as much as me, or he won't be my forever man."

"Got it," I said, nodding doing my best façade of passive interest.

Just like that, she snapped out of her reflection.

"That being said, you are my 'for now' man. C'mon, Tekelius, let's go!"

Her energy was infectious, and I found myself literally running the rest of the way across Emancipation Bridge. We walked another block just past the Gilleyville starting spot for Riverside Graveyard. We turned right on the first street that ran parallel to the Tar River on the Gilleyville side. It was almost pitch-black except for a light about 500 feet ahead. I could make out most of the buildings. They were the same old warehouse style, but they appeared to be abandoned. I couldn't tell if from the storm or just age. The floodwater had not been as bad on the Gilleyville side of the river.

As we got closer, I could actually make out parked cars along the street, and I heard voices. It sounded like a party. I looked at Angela, who squealed with delight and grabbed my hand.

The street terminated at a clump of trees that I was pretty sure led down to the river. At the end of the street was a building that looked like a small two story clapboard house in the front, but had a sizable one-story add-on in the rear. There was sign that read, *HI-SIDE BLUES BAR*.

"C'mon, Teke," Angela said in the exciting female southern accent that always got me going. We jogged through the grass to the back of the building. There was a single door opening, and one older African-American man of about seventy sitting on the stool. There was a single exterior light fixture just above his head, giving him a spotlight effect.

People seemed to come and go as they pleased, and he occasionally spoke to some of them.

"Angela, is that you hiding in the shadows?" the man shouted as we got within 20 feet.

"It's me, Hiram; how's it going tonight? You all getting back to usual?"

As we reached Hiram, they hugged briefly. He was short, about Angela's height, and medium brown skin over a jowly grandfatherly face. His eyes were quick and danced around as he kept his head on a swivel. His eyes danced my way several times, but he continued to speak to Angela.

"We getting things back together slowly but surely," he said. "But what's been going on with you? I can tell you are glowing, Little Sista'. Did you kill it on stage tonight like Uncle Hiram taught ya?"

"You know it," Angela said, her arm still around Hiram's shoulders.

"Okay, I thought you may just be glowing from tall dark and quiet over there," Hiram said, casually acknowledging me.

Angela made introductions.

"Hiram Brown and his brother are famous in blues circles all over the world."

"Who is your brother?" I asked innocently. Angela and Hiram looked amazed.

"Blind Billy Brown of New Orleans, the Famous Triple B," Angela said, and I was duly impressed. Blind Billie Brown was my brother's favorite blues musician of all time.

"It is an honor, sir. My brother has been listening to the two of you for years," I said and held my hand out to him. Hiram gave it a firm shake.

"Before you go kissing my rings, young man, my brother is the superstar. I just share the gene pool, and I manage out a tune or two."

"Bullshit, Teke," Angela interrupted. "All those songs your brother likes? —that smart piano, keyboard, and trombone you hear is this man right here."

"I get the name of the place now— 'Hi' is short for Hiram," I said.

"What else would it be?" Hiram asked.

"At first," I started explaining and feeling things go south, "I thought it was because Gilleyville is on the high side of the riverbank."

"Hey, man, I'm from Benoitown. You saying we low people?"

"Not at all! I see your point," I said, stepping back to remove shoe from my mouth figuratively.

Hiram and Angela had a conspiratorial laugh at my expense.

We talked for a few more minutes. Then Angela and I went inside. It was a dimly lit single room about 50 feet square. Just inside the door to the right was a bar with a few customers. The stage in the back actually had a shimmering curtain around it. There were 30 small tables randomly arranged throughout the room. It was about half full.

"Let's sit at the bar," Angela said, sliding onto a stool halfway down. There was a slim girl with dark brown skin and large beautiful eyes behind the bar. She had light blue and pink ribbons intertwined in her braided hair. She asked us for our drink order.

"He'll have a Jack on the rocks and a tequila and ginger ale for me," Angela said. The two of them shared a conspiratorial look and a smile before the barmaid walked off to fill our order. We turned our backs to the bar and faced the large room and the stage.

As if on cue, Hiram reached the microphone in front of the stage lights.

"Ladies and gentlemen, coming to the stage is the return of our house band,

The Hi-Siders featuring one of our favorite singers, Angela Babineaux!"

She gave me her best, 'surprise' grin, fueled by my surprise. The room was applauding loudly.

"Sit tight, Manion," she said with a wink, hopping off the stool, grabbing her drink that had recently appeared, and walking quickly through the tables towards the small stage. By now the shimmering curtain was pulled back revealing the band, a group of musicians all over sixty years old.

The barmaid handed my drink to me. As I reached behind me to take it from her, my eyes caught someone at one of the seats next to the stage. The stage lights barely illuminated her face, but I was sure it was her.

"Good morning, Mrs. Phillips," I said once I reached them. Nadine was in an animated conversation with two younger men. They did not see me walk up to the table.

"Manion," she said, clearly surprised. She looked around frantically and back to me.

"No, Gerald is not here," I said and took a sip of my drink. "But he is looking for you."

"Hey, Man, this is a private conversation," one of the young men said, getting to his feet. Angela and the band went into a version of BB King's *Made Your Move Too Soon*.

"It's okay, Louis," Nadine said, pulling his six-foot, five-inch frame down to his seat. He was clean-cut, a college athletic type. He had a medium brown complexion, honest and forthright eyes and a fresh haircut. His hand shook a bit.

The other man at the table was just as young, between twenty-one and twenty-five. He never moved, just looked up at me under the brim of his low-slung fedora. He had a slight smile on his face, with lips holding a lit cigarette, but the eyes that stared out from his dark-brown face promised trouble if I didn't tread carefully. He kept one hand under the table, and I was sure Nadine would not be able to pull him back once he got started.

"Gerald is looking for you," I said again, standing very still, not wanting to make a scene.

"How do you know I didn't already talk to him?" she asked sarcastically.

"Did you?" I asked, pulling my phone out to call Gerald. She stared at me, making a show of not being fazed by my gesture. I had nothing to lose. I punched in the number and walked back towards the back of the room so I could hear over the band.

It rang once, twice, then someone behind me pulled the phone from my hand. It was the dangerous one with the fedora, wicked eyes holding a cigarette between his lips. He disconnected the call, made few more taps, and dropped my phone in his jacket pocket. Nadine and the nervous kid were standing there, too. They had followed me to the back.

"Look, Manion, we are leaving, but just believe me. I will call Gerald first thing in the morning. We got some things we are working on tonight. If you wake Gerald up, he's gonna come after me and get in the way."

"That may not be a bad thing," I said to her but all the while looking at her escorts. Wicked Eyes smiled slightly broader. The other kid just continued to look nervous.

"Well, I'm asking you for me," she said. "It's not like you're new to keeping secrets. I just need tonight, or should Stacey hold onto your phone until morning?"

"Okay," I said, not wanting to get into it with Fedora Stacey over a phone. "But what's with all the secrecy? Maybe I can help." All three of them laughed.

"No, Tekelius, you and my husband are too close to the police to be any help to us, but we will keep you posted. I will talk to Gerald by dawn. Deal?"

"Deal," I said.

Nadine nodded to Stacey. He pulled my phone from his pocket. Checking the screen, he smiled.

"There you go! Just like new," he said over the cigarette in his mouth and a tip of his fedora. "Just keeping everybody honest."

He tossed the phone back to me. I suspected he removed the SIM card, but I was wrong. He actually initiated the "factory reset" application. My phone was as damage-free and as empty as the day I bought it. No contacts, no notes, nothing. Even using the cloud to reload my data would take at least an hour with the sketchy cell service in this part of the state.

I sat and downed my drink. Bright eyes placed another one by my elbow. Angela was halfway through a version of *Something to Talk About*, the Bonnie Raitt hit.

I felt things were happening on this case, but at that point in the middle of the night I was at my limit. Rudolph Lemieux, my guru-sensei, cautioned me about not overworking situations and circumstances.

"If you let the world come to you, the answers will be easier to see," he was fond of saying.

It felt surreal thinking of Lemieux and his teachings while halfway around the world. It made me relax, sip my drink, and watch the beautiful singer I could feel flirting with me from the stage.

Then   again,   maybe   it   was   just   the   booze.

Chapter 18
Mayoral Manor
- Gilleyville

His Honor Vergene T. Managualt lay in bed wide awake. Once again he had partaken of the barbeque ribs from Blackbeard's Cafe after 8:00 PM. His stomach, what there was of it, was doing full flips. Mayor Managualt was a descendent of the Tidewater Managualts, a thin, hardworking, rawboned clan with a lot of nervous energy. He weighed 160 pounds and stood just under six feet tall. His sandy brown hair, which he kept cut short and even all over, matched freckles on his face. He had smart gray eyes, but a big smile for everyone he met. People likened him to a better-looking, taller, and friendlier Ross Perot.

That night he had taken Pepto-Bismol for the gas, Zantac for the acid, and chewed mint leaves from his wife's garden to get some needed relief. For now, he was lying in bed wide awake. He could get up and watch television until his remedies kicked in, but then his wife Mary would know he was not well. That would be the last barbeque he would have until next spring.

It was during this mental quandary that he heard it. Voices from outside. Men. More than two. He couldn't make out what they were saying, but they were speaking excitedly and moving through the yard. He could hear their feet dragging through the healthy dewy St. Augustine grass.

"Who is stupid enough to break into the mayor's house?" he thought.

But there were a lot of out-of-towners in the area. Realizing he had lain there listening to them long enough, he slid out of bed, hitting the floor on his hands and knees. Mary mumbled something but continued to sleep. Crawling over to the window, he slowly peered out, hoping to God Almighty that he would not see another face just on the other side of the glass pane. He didn't.

There were at least four of them. Out by the tomb of Sam Gilley. The former home of Sam Gilley was now the mayoral home for whoever held the office for the town of Gilleyville. The tomb holding the remains sat at the edge of the property on the west side of the lawn. Vergene could see one standing outside the tomb appearing to be the lookout. The others were actually inside the six-foot-by-8-foot vault containing the body and several valuable keepsakes of historical significance.

Why would somebody want to do that? he wondered.

They were starting to break the marble and granite with picks and sledgehammers. He could also tell they were drunk. Then he remembered this business about finding gold in the graves that bubbled up from the flood. Could they be here for that? He couldn't let this go on. At this rate, they would destroy the entire tomb.

He turned and crawled out of this bedroom, getting to his feet in the hall. He raced in bare feet, boxers, and a sleeveless undershirt to his office. He didn't turn on any lights so as not to alert them of his presence. Better they think that the house is still asleep.

He fumbled around in the left-side drawer of his large oak desk. He found the keys to his gun cabinet. There was just enough moonlight to see the Mossberg 500 pump action rifle and full-size shells. He picked up the box but thought better of it.

I don't want to kill 'em, just scare them off, he thought to himself.

He picked up several boxes of shells until he found the small round buckshot he used for quail hunting. He quickly filled the chamber. He walked slowly through the dark farmhouse, back down the hall, through the kitchen, and into the mudroom. There he slipped his feet into his black rubber boots. He opened the backdoor and the creak seemed deafening, but they never noticed.

He stepped into the backyard and hid from tree to tree.

When he was forty feet away, he quickly racked the Mossberg and shot his first volley in their direction but well over their heads. The gun boomed in the echo of the muggy night.

"I don't know what you want in that tomb, but if you ain't off this property in the next ten seconds, I will make sure you end up in one of your own!"

He racked the rifle again and sent small round shot in their direction. Now they were cursing and bumping into each other. Trying to figure out which way was the best way out and avoiding the crazy man with the shotgun. Vergene stayed hidden behind the last tree, bracing the Mossberg against his left shoulder. It took a little more than ten seconds, but they did take off running west, jumping the low fence and continuing on foot. Vergene walked up to inspect the damage. The tomb was a mess. At first glance it didn't appear that they got anything. They even left their flashlights. Vergene picked one up and turned it on to get a better look. The compartment that held Sam Gilley's remains was partially damaged. Another minute and they would have had access to the body. Vergene shone the light through the hole in the marble compartment panel, and that's when he saw it and called the police.

River Access Road – Gilleyville side

The access roads to the Tar River were actually gravel trails that ran parallel to the shore between the water and the grassy riverbank. They were a joint venture between the state parks department and the local electric company. They provided a flat surface wide enough to allow egress for service vehicles and vessel launches as well.

Tonight, a lone figure ran down the middle of the service road about a third of a mile north of the Emancipation Bridge. He could see the National Guard lights where the graves were disturbed by floodwater. He slowed to a walk when he saw the shadows of sentry guards ahead. He felt alone and naked.

He was supposed to meet the connection that night, to discuss the plan about the gold and what happened to Lieutenant Perales in the staging room. He barely got out of the hotel with his wallet and his phone.

In the end nobody showed up at the meeting place. That was bad. Also he hoped to get a place to hide. He couldn't stay where he was. Too public. He needed time to figure out his next move and talk to the fucker that got him in this mess. Then he received another text saying to meet on the access trail north of the dig site. He didn't recognize the number, but he didn't know if it was a trick by the MPs to find him. Eventually he decided to go. He couldn't keep roaming the streets in the dark.

Passing a patch of brush between the access road and the adjacent riverbank, he heard it.

"Hey, Corporal, stop," the voice from the bushes said. He didn't recognize it.

"Who are you?" he asked breathing hard, his heart banging in his chest.

"Get off of the trail before someone recognizes you," the voice said.

That made him turn his back to the brush, step into the shadows it afforded, and look up and down the river and the access road. Before he could turn back to the voice behind him, there was a bag placed over his head.

"What the fuck!" he said inside the plastic bag. He felt himself being pulled back into the brush. He was aware of what was happening to him, and he was ready.

With his hands still free, he quickly tore the plastic from around his nose and mouth. He took a deep breath, and he pulled the bag from his head. The exhale came out in a cough. He breathed in again and coughed blood this time. He tried to turn around and couldn't do it. It was like someone was holding him by the back and holding him in place.

He coughed blood again and fell to the ground. He tried to roll and the pain shot through his entire body and made his head go light. Then someone was on top of Corporal McLean and rolled him over onto his stomach, pushing his face into the grassy riverbank. He coughed again, not able to catch his breath. Now the pain came with every cough. He had to get away and get help. He would rather be caught by the sentry than die   there   in   the   dark.

Chapter 19

I did not dream, and beyond about 2:30 AM the previous night, I had no memory.

I woke up to being shaken by Gerald.

"Hey, Manion, get your ass up," Gerald said. "We got trouble."

I sat up; looked around. I didn't recognize where I was. Then I looked past Gerald who was sitting on the bed next to me. I saw Angela Babineaux in boy shorts style underwear and a tight Green Day t-shirt. She was leaning against the bedroom door, in her bare feet, holding a coffee cup. Her hair was mussed; her smile was sleepy; her expression non-telling. My memory was starting to come back into focus.

He rolled over onto his back with all his might, the searing pain ballooning through his chest and stomach. Kicking and elbowing, he freed himself and stumbled to his feet. As he prepared to run, he got a glimpse of the body behind the voice in the brush.

"You? What do you have to do with anything?!" he said, running for his life.

I looked down. I was naked but for my socks. I didn't remember getting undressed, but had foggy mental images of the last several hours. I looked back at her. We both smiled with mutual recollection.

"Gerald, what's going on? What time is it?"

"Its 7:30, and things are getting ugly out there," he said.

"Hey, did you talk to Nadine?"

"No, I can't; at least not until I get her a lawyer," he explained. "She's in custody."

"What?" Angela and I said in unison.

"Yes, and it's got to do with the new dead body in the river this morning. Get dressed, Manion, we burnin' daylight. I'll be downstairs."

When he left, I jumped from bed too quickly and felt the effects of overindulgence squeeze my head like a vise. I found my underwear, got one leg into my pants, and had to give my head and stomach a chance to settle.

"Here," Angela's voice said. She stood somewhere over me as I sat back on the bed. She was holding a paper cup of black coffee. The smell alone restored my consciousness and made me halfway ready to meet the public.

"Thank you," I said, greedily grabbing the cup from her hand. As I sipped, I could smell her scent. It brought back more memories from last night. I finally got my pants on, and I stumbled to the bathroom. I soaped my hands and washed my face, neck, and few other important parts. Then I ran water over my hair, fingering it into place.

After a few more sips of very strong black, unsweetened coffee, I fingerbrushed my teeth as my brain came fully online.

Gilleyville River Bank - Tar River

Each day the floodwater receded, it revealed new, sometimes strange, sometimes horrible things. That morning the body of Heyworth "Mac"

McLean was stretched out along the riverbank, his head and one shoulder in the water. Sheriff Cormac and one of the MPs were setting up yellow crime scene tape. The rest of the party included the other MPs, Colonel Sanchez, and Barry Butto, the forensic specialist, his white hair almost glowing in the natural morning light. The deceased was in street clothes clearly too small for him, tennis shoes the style a break-dancer or skateboarder would wear. In the back left part of his ill-fitting t-shirt was a large serrated-edged knife. The blade was still halfway in. Maybe it hit bone.

Gerald and I found Adam Samuelson at the top of the riverbank with about two dozen onlookers.

"Well, we just got bad to worse," Adam said, wringing his hands. "It's unfortunate enough that we got the natural disaster of the decade along with this graves-of-gold scenario. Now it looks like we got people whispering about serial killers."

"Did the sheriff say that?" I asked. Adam shook his head and rolled his eyes. It was the most composure I had ever seen him lose.

"Come on, Manion, how many people have to get stabbed by serrated hunting knives before we have a bad news story? State is going to have an absolute hemorrhage over this."

"What does this have to do with Nadine?" I asked, turning to Gerald.

"I don't know yet. Sheriff says he will discuss it with me after processing this crime scene. They won't even let me see her, less known talk to her."

"Did he say she was a suspect, actually use those words?" I asked.

"No, just said she has a 'connection' to the dead body, and he needed to detain her for now."

We stood there watching the crime scene process unfold. I focused and tried to think. I looked around where the body was found. Corporal McLean's body was not near the excavation work I watched the previous night with Angela Babineaux. Rather it was further upstream north of the dig site and the Emancipation Bridge. Wearing someone else's clothes made sense. He left all of his when he fled the hotel. Whose clothes were they? The answer to that would probably go a long way to telling what happened. Did the same person who killed Lieutenant Perales also kill McLean, or was that what the killer wanted us to believe? There was something about the crime scene that seemed staged, a little too television-murder mystery.

"You find a lawyer for her yet?" I asked Gerald.

"I'm on my way, but I wanted one of us to stay with the law to report back to WorldSpan."

"I will do that; you see to Nadine."

"That I will do in more ways than one," Gerald said and walked down the street back into town. He was making a call on his phone as he walked.

I climbed over the railing at the top of the riverbank, explaining to Adam Samuelson that I was going down to speak to Cormac. He made a hand gesture as if to say, *Be my guest.*

I was stopped halfway down by one of the MPs. I showed my identification, making a wave to Sheriff Cormac and Colonel Sanchez. They waved me down to them.

"Good morning," Sheriff Cormac said flatly. "You look like the kind of night we have had; but at least you look better than this guy."

I nodded, just watching the scene up close. I could see Colonel Sanchez visibly upset, being argumentative with the affable Dr. Butto.

"She's obviously not happy with two dead soldiers in two days. This was supposed to a humanitarian mission. Her general is all over her ass. They want to send in full combat. Put this town under martial law."

"They can do that?" I asked. Cormac shook his head.

"It would be like killing a fly with a sledge hammer, but that puts me and my deputies under the gun. Either we get this solved, or they will. The US Army wants their pound of flesh for these murders. One way or the other. Hell, I want it to. This is still my quiet little Southern county. I could have stayed in

Baltimore for this."

"Who reported it?" I asked.

"Get this! Patrol found it. We are out in the middle of the night clearing the drunks off the streets, making sure the bars close with no problems. I should have known it was going to be special."

"How so?"

"You know," Cormac said with a shrug as if searching for his words. "It was just that kind of night. There were more than the usual number of drunks, the out-of-town contractors blowing off steam. There were two bar fights between insurance adjusters from competing companies. One of the deputies pulled over a speeder who was transporting four hundred pounds of marijuana in the trunk of his car. Then there was a naked woman found running down the middle of

Main Street, claiming she was almost choked to death."

"What? Who?"

"Had a British accent, obviously not from here. After Deputy Laurie got her calm and dressed in some jail garb, she didn't want to press charges; wouldn't give me her name; wouldn't give the john's name or address. Eventually I had to let her go."

"You run her prints?" I asked.

"Manion, I had a jail full of drunk men; the last thing I need is to throw female fuel on that fire. Anyway, we went back to the area where we found her. We asked around the downtown area, and that's when patrol found our dead corporal."

"Sounds like a wild night, but what does Nadine Phillips have to do with it?"

"I want to wait and discuss it with her husband first, but we picked her up and we're holding her based on evidence we found on the deceased. Information that lets us know they had contact in the last 12–24 hours."

The cell phone rang on Sheriff Cormac's hip. He snatched it off the holster and read the screen.

"This is the rest of the bad news; it's Deputy Laurie," Cormac said, punching the talk button. "I'm here, Laurie; talk to me."

I could hear Deputy Laurie's voice but couldn't make out the words. I took a step closer to Cormac, but still couldn't get the gist of what was being said.

"Send me pictures; I'm still at the riverbank scene. You are going to have to handle things there. I will get there as soon as I can." He hung up shaking his head.

"It appears the whole county has gone grave robber crazy. The tombs of Sam Gilley and Jolly Benoit were raided last night," he explained.

"Did they disturb the remains? Did they see who did it?" I asked.

"The Gilley tomb was hit first. They broke in, smashed a lot of marble, made a bunch of noise."

"But the bodies?" I asked.

"They didn't get anything or disturb anything for two reasons," Sheriff Cormac said, waving me closer so no one else at the crime scene could hear.

"First, Mayor Managualt of Gilleyville scared them off with several pumps of small-round buckshot. Thinks he may have even hit one."

"How did the mayor come to be there?" I asked.

"The mayor's job in Gilleyville comes with the use of a home on what was Gilley estate lands. The house and the tomb sit on the same property."

"And somebody was bold enough to raid a tomb in the mayor's front yard."

"Seems kind of crazy, huh?"

"You said there were two reasons?"

Sheriff Cormac leaned a little closer. I could smell coffee and Listerine on his breath.

"It seems, according to the mayor and Deputy Laurie, there is no body in the tomb for Sam Gilley."

"What?" I said louder than I should. "You mean it was stolen already?"

"No!" Sheriff Cormac said, looking at me as if I were simple. "There never was one in there. The raiders were just starting on the actual compartment where the remains were supposed to be, but when the mayor and the deputy broke it open all the way to see what was disturbed or taken, there was no body. Never was. Just decades of dust."

"So where is the body of Sam Gilley?" I asked.

"I have no freaking idea," Sheriff Cormac said, wiping morning sweat from his forehead. "That tomb was put there almost 100 years ago."

"What about Jolly's tomb?"

"Well, it's actually a small grave site with a simple headstone. It sits on top of a small hill overlooking downtown Benoitown on land that was Jolly Benoit's home and farm. Now it's the Edgewood County Museum."

"But did it get damaged?" I asked, appreciating the history lesson but anxious about what happened.

"No," Sheriff Cormac said, rubbing his forehead again, the warming fall sun giving rise to an earthy muggy humidity. "Without permission from the sheriff's office, Reverend Moten has been stationing college students out at the site each night in case something like this happened. Raiders tried to get into Jolly's grave and got the surprise thrashing of their lives."

I thought about the two dedicated and highly capable young men who were with Nadine last night.

We stood there quiet for a few minutes, in our own thoughts. I was trying to process everything the sheriff told me, but I was still a little foggy upstairs. At some point I was going to have to call Paris. I wanted to be at the police station with Gerald when they did whatever they were going to do with Nadine.

Also, I realized I hadn't seen our Spanish attaché that morning.

I looked back at the body of Corporal McLean, at Colonel Sanchez standing nearby as Dr. Butto and his assistant processed the crime scene.

The colonel was tough, but I could tell just as in the case of Lieutenant Perales, this was personal for her. They were her people, an extension of her, her responsibility. These murders would also be a reflection on her command in some way. This line of thought brought a question to mind that I had been pondering since I arrived.

"Sheriff, where are the descendants of Benoit and Gilley?"

"I read about that years ago," Sheriff Cormac said. He looked upward as if trying to recall facts. "Benoit had no children; I believe something about the wife couldn't conceive. Gilley moved to New York; had a daughter who got married so she got a name change. But none of them came down to claim the fame. I'm assuming Gilley took his share of the gold to New York and made more money with that."

I nodded, just acknowledging that I heard what the sheriff said. Clearly, I had some more reading to do.

Chapter 20

Darryl "Lemon Boy" Phillips was working in his office—which was the front bedroom of his brownstone tenement building in St. Louis, Missouri. He got the nickname "Lemon Boy" as a kid growing up just across the river in East St. Louis. The kids thought his light-brown complexion and freckles were worthy of a nickname. As is the case of many childhood nicknames, "Lemon Boy" stuck even into adulthood. It didn't bother him. Now in his forties, he still thought it was pretty cool.

For the past several years, and after a stormy departure from the St. Louis County Police Department, Darryl had been running a small security company called Paladin. His partners included his former partner on the force, Bobby Farr Sr., a tough-minded Irish man who wouldn't let his wheelchair confinement stop him or slow him down. There were also the two younger partners: Bobby Farr Jr. was a twenty-three-year-old ex-college tight end, pretty quick with his fist and his snub-nosed 38 revolver. Terri Lovejoy, a diminutive ball of energy with a PhD in clinical psychiatry and a black belt in taekwondo. That morning Lemon Boy got a call from first cousin Gerald, the lawyer.

"What's good, Counselor? Where you calling from—Morocco? Shanghai?"

"Very funny," Gerald replied wearily. "Look Man, I got some real trouble down here in North Carolina, and I need some real help. Your kind of help."

~ ~ ~

Benoitown City Works Building - Early Afternoon

Eventually the processing of the crime scene at the riverbank was finished. As they removed Corporal McLean's body from the river's edge, it didn't seem human, but more like a dead water creature that washed up on shore and died. Grass and sand stuck to his face and hair and clothes as if he were a human drift log.

Sheriff Cormac, Adam Samuelson, and I retreated back to the sheriff's office in the city's works building. There, the hits just kept on coming. As we entered the lobby, we were met by the media. The first one to reach me was the young reporter Al Harrison.

"Sheriff, do you have a comment on this morning's press conference?"

"What press conference? By who?" Sheriff Cormac asked, clearly bewildered by the throng of people in the lobby of the building.

There were media, staff personnel, and curious bystanders. It was obvious the Sheriff was caught totally off guard and showed it. I grabbed Al, pulling him close.

"All right, what the fuck is going on here? Who called this press conference?" I asked.

"Um, all I know is that Reverend Moten told me to be here," Al explained.

"He has an announcement."

"It seems like there were more people here than at a usual Reverend Moten press conference."

"I agree," Al admitted. "I think there are others speaking as well."

Right on cue, a group moved up the hall from a side door. It was Reverend Moten and about six of his young collegiate volunteers. Right behind him was Val Cedars and his sweater-vest youth bullies— and to round out the bizarre circus was Fedelito Gaspare.

They walked past Sheriff Cormac's office, headed to the center of the building where all the hallways met. There had been very few press conferences in the county works building. This portion of the hall was used out of necessity when the flood waters rose.

"First, as the leader of the Citizens for the Ethical Treatment of the Ancestry, the CETA, I want to express our continued concern for the lost souls of the slave ancestors," Reverend Moten started speaking immediately, taking charge of the location.

"Recent activities by persons unknown continue to illustrate the inability or lack of desire by local law enforcement and the National Guard to provide the protection we need. Grave raiders tried to violate the tombs of Jolly Benoit and Sam Gilley just last evening. Both attempts were thwarted."

He paused to let the bystanders respond and murmur. The reporters scribbled.

"I have reached out to the US Justice Department to start an investigation into this entire matter. We have members of the US military grave robbing for gold and ending up dead. I have contacts with the US

Attorney General's office, and our plan is to pursue this to the final answer."

The reporters were raising their hands now and calling out questions. The Reverend Moten took a large step back as if rehearsed. Val Cedars stepped forward. For a few seconds he looked out at the press gallery and citizens. He gave his stern, unblinking, stare for several seconds. The questions and murmurs died down to silence.

"The historical significance of our region is being compromised by grave robbers and vandals. Local law enforcement is powerless to protect the treasures that make this area unique. The Benoitown/Gilleyville National Historic Society will be making a request through the National Historical Society to get additional protection and investigation from these grave robbers. We, along with members of the CETA, will take over the protection of these sites."

That sent an eruption of questions from the press. Sheriff Cormac and I stood down the hall by about 50 feet. He stepped forward to address the crowd, but I held his arm. He looked back at me and my hand on his arm. His eyes said he was ready to assert some order to this circus.

"Sheriff, don't play into it," I whispered to him. "This is a rehearsed and planned show. If you go in there with the muscle of the law, they will play the victim, focus on our frustration and make it look like incompetence, and it will all be about that, not who is killing these people and desecrating the graves."

"So I am supposed to let this go on with no response?" Sheriff Cormac whispered back. I could feel the muscles in his forearm flexing, with the vein forming in the middle of his forehead.

"No, but right now it is just words. We will respond, but not off the cuff. At worst we will have a bad press day. Think about your response;

focus on the dead body in the river. That should be your focus, not what a bunch of talking heads are saying."

He snatched his arm away, but stayed beside me.

"Just think about it," I continued talking. "It is never too late to confront something; sometimes it can be too soon."

He nodded and took a deep breath. Looking at the press conference he pointed to it, urging me to follow his gaze.

"Hello, I am Fedelito Gaspare, and represent the country of Spain. I am here to make Spain's claim on any gold recovered during this process."

It was Gaspare in a shiny silver sharkskin suit. His hair was slicked back, and he was recently in a tanning bed.

"The country of Spain stands in lock step with the Reverend and Mr. Cedars. These dark elements that are killing American soldiers and raiding graves have no respect for these dead souls, the historical beauty of this area, and the right and proper claim of the country of Spain."

"Is that Gaspare up there? What is he saying?"

It was Gerald who had just walked up behind us. He looked more upset than the sheriff did. Gerald and Gaspare had been locking horns from the beginning. With the stress of his wife's arrest, Gerald's patience with Gaspare's histrionics was about gone.

"It's not worth it, Gerald. Let's get with the sheriff and talk about getting Nadine out of custody," I whispered to him. He nodded, but I could tell he was barely keeping it together. The three of us retreated to the office. Cormac put one of his deputies on the door to make sure we were not disturbed. Adam Samuelson was having a quiet conversation with a stately gentleman of about sixty. He was short, stout, but well-dressed with perfectly cut and styled black hair with gray streaks. He reminded me of the television character lawyer Matlock.

"Sheriff, this is Nadine's attorney, Mr. Bunkton," Gerald started.

"I know who he is," Sheriff Cormac said. "How ya' doin', Howell?"

"Doing good, Sheriff. Still getting pretty good peppers and tomatoes this year."

"Really?" Sheriff Cormac said, coming out of his funk. "This late even after the storm? Mine burned out back in the summer and then blew away with Hurricane Chester." They both laughed.

"I told you," Howell Bunkton said with a chuckle and a point of his pudgy manicured finger. "You're still trying to grow those delicate juice tomatoes from up north. You got to switch varieties."

"I know," Sheriff Cormac said, shaking his head. "The Marzano tomatoes just make great sauce."

Adam Samuelson, who all but disappeared in the corner, made a slight throat clearing sound. Gerald was a second from losing it.

"Um, well, I will … um … send you some of my prized beefsteak varieties.

You won't be sorry," Howell Bunkton said quickly. "Shall we talk about Mrs. Phillips? Sheriff, have you charged her at this point?"

"No, I have some questions for her, and she has been less than cooperative," Sheriff Cormac said, also turning serious.

"About what?" Gerald asked impatiently, but Howell Bunkton Esquire kept talking as calmly and sweetly the way he spoke about his prized produce.

"How about it, Sheriff? My client has rights. You can't hold her unless she has a connection to the case."

"True, and we haven't charged her, but she has a connection to the dead man in the river."

"Okay, what is that?" Howell Bunkton asked.

Sheriff Cormac leaned back in his chair and unlocked his desk. He reached into his left side drawer and pulled out several plastic evidence bags. He spoke softly as he laid the bags out on his desk.

"Um, maybe we should excuse Manion and Adam. This does not really concern them personally."

"No, I want them to stay," Gerald said. "We need as many eyes on this as possible. In case we all end up in court over this later."

"Mr. Phillips, we are not charging your wife, but we just have to follow up on every lead and.... "

"You're not charging her, but I couldn't see her? Sounds like two-sided business to me, Sheriff."

Sheriff Cormac turned to Howell Bunkton seeking help with his client, but the stately old lawyer just shrugged. At first glance, it seemed like Sheriff Cormac was being cautious due to his dealing with lawyers, or in response to Gerald's allusion to the possibility that Nadine's civil rights were being compromised. However, the sheriff seemed to be made of sterner stuff. I sensed his verbal light stepping had to do with something else. He took a deep breath and continued.

"First, Howell, I need to ask Mr. Phillips about his whereabouts between two o'clock and six o'clock this morning?"

"What?" Gerald blurted out, but Howell Bunkton placed a calming hand on his arm. My partner continued in a calm tone. "Um, I was at the bar of my hotel until it closed at midnight. I was in my room watching the West Coast baseball playoff game that was in extra innings. Then, I went to sleep."

"Can anyone verify that?" Sheriff Cormac asked, sternly now.

"No," Gerald said irascibly. "Am I a suspect or not?"

"Not right now, but it would be great if we had confirmation of your whereabouts throughout the night."

"Personally I don't know how you got any sleep last night, Gerald," Adam Samuelson said. "There was a rowdy group of contractors in the hotel last night running through the halls creating quite a raucous."

We all looked at the State Department operative after the off-subject comment, but Gerald spoke first.

"That's right; it was crazy last night. I called the front desk several times from my room."

"Okay, we can check that," Sheriff Cormac said, showing obvious signs of relief.

"Damn right you can check it," Gerald said, a triumphant look on his face.

"Okay, I will show you what we got," Sheriff Cormac started. We all stepped or leaned in a little closer to his desk. He held up the first bag.

"These are the contents we extracted from Corporal McLean. First are peanut shells, just like the ones we found near the body of Lieutenant Perales." "So Lieutenant Perales was killed by McLean?" Adam Samuelson asked incredulously.

"No, but he was likely in the room that night and has some contact with the killer," Sheriff Cormac explained. "Next we found his cigarettes; physical inspection shows they are chemically laced. We suspect this will be what they used to subdue the Guards at the forensic facility."

Sheriff Cormac held up another bag with a plastic key card.

"This key card is for a room at the Jasmine Plantation Hotel. We believe he was hiding out there since he eluded the police. This key and the room it opens is registered to Mrs. Phillips."

The room was quiet as a post office on President's Day. I looked at Gerald. His face was unreadable. Sheriff Cormac was now in full investigator mode, staring straight into Gerald's face for any sign that may give him a clue.

"And you have questioned Mrs. Phillips about this key?" Howell Bunkton jumped into lawyer mode.

"I have, but she refuses to say anything; even says she has no knowledge of setting up any room."

"Well, maybe she's a victim of identity theft, Sheriff," Howell Bunkton said.

"Um ... I doubt it. Deputies confirm that a person matching Nadine's description made the reservation in person at the hotel earlier yesterday. That same person matching your wife's description returned to the hotel throughout last night asking about the comings and goings of the occupant of the room."

"Did she offer any explanations at all?" Howell Bunkton asked.

"Only that she did not have anything to do with the killing. Says she has several witnesses that saw her throughout the night, including Manion." The room got small and hot as all eyes turned to me.

"Gerald, I was gonna tell you, but I just have not had a chance. With the dead body and...."

He just stared at me with amazement.

"So you did see Mrs. Phillips last night?" Sheriff Cormac asked. "Yes, and she was with two other gentlemen; neither were Corporal McLean."

"What time was this?" Sheriff Cormac asked.

"Between one and two o'clock last night," I said.

"And you didn't call me?" Gerald asked irritably. "You knew I was looking for her."

"Gerald, I know, but my phone went dead, and I...."

"Oh, I know, Manion. Angela Babineaux happened. Thanks, partner," Gerald said, waving me off and turning back to the sheriff. "Can I see my wife now, Sheriff?"

"In just a minute; we want to check your story. See, I just want to rule out that you did find your wife and Corporal McLean in the Lovers' Suite and then...."

"Lovers' Suite?" Howell Bunkton asked, sensing the rising tide of emotion and placing a hand on Gerald's arm.

"Yeah, the room that was rented was the Lovers' Suite, a high-end accommodation usually reserved for honeymoons, major anniversaries, things like that," Sheriff Cormac continued, maybe taking a small bit of pleasure in Gerald's discomfort.

"You know what, Sheriff?" Gerald said, standing up. "Good thing Manion didn't call me last night, or that theory may have had some merit."

Gerald walked past me and out into the hall. Howell Bunkton was mumbling something to Sheriff Cormac about not taking that last comment as a serious evidentiary of anything. I felt my headache come back.

In about ten minutes, Gerald's whereabouts for last night had been confirmed. He and his attorney were taken to an interview room where

Nadine was waiting. For my punishment, I was subjected to bad coffee, no food, and some intense questioning by Sheriff Cormac.

Interview Room - Police Department; City Works Building, Benoitown, NC

Gerald Phillips was pissed. Ordinarily a cool customer in stressful situations, this was just the opposite. He knew this idea of Nadine getting involved was not a good idea, and he had explained as much.

It aggravated him to no end when people did things despite being warned off, only to have the things go bad in just the way he said. It also aggravated him that he was acting out of character. As opposed to being the calm eye of the storm, he was allowing himself to be tossed around like the debris, feeling like he had no control.

But what put him over the edge was when he walked into the interview room, he saw his wife, Nadine, calmly applying lip gloss in the reflection of the two-way glass set in the wall of the room.

"Baby!" she said louder than normal. She stepped quickly over to hug him.

He didn't hug back. She kissed him. He didn't kiss back.

"Sit your ass down, right now," Gerald said to her. His eyes were dark brown daggers. In her defense, Nadine acquiesced to her husband's request, but still kept a small look of defiance on her face.

"H- hello, Mrs. Phillips," Howell Bunkton said softly as he stepped from behind Gerald and extended his hand to Nadine. "I will be representing you on this matter. Now, if we could just get some...."

"What the hell were you doing hiding a fugitive from the law?" Gerald said, his voice reaching a level that could be considered loud.

Howell Bunkton motioned for him to stay calm. He motioned back and paced the room.

"I didn't hide a fugitive," Nadine said seriously. "But it would be just like this white law to assume the worst before they get the facts."

"Nadine, please, half the sheriff's staff is black or female," Gerald said.

"But that's not who I dealt with on my case. It was Cormac. Just wait 'til Reverend gets a load of this…."

"That slick preacher will not be involved in this," Gerald said through clenched teeth.

"But he has to be. Our rights are being stomped on and ignored, just like those slave graves," Nadine said, her emotion mounting. Gerald wondered how he let this get this far. She was talking like a revolutionary.

"Nadine," he started carefully. "I need you to explain to Mr. Bunkton and me how the dead man came to have your key to the Lover's Suite at the Jasmine Plantation Hotel."

There were a few starts and stops as she strayed off subject. Eventually her rendition went like this:

Yesterday morning, I was working at the reverend's house. I was approached by someone who said they had a witness who would have useful information about the bad business going on at the graves. The witness needed a place to hide because they feared for their life.

The reverend was interested but did not want the person staying at his house. The reverend is an important man, and can't have scandal attached to his name.

Well, it just so happened I had this room already, and I wasn't using it. I told the informant that the witness could use the room for a couple of days, long enough for the reverend and his team to interview them.

Later that afternoon, I heard about the two soldiers arrested in connection with the murdered forensic scientist and the one that escaped and was never caught. It was about then I put two and two together.

I went to the hotel with the informer and the reverend. The witness had left without a trace. By that time, we had confirmed who he was. The plan was to find him and convince him to come back and tell us what he knew. Also, we wanted his help in getting Private Jackson out of custody.

I enlisted the help of two volunteers and we searched every place a soldier could hide on both sides of the river. We looked well into the night, running into Teke at the Hi-Siders Club, but we never found Corporal McLean.

When we ran into the totally naked woman running through the street and the groups of brawling drunks, we figured it was time to head back to the reverend's house.

I fell asleep until the deputies came for me this morning requesting that I accompany them down to the station. The sheriff asked me a bunch of questions but never told me that Corporal McLean was dead until after I was detained. It was then that I asked for a lawyer.

Gerald just looked at Nadine like she had two heads. He could not believe this was his wife. Did he really know her at all? Howell Bunkton just took notes as she spoke. He was still writing after she finished speaking. Nadine sat there with an expression that was hard to read. She seemed unaffected by all that was going on around her. Gerald wondered how she could be so unaware. Or was she aware but did not care?

"And the informer?" Gerald inquired. Nadine looked up as if deciding if she would divulge the name.

"Albert Harrison, the young reporter. He smuggled Corporal McLean from the truck stop in the trunk of his car."

Gerald thought back to the conversation he had with the reporter on the parking lot of the truck stop, him asking all kinds of questions when he had the guy all along. He must have been trying to decide what he had in his trunk.

"Listen," Gerald started but she cut him off.

"Gerald, I know what you are going to say, but I am not leaving. I still have work to do with the CETA."

Gerald and the lawyer Howell Bunkton looked at each other and chuckled.

Then Gerald continued.

"You damn right you are not leaving. You can't. You're a person of interest in a murder case."

Chapter 21

Figuring I had caused enough trouble for one day, I walked back to my hotel room. I showered and changed clothes. I called Camille and gave a general report, leaving out non-pertinent information about Angela Babineaux.

Camille was no fool, and her skeptical expression of my freshly washed but haggard appearance spoke volumes. Nevertheless, it was the middle of the afternoon in Paris. She would brief the partners, and we would talk later that evening.

Afterwards I picked up the *Journal of Jolly Benoit* and did some more reading.

Date: June 1863

The War over slavery rages on into its second year. It has changed our world but not always for the better. Slave revolts and runaways seem commonplace. Citizens from Benoitown and Gilleyville have provided sanctuary to those in need, subjecting themselves to substantial financial and personal loss. There is a group of former slaves and white and Negro free men from up north that travel down south to aid runaway slaves, an insane but brave endeavor. Sama informed me of this group, and has provided them support in terms of money and more importantly the names and locations of anti-slavery farmers and city dwellers that will assist these underground agents as they are known.

For my part, it is important that I appear impartial to the war, not favoring one side or the other, but fussing over the well-being of our sister cities. This has brought about some disdain from my brothers who want to take up the revolt charge. They have heard the stories of Haiti's revolution and my part in the aftermath. They ask, "Papa Benoit, why you no lead us like General Toussaint? We stand ready to fight like the Haitians!"

My brothers and sisters are bold, strong, beautiful people with amazing gifts bestowed by the great creator, but they are children in the ways of man's beastly side. They think they know war from the songs and fables of the survivors. They do not know.

Recently, the southern army exercises their cannons from the ships in the tidewater or from the large fields to the north and west. The roar of cannon fire makes the men stand uneasy and close together. The women and children cower inside for the rest of the day and night. Eventually the fight will come up and down the Tar River. I pray to the great creator that I am smart enough and leader enough to keep them all safe.

I have done my part. I continue to do things as I have always done. I work my land, visit the stores, churches, and medicine people. I even continue to commune at the top of the morning at the spot up stream where Sama and I first laid out plans for these cities. At each spot, I have exchanged information for the northern army. I agreed to give them information about troop movements and ship positions in and around North and South Carolina. I give information to other blacks and sympathetic whites working for the Northern cause with the point that I will never ever meet with a member of the Northern army. At first this was met with suspicion but Sama Gilley, who has earned influence in New York in these past years, vouched for my integrity with the right people. I never know how much good my efforts are doing for the war effort, but the new mayor of Gilleyville tells me it is invaluable. He is a hardworking young man with strong Christian leanings. He is the son of one of the first families that Sama met in New York. I had my doubts in the beginning even over the assurances from my friend. However, Algernon Barklay has won me over in time. Among his first contributions was his introduction of Mr. Fisk, who eventually took care and control of the remaining gold supply left in North Carolina. The uncertainty of war and the lingering legend of gold have kept me up through the night with worry.

Date: September 1864

The rages of war loom closer and closer. The cannon fire we hear now are not exercises but real battle. Some families from both sides of the river have departed to what they feel is safer ground. There is no safer ground in a war.

We have been able to acquire additional lands for very little paper money and even less gold. It has not been as easy to do things in secret with Sama gone to the north, but the pretense of secrecy seems less important when people are wide-eyed | with constant fear. I have even bought property directly without a go-between using gold. I expected to get questions or surprise at the site of gold in my African hands. Quite the contrary. The fear of escaping the cannon boom and the danger it represents makes white landowners blind to the unnatural sight of a Negro with a hand full of gilded coins.

Algernon and I have regularly met at the twin cedars to engage with Mr. Fisk. The same ground Sama and I stood on many mornings talking our dream into bricks, streets, and glass. Fisk has never failed to respond and prove an iron strong protector of our treasure.

I reread the passage. The Jolly Benoit story was getting thicker. I knew the names Benoit and Gilley, but who were Fisk and Barklay? I wondered if they still had descendants in the area. Those were fairly common southern names. I thought I would make another visit to the bookshop and ask Teresa Dorterre'.

In the meantime, I updated my own notes.

Was there gold somewhere in this town? A lot of people thought so. So much so they would kill for it.

What is the connection between Lieutenant Perales and Corporal McLean? They obviously knew each other, but were not close. The lieutenant was obviously onto something, and someone killed her for it.

Did McLean kill Perales? Highly doubtful, but evidence shows he was there.

If someone else killed Perales and knew McLean was there, then that would make sense.

This person, X, would kill Perales for what reason? She found him or her raiding the graves looking for gold? That would do it, but that seems like it was someone who couldn't leave the area. Someone local?

Was the person who killed Perales in partnership with McLean? Were the parties there at the same time for the same reason but not working together?

Doesn't seem likely.

More likely they were working together. That would explain why McLean, a decorated veteran, could be caught off-guard and stabbed in the back. It had to be someone he knew. That was why he came out of hiding in the middle of the night.

But what was Perales researching? Something sent her to the bookshop to research Jolly Benoit. Something sent her back to the lab at that hour, surprising the others.

I figured it was time to head back to the jail to see what they learned from Private Jackson. Now that his friend was dead, he may be in a mood to talk. Also, I need to ask Sheriff Cormac and Colonel Sanchez about anything in Perales' personal effects.

Maybe by then Gerald will be on speaking terms with me.

Main Street – Benoitown

I found the small riverside town alive with protest. As I walked down Main Street towards the river, I saw twenty-five of the followers of Reverend Moten picketing in front of the City Works Building. They wore CETA t-shirts and were holding signs that read, BLACK SOULS MATTER, RESPECT THE DEAD, and FREE PRIVATE JACKSON. Instead of chanting at the city officials held up inside the City Works Building, they were directing shouts at other groups.

Val Cedars and members of the BGNHS were chanting back at the CETA. Dressed in various vests all red, they held signs that read, RESPECT THE HISTORY and PROTECT OUR TREASURES.

"Val, what is this about? You already filed your injunctions with the court," I asked, stopping in front of the groups. I had to shout to be heard.

"Its civic activism, Insurance Man," Val shouted back. "We have been in touch with the National Historic Registry. In a day or two we will have 1,000 preservation soldiers here to protect our treasures."

"What treasure? We only have three coins, and Spain has a claim," I said, almost laughing.

"Well, we will see about that; I think the original claim is with the tribes of the Yucatan. Therefore, it might as well stay here."

"Yeah, where is that Spanish Floppy-Doo?" asked one of the big male drones of his.

"I don't know, haven't seen him," I answered, never taking my eyes off Val Cedars who never took his eyes off me.

"Well, I hear he has a love for knives, and we got two dead bodies from stabbing," the young man said. He was sweating and breathing hard.

The sweater vest he wore was at least two sizes too small. The material was stretched so thin I could see the shirt underneath.

"That's enough, Bo," Val said, cutting off the young man. Bo Boulage started as if coming out a trance. He mumbled what sounded like an apology and took a step back.

"Your boy seems to know a lot about facts not reported in the paper yet," I said to Val.

"Yes, he does," Val said, a smug smile on his face. "But where is your master?"

"Who?" I asked.

"Oh, I mean your principal, the little Spaniard you work for?"

"Haven't seen him," I answered as I walked away and ignoring the obvious attempt to goad me. "I'll tell him you're looking for him when I see him."

"You do that," Val said to my back.

I found my way inside and down the back hallway leading to the jail cells. When I found the MPs stationed outside a cell I slowed, figuring it was the holding unit for Private Jackson. I held my hands up to the MPs who gave me looks that said, *Not another step closer.*

I stood about five feet away. I could hear Private Jackson being interviewed by Colonel Sanchez and Deputy Laurie. He was sobbing heavily. Obviously, he had been told about his friend lying dead on the riverbank less than six blocks away. I couldn't make out what they were asking him, but I could hear the grief stricken private very well.

"I swear the first time Mac and me talked about the gold was two nights ago," he stated through a voice garbled with emotion and nasal sniffs.

"See, he was having money troubles back home; about to lose his car, credit cards maxed out, and stuff like that. So he said we would just look around in the graves a little bit to see if he could just get one more piece. I told him I didn't want to do it, but he was my buddy so I kind of went along with it. He said he knew someone who could take care of it. Would get him cash quick. We tried to start up a conversation with Lieutenant Perales because her team found the first coins. Mac pissed her off, and she left before we could ask her anything. Later that night, I guess he went out but that wasn't unusual.

I figured he was going out to smoke or flirt with the girl behind the desk in the lobby. I didn't think anything about it. When I woke up the next morning, he was already up and in the shower. That's when the MPs showed up and Mac jumped from the window. We never had a chance to talk about what happened that night."

I heard Deputy Laurie's voice. Then Private Jackson answered.

"No, I have no idea who he was meeting to pass off the gold coins to. He never said anything, and I never met them."

The rest of the interview involved the private crying pitifully. Colonel Sanchez was obviously instructing him of his fate from a military standpoint. A few minutes later, Colonel Sanchez and Deputy Laurie emerged from the cell. They saw me and walked past. I turned and caught up with the colonel.

"Manion, I don't have time for you right now," she started, not looking my way.

"Just a couple of questions about Lieutenant Perales," I said.

"For the life of me, I don't know why the sheriff gives you so much access, but this is a military matter and off limits to you," she said, not missing a step.

"The lieutenant was investigating something about the gold discovery," I said, and she stopped.

"How do you know this?"

"One, she was at the lab late at night after having a drink. She was troubled by something having to do with the dig. Second, she went to the local bookshop specifically to buy a copy of the Jolly Benoit journal."

"So she went and bought the number one tourist item in this area," Colonel Sanchez said.

"True, but she has been here almost a month with the cleanup and then the graves. She is just getting around to buying it now, only after the discovery of the gold."

Colonel Sanchez stopped and fully turned back to me, her eyes dark with emotion.

"You saying my forensic officer caught gold fever?" Colonel Sanchez asked, her voice on edge as she stood inches from me.

"No, not at all. I don't know what it was, at least not for sure," I said, choosing my words carefully. "I think she had questions about the gold, but you knew her? How she thought?"

"I did know her, Manion. Like a younger sister," Colonel Sanchez said, her eyes fixing on my face like two dark marbles. "I want the motherfucker who did this. I am going to gut the son of a bitch with his own knife. And I am going to gut anyone associated with him. You understand me?"

"Clearly, so go back and look through her things, maybe there are some notes, some indication what she was concerned about. That is the clue we need.

I can come with you."

"No—I will do it," she said, seeming to think about my words, turning it over in her head. Her eyes became more thoughtful and less predatory. "Thanks,

Manion. If I find something, I will let the law know."

I raised my hands indicating no problem with that plan. After that, she walked up the steps at the end of the hall?

~ ~ ~

Hillside Plantation Inn

Returning to my hotel, I found Gerald and Fedelito in the lobby. They were in a corner sitting in chairs separated by a low table.

"What the hell, Gaspare?" I started. "I thought we were a team."

"No, I have tried to be a part of the team, but you and Señor Phillips have thwarted my efforts every time," he said. He was standing now, pointing his middle finger bejeweled with the ruby ring.

"What are you talking about?" Gerald asked, rising from his chair.

"What is our mission? To recover gold for the country of Spain," Fedelito started, pointing his finger at both of us. "Now we have dead bodies and getting no answers. I have never been so disrespected by employees in my life."

"We are not your damn employees," I explained for the tenth time. "And we can't include you in murder discussions because the sheriff doesn't trust you."

"No!" Gaspare replied loudly. People behind the front desk about 30 feet away looked up in alarm. I raised a hand, assuring them there was no reason for concern.

"I am not talking about the sheriff," Fedelito said. "I am talking about my briefing from you two."

"We don't trust you either," Gerald said with a deadpan expression. Gaspare clapped his hands once and pointed at Gerald.

"That's not true," I interjected. "But Gaspare you have been a loose cannon. I mean what is your embassy saying about the moves you've been making, getting engrossed in local politics? I thought we were supposed to be low key here."

"That may have been your instructions," he said, leaning over to bang his fist on the table again. "The country of Spain gave their favorite son one instruction: if there is Spanish gold there, secure it and bring it home where it belongs."

"You boys need to keep it down over here," came a woman's voice behind me. I saw Gerald whip around in the direction from which it came. I turned around and saw Nadine standing smiling. She looked even better than during her time in jail. She was wearing one of her signature sundresses that Gerald always bragged about. She seemed more relaxed. Her face was made up, and her long braids were curled and styled. Her medium brown skin was radiant from her face to her runners' legs. She looked ready to go on vacation. The other lady was also African-American, with dark-brown skin and a small athletic frame.

She was not smiling but had intelligent eyes set in a cute pixie face.

"Babe, how you doing?" Gerald asked as he took her in his arms. He kissed her on the cheek.

"I knew if there was noise or trouble Teke Manion would be near," Nadine said.

"Yet the last time I saw you, I got my phone taken," I said, giving her back as much as she gave me.

She was teasing me, but I was aware Nadine Charleston-Phillips did not list me among her favorite people. I was a member of the out-of-town, globetrotting world citizens of which her husband, Gerald, had been a member.

She was always anxious that working with me would spark that wanderlust in him, taking her husband away from her. I was no threat, but she was a careful character when it came to those things close to her. I actually liked that about her. Too often people failed to fight for the things they should.

"Come on you two, play nice," Gerald admonished.

"It's cool, Baby," Nadine said to Gerald. "I owe Teke an apology. We were pretty rough on him last night. If I had worked with him, maybe I wouldn't be a person of interest in a murder investigation."

"No problem, Nadine. I'm a big boy, and I know you really love me," I said disguising my surprise.

"Don't push it, Manion."

"Uh, who's your friend, Nadine?" Gerald asked as he pulled from his embrace.

"This is a new volunteer, Terri Paladin, from St. Louis," Nadine said.

We all waved.

"So, Little Terri, are you here for the cause of the poor black slaves or you trying to get close to the gold?"

We were all stunned by Gaspare's nasty remark on someone he just met, but before we could respond, Terri crossed to stand inches away from Gaspare.

"You know, the truth of it is you and I are really the same height. But those are some pretty good lifts in your shoes" she said, and we all erupted in laughter. All except Gaspare. Terri turned away from him and continued talking.

"I'd been watching the news about Benoitown while working on my job at 7-11. Finally, I had to come and do my part."

"This is what happens when the people mobilize. This is going to be a nationwide movement before we are done," Nadine said with renewed energy and pride. "We will leave you gentlemen to … whatever you were doing."

After the ladies left, Gerald and I turned back to Gaspare.

"Listen, I got work to do," Gerald said. "Gaspare, you on your own, but getting mixed up in the local politics will not get gold for Spain. If there is any gold."

"There is gold," Gaspare said and placed a hand on his chest. "I can feel it."

"Another thing," I remembered. "You may want to pause the knife throwing workouts. Since we have a knife-wielding killer on the loose."

"What? They plan on arresting me? I would like to see them try it," Gaspare said.

"Manion, come with me for a minute," Gerald asked as he walked for the elevators.

We left Gaspare gesticulating and pontificating to no one in particular.

We jumped on the elevator saying nothing. I followed Gerald as he motioned for us to exit on the seventh floor, which was not the floor for either of our rooms. We walked down the hall until we got to room 711 and knocked on the door. I started to ask, but Gerald held up a hand for me to hold my questions.

In a few seconds, a well-built man in his early twenties answered the door.

He was about six-foot three inches with broad shoulders and serious brooding eyes. His brown hair was cut short on the sides and long on the top. I remember thinking how serious he looked to be so young. He waved us into the room with the largest calloused hands I had ever seen.

"Gerald? How are you? Bobby Farr Jr. of Paladin Security," the serious young man said. His skin was fairly tan for someone who just got to town. Looking around the room, I noticed metal cases open to reveal several size handguns and what appeared to be Kevlar vests.

Gerald shook his hand and introduced me.

"Where is my cousin?" Gerald asked.

"With my father back in St. Louis," Bobby Jr. explained. "He thought it was best."

"He did, huh," Gerald said, pulling his phone out and clearly upset. Bobby Jr. placed one of his big hands over the phone.

"Gerald, hold off on the call. When Terri gets here, we'll call Uncle Lemon and my dad and discuss strategy."

In a few minutes, the diminutive Terri we met in the lobby came walking into the room.

"Gentlemen, I want to introduce Terri Lovejoy, Paladin Security," Bobby Jr. said.

"Gerald, glad you got the verbal clues," she explained with a devilish smirk.

"Yeah, I have seen pictures of you on my cousin's website. You move fast. How did you befriend my wife so quickly?" Gerald asked.

"Not too hard," Terri explained with a shrug. "I acted eager to help and lost as to how to start. Nadine is being given a wide berth. A lot of volunteers are spooked by her involvement in this latest murder business. She welcomed my company."

"Excuse me?" I finally said. "What is all this?"

"Teke, let me get my cousin on the phone, and I will explain," Gerald said.

In a few minutes Gerald, Bobby Jr., Terri, and I were sitting around a laptop with an oversized screen. Gerald's cousin, the one they called "Lemon Boy" Phillips, appeared on the screen via Skype video conferencing. A former police detective, Lemon Boy now ran the Paladin Security Company with his former partner Bobby Farr, Sr., Bobby Jr., and Terri Lovejoy.

"Hey, man, I told you I needed the cavalry; that means you *and* your team," Gerald said, his irritation showing.

"Cuz, hear me out," Lemon Boy started. I didn't think he and Gerald shared much family resemblance. "You and Manion are trying to find gold, keep the beautiful Nadine safe without her knowledge, while staying out of the way of the police who are trying to find a killer. Now, if we come down there in the bulletproof black Chevy Tahoes, full artillery display, and digital satellite connected drones, we will never get to the bottom of this. Along with the fact we would piss off the military presence."

The room was quiet as we all thought about that. Terri took up the explanation.

"Gerald, the plan is for me to infiltrate Reverend Moten's group. Bobby Jr. will blend into the group in Gilleyville protecting the Sam Gilley tomb as well as Val Cedar's BGNHS. From there we can keep our eyes open and feed intel back to you and Manion."

"The two of them are already on the job after only 24 hours. Terri is on Nadine's hip like a groupie," Lemon Boy explained.

"And I have already joined the group repairing and guarding the Gilley tomb. Got the scars to show from it," Bobby Jr. explained, holding up his hands. That explained the calluses I saw earlier.

"What do you think, Cuz?" Lemon Boy asked from the Skype screen.

Gerald thought for a second. He looked at me. I nodded.

"Okay, Man," Gerald started. "Sounds like a plan. You know this stuff better than me."

"I do," Lemon Boy said with a laugh. "That's why you called my bad ass. Bobby Jr. and Terri are the best. They know how to handle themselves. Nadine is in safe hands."

Gerald thanked his cousin again and ended the call. Bobby Jr. and Terri Lovejoy promised to check in every day. However, they felt it was best that we never meet in person again. No one needed to connect them to us.

Gerald and I returned to the lobby.

"So what now?" I asked.

"I'm going back to the lab to see if they made any headway on that video from the lab," Gerald explained.

"The way I see it," I started, "if bodies keep piling up, the military will shut this operation down. The graves will get reinterred, but no additional gold will be found."

"If it's even there," Gerald said.

"And there is that," I continued. "There are some things I want to check out. Who had a motive? Someone is willing to kill for the gold. I think Perales was killed because she was close to discovering who it was. I think McLean was killed because he was somehow in bed with the killer. When McLean was on the run from the police, the killer thought he was a liability, lured him out in the open, and killed him."

"Teke, you got any proof of all that?" Gerald asked, a sideways grin on his face.

"Not yet, but doesn't it make sense?" I asked.

"So who is on our short list?" Gerald asked.

"It could be any one of these gold chasers running around town," I said.

"No," Gerald responded. "It has to be someone who McLean would have been comfortable taking into the lab, who knew their way around the lab, and who has knowledge of the use of deadly weapons."

"Yeah," I said, thinking. "I feel like it's someone just under our noses."

Chapter 22

Moving back through the main street, I was not sure where I was going first. I felt we were close. The killer had struck twice. That meant they were desperate. But desperate for what? We needed to find answers quickly. Any more bodies and they would declare martial law in the town, and the boys from WorldSpan would find themselves on the outside looking into the game. There was a part of me that kept saying I should be scared out of my skin. However, the Eastern meditation from Rudolph Lemieux was kicking into my thought process.

No fear until there is something to actually fear.

I saw Baliles standing on a corner, and I had an idea from last night.

"Excuse me," I said. Baliles turned his gaze to me, but his eyes were blank.

I wondered if he was drunk, but I did not smell anything.

"Young Manion, what can I do for you?"

"Why didn't you tell me you wrote *The Journals of Jolly Benoit*?" "I didn't write it," he said in a matter-of-fact fashion.

"Teresa at the bookshop says you did," I answered.

"Not true," he said with a sigh and actually looking at me for the first time. "The man that inhabited this body ten years ago wrote a piece by that name and submitted it to the money devil publishing world. They replaced my words with the words you and countless others have spent your nights driveling over."

"I think it's pretty good; how much did they change?" I asked.

"Enough that I no longer wanted my name attached to it. They refused to change the author credit, so I changed my name, my work, and all attachments to academic life to separate myself from that deceptive text."

"Wow," was all I could say. We stood in reflection for a moment. Then I continued.

"The journal mentions a guy named Fisk who starts to help with moving some of the gold during the war. Did you ever get a line on him?"

"No!" he snapped loudly. I jumped back and a nearby passersby reacted. He caught himself and spoke in his tone of the calm, sage, and wise street philosopher.

"During that time, Jolly Benoit was essentially a spy for the Union Army. There were a number of go-betweens he met with. This Fisk, if that was his real name, was probably one of them. In my manuscript I was not going to mention the name Fisk at all."

"Why?"

"Because we didn't have support based on the data we had to establish whether it was a man or a woman. His original journal just kind of mentioned the name in passing. The original journal mentions a lot of names and long passages in French patois."

"So why did Fisk get elevated in the final manuscript?" I asked at the risk of riling him to anger.

"Sensationalism. It enriches the treasure part of the story; makes more compelling reading," Baliles explained, making air quotes with his huge hands. I noticed for a man who spent half of his nights sleeping on the streets of Benoitown, he had very clean hands and nails.

"Two last questions," I said, then pouring forward before he could say no. "Where is the original journal?"

"The original is at the museum in Benoitown. It would take a year to get access. There is a copy at the archives in Gilleyville. I would suggest you go there. By the way, how is your patois?"

"Not too good," I answered.

"You said you had two questions?" he asked.

"So do you think there's more gold down there?"

He thought for a moment and smiled, looking down towards the river.

"I think there is gold in a lot of different ways and means."

"You mean like your 'golden' tales of pirate adventures," I said, smiling.

"Precisely," he answered and walked towards a group of people standing in front of the bookshop.

My phone rang. It was from my office in Paris. I stepped around the corner to a side street.

"Bonjour, Monsieur Manion." It was Lisette Fournier, one of Camille's assistants. This one was a perky little ball of energy who mimicked Camille all the way down to the pencil skirts and spiky short haircut.

"Good afternoon, Lisette," I answered. "What's up?"

"Madame DeSoronne would like a status," she said expectantly but cheerfully. I gave her an update for the last few hours.

"And she would like to know how you are doing personally, Monsieur?" she asked.

"She could call and get that herself, Lisette" I said.

"Well, you know she is very busy as we all are, but she is thinking of you as much as always."

"Okay," I said, returning the laughter. It was an inside joke. When Camille got busy, she can be guilty of things like this … sending her regards through her staff. I didn't take it personally. It was just her way.

"Would you like me to do research on the name?" Lisette asked, but I had not been listening.

"Come again?" I said.

"The name Fisk? I can do research through public records and other sources?"

As crazy as it may seem, Lisette was a phenomenal internet researcher, and besides it would keep her from calling me for updates every three hours.

"Sure, go ahead," I answered and prepared to end the call, but Lisette kept making noises like she was not finished.

"Lisette, what is it?"

"Well, I was doing some research on your situation, and, um … I uncovered something that may be important. Uh, maybe it's nothing. Can I send it to you?" "Yeeesssss," I said, making it clear I was ready to go. Lisette just giggled. We said our goodbyes.

In a few minutes I received an email from WorldSpan Secure. It had an attachment. I clicked on it, and it slowly opened. It appeared to be someone's Twitter page entry.

Chapter 23

Throughout the annals of history, many a life has been saved by the timely intuition of women. Deborah Sampson in the American Revolution, Grace O'Malley of Irish folklore, and Harriet Tubman of the Underground Railroad.

Tonight Mimi Boulage had a premonition. Something about the two deaths, the knives, that made her nervous. She logged into Twitter and conducted the search to his account. She had mixed emotions as the most recent tweet came onto the screen. When it fully loaded, she sat at her kitchen counter and looked at the still photo.

It was a surreal moment. All her silent trepidation came to fruition. Her son, the big playful, energetic, and misunderstood kid posing on Twitter. He was on his knees with his shirt off, his skin glistening with sweat. He wore a camouflage-colored headband. In each hand he held knives very similar to those found in the back of the two most recent murders. Below the picture was his 140-character proclamation.

I swear mortal allegiance to the history and heritage of my home. Gold mongers and outsiders be gone!

The tweet was posted two days before the death of Lieutenant Perales. Mimi noticed her hand shaking as she worked the mouse. The fear that gripped her made it hard to think. For not one minute would she believe he did this, but he had already spent time behind bars. She had thought that would kill her. She swore she would never let that happen again. She pulled her phone out and dialed a Gilleyville number.

"Hey, it's me," she started when the other party answered. "No, it's not work. It's about Bo. I'm sending you pictures. After you see them, I need a favor."

Sheriff Cormac's Office

I felt bad about showing the tweet to Sheriff Cormac, but it was compelling. I didn't think Bo Boulage was guilty of murder. At best he was a bored, boisterous kid looking for something to believe in. I was worried that Val Cedars had his merry band of miscreant youth ratcheted into a hot lather.

"Manion, you do know this is my secretary's boy?" Sheriff Cormac said as he looked at the screenshot of the tweet. He took a deep breath and rubbed his face. I shared my feelings about possible suspects.

"Well, good for you and your feelings, but I don't get to have that luxury. I

have a killer running around Benoitown and Gilleyville."

"Where is Mimi?" I asked, noticing her unoccupied desk just outside the sheriff's office.

"She left for lunch and didn't come back."

It was about 4:00 PM. He called Mimi. Her phone went to voicemail. He called Deputy Laurie who was out on a call. He instructed her to go by Mimi's house and request Bo come in for questioning.

Just then Colonel Sanchez and Gerald came into the office.

"We've made some headway," Gerald said, very excited. "We can hear some of the audio on the video. We can't make out words, but there is definitely a struggle that takes place. You can hear it."

Colonel Sanchez placed a small laptop on the sheriff's desk. The screen shows the video feed I saw earlier. She pressed play. There was a high-end distorted hiss. I could hear Lieutenant Perales talking into her micro recorder. We could not make out the words, but it was her voice.

Then the struggle started. A man grunting and breathing. We heard Lieutenant Perales react. The video camera is knocked to the floor and only showing the tile floor inside the staging cooler.

You clearly hear Lieutenant Perales say, "Hey!" Then we heard the grunts, groans, and snorts of her and her attacker interchange. There are shadows moving around the room, picked up by the camera feed and now coinciding with the audio of the struggle taking place.

"Listen here," Colonel Sanchez said. "This is where she fights back."

There was about three seconds of silence save for the hiss of the amplified audio. Then what was obviously a man's grunt, followed by another and a third. Then we hear heavy breathing like someone coming up for air from underwater. There are footsteps while the breathing continues. It seemed like a woman's breathing. There are some attempts to speak, but we couldn't make it out.

Then we heard tables scraping the floor followed by two quick low-level thuds and more manly grunts. They were clearly fighting, then rapid steps getting fainter; someone was running away.

Then there was only breathing for several seconds. It was Lieutenant Perales, because for the first time we could hear her voice clearly but weakly calling out for help. A few seconds later we hear the alarm near the door to the lab. Before I could process what my brain knew was going to happen, we heard a long agonizing cry. It stopped and started like a small child who had been badly injured and was scared and hurting. It was Lieutenant Perales being stabbed from the back. I felt my scalp get tight.

I looked around the room. Gerald looked sick and shook his head. Colonel Sanchez's face was stone, her eyes dark orbs of vengeance. Even Sheriff Cormac was clearly affected by the audio. He was looking up at the ceiling with wet eyes that he rubbed every few seconds.

Each one of us reacted with a different physical action, but our thoughts were the same. We wanted blood from whoever did this. This person was still among us, living, breathing, acting normal, with blood on their hands. We wanted that person. We wanted that person badly.

We all had our motivations. Sheriff Cormac was sworn to bring them to justice. For Colonel Sanchez it was duty and personal. Gerald feared for his wife. While pursuing a noble cause, she was too close to a killer.

I found my mind back in White Sand Island. Recently a trip back to my home in Florida landed me in the middle of murder, theft, and betrayal. I barely escaped with my life. There was a time on the island, I wasn't sure I would live, that it may be easier to lay down and let it happen. Then something deep inside me kicked in, and I made the moves to get home alive.

I felt that way right now. I was determined to find the son of a bitch who did this, so the rest of us can get home alive. It's why I was given this job, the *Expeditor*. They saw in me what I couldn't see. I was scared, but I wasn't running.

"Okay, what's our next move?" I asked.

"Gerald and I are going back over the evidence," Colonel Sanchez explained. "We are going over the clothing, the knives, prints, and samples. Sheriff, I need to see the gold coins and the chest found by the forensic team."

"What are you thinking?" I asked.

"Just following up on your theory. Lieutenant Perales had questions about that gold. That's why she was in the lab that night. I checked her diary. She makes mention of it. I checked her phone. She made a number of calls to the same number, her sister out west. I'm going to call her, but I want to look at those gold pieces before I do."

"Okay, I can do that," Sheriff Cormac said. "But I have a question for just those of us in this room. Based on this audio, there are two gold thieves/killers out there. I think about Corporal McLean. He was there. We know that by the doped Guards and the peanuts on the floor. It feels like there is someone else out there. Someone we know. Who?"

"It could be any one of these gold hunters rouging around the city," Gerald said.

"No, I think it's someone close," Sheriff Cormac said. "For instance, I have heard that your friend from Spain has an affinity for knives."

"What?" Colonel Sanchez said, looking back at me.

"Yep, the manager at the hotel has holes in the wall to prove it," Sheriff Cormac said.

"Manion, is this true?" Colonel Sanchez asked. "Is that little Spanish prick a knife freak?"

I nodded. Colonel Sanchez rolled her eyes.

"Colonel, that is not enough," Sheriff Cormac said. "We need proof?"

"Oh, I will get it; Gerald, you coming?" Colonel Sanchez asked. Gerald looked at me, and I nodded. I needed him to stay on the evidence trail and be our eyes and ears there.

Sheriff Cormac's phone rang.

"Deputy, what's the story at Mimi's house? Oh, he's not there? Oh, she won't, would she? Stay there, I am on my way."

He addressed us as he locked his desk and prepared to leave.

"Bo is not there. Mimi claims she doesn't know where he is, an obvious lie. She also won't let us in to inspect the house. I was afraid of that," Sheriff Cormac said, walking towards the door to his office.

"So what are you going to do?" I asked.

"The same as all of us: follow the evidence," he said and crossed out of his office past Mimi's desk, and into the administration room. He pulled a document off the fax machine. He walked back into his office holding the paper up to us. "This is a search warrant for Mimi's house. I got two dead bodies; no more country cop routine. I will go up a bear's ass looking for clues if it means finding the killer."

"Good. Keep me posted, and I will do the same," Colonel Sanchez said and left the room. Gerald followed right behind her.

"So Manion, what's your next step?" Sheriff Cormac asked as he moved to leave his office.

"I got a few things to follow up on," I said.

Chapter 24

The more I thought about Fedelito as a possible suspect, I had to admit it made sense. He was a poser, a schemer, an opportunist, totally amoral, but above all, a coward. However, he was fond of knives, and he was desperate to find gold for Spain.

Things were clear in my head. I thought about the audio, the struggle, and I thought about what I had seen for the last few days. I matched up one with the other and came up with a plan.

I found who I was looking for at the local YMCA. He was working the jump rope just to the left of the body bag.

"Xanadu Waters, you remember me? I was a friend of Mr. Gaspare."

"I remember," Xanadu answered with the same infectious smile across a hard sweaty face. "He's not here right now."

"That's cool, because I wanted to talk to you."

"You want lessons, wanna spar a little?" he asked excitedly, playfully taking a fighter's stance.

"No, nothing like that," I said. "Uh, when was the last time you worked out with Mr. Gaspare?"

"It was just the one time, when you saw me. He paid well, so I was hoping to hear from him."

"And what all did you do?" I asked.

"The usual stuff. We worked the bags, some rope work, and sparring." "How good is he?" I asked.

"Not bad for an amateur," Xanadu explained. "Only thing was, he was lousy at defense. Almost seemed to love getting hit."

"Weird," I said for conversational spacing. Xanadu nodded.

"I remember when I saw him that night, during your session. He had some pretty bad bruises across his chest and stomach. You did those?"

"I noticed that too. I figured it was from some of his previous sparring partners, maybe back in Spain."

"So you didn't do it? He had those bruises when you started?" I asked.

"That's right?"

"You ever see any punch bruises that look like that?"

"Not really now that you mention it. They were smaller but darker. The kind of bruises you see in street fighting."

"Did he favor them when you sparred?"

"Yes, but he didn't complain. Mr. Gaspare is very, uh, kind of proud, you know, but the bruises were fresh, and he felt it when I hit them."

"Thanks, I appreciate you," I said and turned to leave.

"So, you gone ask me a lot of questions but not tell me what's going on?" he asked.

I turned back to Xanadu, pulled out my wallet, and placed two $100 bills on the bench next to him.

"And I expect you to leave the conversation here with me and you," I said and turned to leave. Xanadu made verbal sounds showing he agreed to the terms.

When I left the YMCA, I started thinking about everything unusual that had happened in the last 72 hours. Sheriff Cormac said on the night of Corporal McLean's death there were a lot of fights and disturbances. I called Fedelito, and it went to voicemail. I left no message. I was not sure what I was going to say to him if I did talk to him. I wanted to get an idea where he was. His absence was another peculiar happening in the last 24 hours.

~   ~   ~

There was a place that had no name, three blocks north and two blocks west of Benoit's bar. I learned of it by returning to Benoit's. I found Francina.

I asked her where someone would go to score – weed, pills, and sex for money. I promised her I was not working for her father, and I would not tell where I got the information.

It was an abandoned storefront that was opened by a local resident. He started off providing donated water and food for displaced flood victims after the hurricane.

Once it had established a following, he and his wife turned it into a funky, rustic hole-in-the-wall restaurant selling burgers, chicken fingers, and tacos. The furniture was all donated, mostly rough sewn wood outdoor furniture. It only sold beer and wine, but it did allow patrons to bring their own booze. I wondered about the legalities on this. Francina told me her father did not want to limit a distraction to the already beleaguered folks along the river. For now.

Despite its noble beginning, this place soon became the hangout for a rough crowd of out-of-towners.

The smell of grease, stale beer, wood, and vomit combined to greet me at the door. The place was about half full, a daytime hangout for second-rate contractors, boozy handymen, and freelance insurance inspectors. I walked in and went straight to the opening in the back wall. It was about four-foot square, with a sliding acrylic glass door.

"Let me speak to the person in charge," I said to the young woman who, with a tired expression, slid the window open. I put a $100 bill against the window, and her expression changed. She held out her hand, and I slipped her two twenties from other hand.

"This don't look like no hundred," she said plaintively.

"And you don't look like the boss?" I said then paused. "You get the rest when I see the boss; or did I mistake you for the help and owe you an apology?"

She rolled her eyes and stroked her hand through greasy blonde shoulder length hair with brown roots. She walked away. I heard her speaking to someone in the back. In a few seconds a small frame, redhead man came out from the back. He walked up and stood within inches of me saying nothing.

"I'm looking for a girl," I said, no nonsense. He smiled, clearly relaxing.

"She's a working girl, hangs out here. Brunette, athletic, got attacked by a crazy last night and was picked up running through the streets naked.

"Yeah, you serious about the rest of that hundred?" he asked. I looked at the girl still behind the window. She was looking anxious and stuffing the first two twenties in her bra. I turned back to the boss and held up the last three twenties. He snatched them from me, put two in his pocket and gave one to the girl behind the window. He slid the window closed so we could not hear her complain about not getting the whole amount.

"You want Glynis, but she not here right now," he explained.

"Yeah, I see that, Red," I said, my patience getting thin. "Where can I find her?"

"She's pretty scared right now; I have to be careful about giving her information out," he explained.

"Be serious: she's working as a hooker, and now she's scared?"

"Hey, Man, this ain't New York City," he explained. "We take care of our own down here."

"Look, I just want to ask her some questions about what happened to her. I can even pay her for her time."

"No problem, I can get her on the phone now. Ask her what you want?"

"I'm gonna need some face-to-face time," I said with an expression showing no compromise. The short little man started rubbing his face like he was thinking about things.

"Listen, Partna, I'm gonna order one or two of your no-name beers while you give your friend a call and see if she wants to spend time with me. I get that she's scared, but if she helps me maybe I can make things safer for her on the street."

Halfway through the first beer, he came from the back. He was holding an old cellular flip phone out to me. I stayed seated, took the phone from him, and held it up to my ear.

"I've seen you around town; you with the police," the female voice said.

"Not really, but I did have a question about the guy who attacked you. Just give me two minutes."

"You said you were willing to pay?"

"Fastest $100 you will ever make," I said.

"I don't know; I can be pretty fast," she said jokingly. I laughed as well. She had the British accent the sheriff mentioned. I had assumed that was fake.

"Give me an address?" I asked. The number and street she gave me was less than four blocks away. She also gave me her name—Glynis James.

I placed the rest of my unfinished drink on the table in front of some half asleep regulars in the corner who slurred their thanks and then proceeded to fight over the half bottle of beer.

Her address was further off the main street. It was an older, run-down block with overgrown poorly groomed oak trees. Their canopy made the street dark as dusk. The houses were narrow, two-story frame units with porches that stretched across the entire front. They were fortunate to be spared from the floodwaters, but unfortunate in that they all could sorely use the tens of millions of federal assistance pouring into Benoitown and Gilleyville.

Her place was in the middle of the block. As I approached via the long walk, two men came out the front door.

"Can I help you, Dawg?" one of them asked. He was six-foot four, 300 pounds, with a patch over one eye and a pale freckled baldhead and sported a lightning bolt tattoo. As we got a few feet apart, I could smell the body odor they had obviously been growing for at least a week. The other one was just as tall, just as smelly, but skinny, with a raw bone face under stringy blonde hair, and missing most of his teeth. Both were hefting baseball bats.

"I just came to speak to Glynis. I just talked to her on the phone."

"How do we know you ain't the one who tried to hurt her?"

I was getting tired of the roadblocks. I was under the gun. People were dying, and these rednecks wanted to play *Pop Quiz*. They kept walking towards me, and I backed up towards the street to keep a safe distance from the bats.

"Just have her come out," I said. "You guys can stand here while I ask her my questions. I will make it worth your while. I assume you two are the pimps?"

"Pimps?" Patcheye said and spit on the ground. I guess I said the wrong thing. "You think we's pimps? That mean you calling our cousin a prostitute?"

"You lookin' for pussy, Boy?" Skinny asked sardonically and hefted his bat. "I got yo fuckin' pussy right here."

"No, no, I didn't mean any disrespect. I guess I was mistaken," I said, holding up my hands.

Skinny grabbed one of my wrists, spun me around, pulled me close, and pulled the bat against my throat in a choke hold. For a tall guy, he was quick. I was trying to apologize, but it came out as coughs. I don't know what cut my wind more, the bat or the noxious odor coming from every pore of Skinny's body. They found my struggling, amusing and distracting. They did not notice my left leg as it curved around Skinny's left leg.

I dipped as low as I could with the bat against my throat, wrapped both hands behind me and around Skinny's butt and thighs, then threw myself back against him while lifting his left leg up with mine.

Just like Lemieux taught me, I landed on top of Skinny, knocking the wind out of him with an elbow to his middle.

His breath came out with a whoosh, and he released the bat. I bounded up to my feet, grabbed Skinny's bat and put my foot on his neck. Patch was ready to swing, but I stopped him.

"Drop your bat Muthafucka, or I will crush his throat under my foot," I said. Skinny was squirming, but the more he moved the more my foot dug into his neck, his chin scraping against the side of my shoe. He was waving at his one-eyed relative to back up.

"That's enough!" a woman's voice came from the second floor of the house.

"Let my cousin up, Insurance Man; they won't bother you no more."
"I don't know that," I said, giving no quarter.

"Well, if you crush his throat, the big one will kill you, and you'll never get to ask your questions," she said, sounding like a character from a production of *Pygmalion* or a movie based on a Charles Dickens' novel. "That is - if I don't put a rifle shell in your arse first."

I heard the rack of the rifle from the porch. After a second, I stepped back off Skinny's neck, but held his bat up ready for what came next.

"Fin and Ben, git your bloody arses in here, right *now!*" she shouted. Patcheye and Skinny eased back toward the house, giving me deadly looks the whole way.

"Give me my bat, Man," Skinny demanded.

"I'll give it to your cousin," I said. He pointed at me as if to say he would remember this.

Just as they reached the front door on the first floor, Glynis came out. She handed the rifle to Skinny and said something to them I could not hear. They proceeded into the house, and she walked out to me.

"Sorry about that, Love," she said as she reached a conversational distance to me in the middle of the yard near the sidewalk.

"Really? That's all you got?" I asked, trying to bring myself down from fight mode. My heart was beating so hard; I could barely hear. I was sweating from every pore, and I couldn't get the stink out of my nose. There was a part of me that wanted to show her how it felt to be choked with a Louisville Slugger, but that was raw emotion born of the primitive that still lived in all of modern man.

I took deep breaths and let it subside.

She had reddish-brown hair, smooth skin with light freckles in just the right places. She had light gray eyes with light brown flecks, a prominent nose and full lips that slipped into an easy smile. She reminded me of a shorter Cameron Diaz.

"How are you?" I asked trying to bring myself and that conversation back to normalcy. She shrugged and smiled as if to say she was okay. Her eyes never left my face. She was charming and shrewd, and she knew it.

She was wearing a short rainbow-colored blouse with spaghetti straps and a denim skirt. She was barefoot, but her toenails were freshly painted. I could see the lingering bruises on her long slender neck. Maybe it was the effects of my adrenaline, but nothing about this girl seemed to go together: her nose was too long, her neck too long, her mouth too wide, and her eyes too spooky, but it all came together to produce an organic sexiness I felt to my toes.

"So about the john that attacked you," I started.

"My *date*; I am not a hooker," she replied.

"Okay, just going by what the police told me," I said.

"So are you here for the police or for yourself? What does the greedy insurance company want to know about me?"

It was a valid question. Initially I thought about coming up with a convoluted story to hide what I was doing, but I didn't have time. Besides, there was something candid and unapologetic about Glynis. In the last 48 hours, she had been so frightened that she went running through the streets wearing no clothes. I didn't want to insult her with poorly and hastily crafted subterfuge.

"Take a look at this picture," I said as I pulled up an image on my smart phone.

Her expression did not change, but her eyes went dark upon seeing the picture of Fedelito Gaspare. She kept her eyes on the picture as she pulled a pack of Dunhill Cigarettes from her back pocket of her skirt and lit up.

"What's his name," she asked. I told her, along with his purpose in Benoitown. I told her my play in all this. We sat down on some steps at the end of the walkway leading from the house, just before it met the public sidewalk. She said she didn't want to press charges. That kind of publicity and headache was not in her plans.

"I'm a journalist," she started by way of explanation. "I came over from Britain to produce a story about what's happening here—the storm, the graves, the gold, the people. I'm doing it on my own dime, but I roomed with my crazy US cousins to cut down on cost.

Anyway, I was hanging out in the bar two nights ago looking for sources or just interesting people to interview. I ran into your friend. He explained that he had ties to the search for gold. He dropped the right names, and I remember seeing him standing near the police and that bloke from your State Department. We had some drinks, and he made me a lot of promises to get me access for my story. I realize now that he drugged my champagne with something.

When we got back to his hotel, we are getting into it. Then he started getting rough, throwing me around and smacking me. I sobered up quick. He brought out a plastic bag to put over my head. He said it would heighten my orgasm, but I pushed him off and threw off the bag. That was when he started choking me. There was no sex, just him choking me and laughing. I was about to go out, but at the last minute, I put a knee in his balls. I didn't stop to grab clothes. I lit out of the hotel room, down the steps.

There was no one in the lobby so, I kept running into the street. I kept running and screaming until I got around people again. Soon after I ran into the deputies out on patrol, and they took me into custody."

When she finished her story, she was on her second cigarette held by a shaky hand. Now that I had confirmation of what I feared, I wasn't sure what to do next. I asked Glynis not to leave town. She assured me she wouldn't be leaving without some kind of story. She cleared her bank account to get here, hired her cousins as her camera crew, so she must do this. I asked if she was afraid of running into Fedelito again. She reached into her back pocket and pulled out a small wide blade knife.

"He better be afraid of running into me."

I thanked her, and we exchanged cell phone numbers. I promised to keep in touch.

As I walked back towards the center of town, I kept looking over my shoulder to see if her crazy cousins were coming for revenge. I saw I had a text from Gerald. I called him.

"Hey, where are you?" he asked when I answered the phone.

"Three blocks from the center of town, walking that way," I answered.

I told him what I learned about our friend Fedelito.

"I hate that guy," Gerald said. "Do you think he's the killer?"

"Not sure," I said, walking at a quick pace and looking back over my shoulder. "What did you and the colonel find out?"

"A lot, but I want to tell you in person," he explained.

"When and where?" I asked.

"Later tonight. We gotta meet Bobby Jr. Says he has some information for us, but he can't be caught sharing it by phone. He's been pulled into some secret stuff over in Gilleyville."

"Where are you?" I asked.

"Having dinner with Nadine," he said, sounding in a good mood.

"Where is Terri?" I asked.

"Not far away," he explained.

"You ever gonna tell Nadine about your moles?" I asked. "Not likely," he said with an audible grin.

"She sitting right there in front of you?"

"You know it," he responded.

"I'm going to Benoit's for dinner; call me when Bobby Jr. is ready to meet."

I ended the call just as I was turning onto Main Street. The sun had fully set, and once again Benoitown took on a dreamy feel of Southern days gone by. Gas lanterns dotted the stone streets. There were sounds of people having casual conversations, greeting each other politely as they passed on the street. The theatrical baritone of Baliles, the professor turned storyteller, regaling out-of-towners with stories of local heroes, could be heard in the distance. With every passing day, I got a sense of what Benoitown and Gilleyville were like before the storm, two small towns with proud histories they love to share with the world.

All this small town peacefulness belied an ugly underbelly of death and betrayal. I am sure the locals would blame it on Hurricane Chester and all the strangers it blew into town. If I were them, I would want all this gone.

I wasn't fooling anybody. I was headed to Benoit's because I needed a friendly face, hopefully the one with whom I recently spent the night.

I found my familiar seat at the bar. I didn't see Angela Babineaux or Sheriff Cormac's daughter Francina. The bartender was a tall slim guy about my age. He wore a long slim chin beard like a character from a Washington Irving novel or the reality show *Appalachian Mafia*. The rest of his head was hairless, none up top, no eyebrows, nothing. He wore gauged earpieces like the Masai African Tribes, large pierced holes in both lobes.

I ordered a shrimp po'boy and Tipsy Tea, a brewed concoction with white rum. A few minutes later I was eating and watching the ESPN talking heads, a man and woman quipped and quoted about the NFL and College Football news of the day. Living in Paris, I had all but forgotten how serious football was in this part of the country. It made me miss the US of A. Big European cities had their traditions, but they were not my traditions, no matter how long I lived there.

"Hey, Insurance Man, looking for your girl?"

It was Francina, Sheriff Cormac's daughter. With every passing day she looked more like a well-bred, wholesome kid from the Midwest and less like the dried-out, drugged-out, hungover subhuman from the other day. She was even wearing makeup.

"What's up?" I said, trying to show I wasn't as anxious as I felt inside. "Is she around?"

Francina gave me a playful sorrowful face and shook her head from side to side.

"She took a few days off, went up to her mom's place in Washington," she explained.

"Oh, yeah, she told me about her mother," I said as if I wasn't disappointed. "She took the boat? I heard they go out on it sometimes."

"All I know is she better come back with some seafood sauce, because we are almost out."

"Sauce?" I asked.

"That's right," Francina said. She reached down below the bar as if searching for something. She pulled out a small squeeze bottle of an orange sauce. "We use it on everything here. Angela's mother makes it in Washington at a small commercial kitchen."

I read the label out loud, "Ma' Barklay's Seafood Sauce," and the top of my head exploded. Figuratively speaking.

"Angela's mother makes this sauce?" I asked, trying to hide my sense of alarm.

"Yeah, has been for about ten years but we only started using it in the last two. I'm sure they will sell you some to take back home," Francina said, mistaking my emotion for excitement over the homegrown condiment.

"Barklay?!" I said louder than I meant. "Who is Barklay?"

"I told you, Manion. Angela's mother, Sara Barklay. Now I don't know if she is the 'ma' in the name or if the recipe is based on something from someone else's ma."

"Barklay—Angela's mother's maiden name is Barklay?"

"Yes," Francina said, wondering where I was going. "Sara Barklay is Angela's mother. She makes the sauce we use in the store. Angela went to see her for a few days because it was getting crazy around here—the gold hunters, the graves, the murders, and you."

"Me?"

"Yes," Francina said and leaned in closer. "She told me you all got busy the other night. A girl's got to go somewhere and figure that shit out when it happens during a drunk night with out-of-town talent."

I couldn't hear anything else she had to say. All this time, Angela Babineaux may very well be a direct descendent of Sam Gilley on her mother's side. Everyone is running around here looking for gold and looking for killers. I slept with a major source of information.

I pulled a couple of twenties from my pocket and threw them on the bar. I waved off the bartender and Francina as I walked out the door. I was mad, but I wasn't sure of the source—Angela for not being forthcoming, at myself for letting my penis do all the thinking when it came to her, or at the genteel façade of Benoitown and Gilleyville. Just as I got close to falling in love with this place, I stubbed my toe on a rock of deception and misdirection.

I walked past Serendipity Books and Gifts. Teresa was standing outside her shop, locking the door.

"Good evening, Mr. Manion," she said in her smoothest voice.

"Ma'am," I said in my flat, no-nonsense, business tone. There was the scent of jasmine and sugar cookies in the air when I walked past her. I was not in a mood to be seduced by a natural holistic. I was on a mission.

"Is that all a woman gets from you is 'ma'am'?" she said as I walked past her.

That and the scent was enough to get me to turn around.

"Teresa, I got business in Washington; I need to go right now," I said, forcing my best manners.

"You know," she started as she walked up to me, put her arm in mine, and continued down the street in the direction I was headed. "I am overdue for a trip there as well. I have some business and some friends I need to call on in Washington."

"Good for you," I said.

"Funny thing about this part of the world, Tekelius," she continued. "Some places, like Washington, you can get to quicker by boat than by car.

"That so?" I said.

"Mmm-hmmm; also, the road between here and Washington? Got a lot of cops on it. Cops like my second ex-husband who makes a living pulling over cars he don't know hoping to catch out-of-town drivers with liquor on their breath."

I stopped walking and gave her my full attention. Teresa was charming and fun, but at times like this she was also scary.

"I don't have a boat," I said.

"I do," she said as she swung me left heading down a side street. "She's small, but the engine is fast. We can be in Washington safe and sound."

"I have to be back in a few hours," I said, feeling myself give over control.

"Whenever you need to leave, Handsome. My business there won't take   long."

Chapter 25

Sheriff Cormac pulled up at a house he knew very well. Mimi Boulage was the dispatcher and police chief's secretary for the last twenty years. She was the first person to befriend him when he moved there from Baltimore. She was no-nonsense but with a big heart like the women he knew growing up in the Chesapeake crab country of Maryland.

As her son, Bo, grew up, Sheriff Cormac helped her get a handle on his trouble of staying focused. The kid wasn't bad or malicious. He had the same emotions other kids had. He just had poor coping skills. For years, Mimi wouldn't admit he needed help; she didn't want him to be labeled. Then he was arrested and sent to the Youth Detention in Fayetteville for seriously injuring five classmates who damaged the paint job on his car.

That was four years ago including the run-in with the trucker and his antique pistol. Mimi put him in counseling and put him under the guidance of her friend from childhood, Val Cedars. Val kept his energies channeled, taught him to be a southern gentleman, and satisfied the court order that he be mentored.

There had been no problems since then.

Sheriff Cormac didn't believe for one minute that Bo Boulage entered into a deal with two soldiers to raid the graves of slaves for gold.

Moreover, Private Jackson said his buddy, the late Corporal McLean, had a connection to help sell the gold they found. He doubted that Bo Boulage had that ability. So why make this trip out to talk to him? He mentally prepared himself to answer that question.

It was police procedure. Bo may not have done it, but he may know something about it. Secondly (and this was first for the sheriff), he already had two dead bodies of people he didn't know. He would be damned if he let Mimi's misguided boy be killed by some gold-crazy maniac.

When he pulled up at the house, he saw Deputy Laurie waiting outside. He also saw Mimi's old red Chevy S-10 pickup and the sky-blue Ford Thunderbird convertible owned by Val Cedars. The fastidious historian was a general pain in the ass, but he was Mimi's closest friend. Sheriff Cormac was glad she had him there.

"You believe she told me to wait outside?" Deputy Laurie said as Cormac got out of his squad car and walked over to her. "I used to baby sit that little crumb catcher, Bo."

"It's okay, Laurie. She's not one of us on this. She's the relative of a person of interest with inside information about how this process works. She's scared for the boy."

"You got the warrant?" she asked. Sheriff Cormac held it up, and she snatched it out of his hand and headed for the front door.

"Deputy!" Sheriff Cormac shouted. Deputy Laurie stopped and turned back to him, an exasperated look on her face. "She is still one of us. We don't have to go all SWAT team here."

"Sheriff, this is going to be fucked up no matter how delicate you try to be. I been sitting out here watching her house, having to pee. My cell phone battery died, and I didn't bring my charger. I'm doing this."

ROD SANFORD

Sheriff Cormac ran to catch up with his deputy as she walked up to Mimi Boulage's front door.

The door opened before they reached it. Mimi stood by the door. Her eyes were puffy and sad. As Sheriff Cormac looked behind her, he saw Val standing in her foyer.

"It's a warrant to search the house, Mimi. Now let us in," Deputy Laurie said.

"Deputy!" Sheriff Cormac said admonishingly. "Mimi, I'm sorry, but we got to do our job."

Mimi, the tough-minded dispatcher, looked as if she were going to cry in the doorway. Val came forward and took her by the shoulders.

"Mimi, the sheriff has to do his job. We won't let anything happen to Bo. We all love that boy," Val explained as he pulled her away from the doorway.

Deputy Laurie slipped inside and went directly to the bedrooms. She peeked into a couple of doorways just for extra measure. She already knew which room belonged to Bo. While the deputy went to work searching the room, the sheriff stood in the front of the house with Mimi and Val.

"I'm going to ask both of you," Sheriff Cormac started. "We need to talk to Bo. Do you know where we can find him?"

Mimi just looked down at the floor, not making eye contact with anyone.

"I'm sorry, Sheriff," Val Cedars said. "I have not seen Bo in the last 48 hours."

"Did you see his Twitter entry?" Sheriff Cormac asked.

"Yes, but really, Sheriff, this is what kids do. Bo is not a murderer," Val Cedars entreated.

"It's very important you both understand," Sheriff Cormac explained. "We have two members of the US military killed in our town. Now it's just a matter of time before they take over this investigation. I know Bo, but they do not."

"You saying because my son got in trouble a few times he is going to be railroaded for this?" Mimi asked, speaking for the first time.

"That's what I'm trying to avoid," Sheriff Cormac said. "But Mimi, I am up against it here. I need to talk to Bo as soon as possible."

She didn't respond. Val Cedars put his arms around her and held her close.

"Sheriff, we can't find the knives," Deputy Laurie said and returned to Bo's bedroom. Sheriff Cormac turned to Mimi.

"Mimi, what did you do with the knives from the picture? If you don't turn them over to us, people will assume the ones we found in the back of the dead people are the ones from the picture. Now where are his knives?"

Mimi thought about it for a few seconds. She looked at Val Cedars who gave a slight nod. Then she went into the kitchen and returned a few seconds later with the hard cedar wood case. She opened the case in front of the sheriff, showing him the full set of Italian hunting knives belonging to Bo Boulage. "Thanks, Mimi," Sheriff Cormac said and took the case from her.

"Sheriff!" Deputy Laurie called.

"What is it, Deputy? Let's wrap this up."

"One moment, please," Deputy Laurie said in an uncharacteristically sweet voice. Sheriff Cormac excused himself.

When he reached the bedroom, he found Deputy Laurie standing in the middle of a sea of opened dresser drawers, upturned seat cushions, and stripped bed linens. Wearing latex gloves, she had a serious but triumphant expression on her face.

"What is it, Deputy?" Sheriff Cormac asked.

Deputy Laurie pointed down into an open drawer at the bottom of the dresser. Sheriff Cormac stepped slowly into the room. He glanced down in the drawer. Inside a white handkerchief, stained with what appeared to be blood, was a small micro-recorder in a camouflage green cover.

Chapter 26

The boat ride to Washington, North Carolina was the darkest ride of my life. We reached Teresa's boat, a 22-foot Bayliner with twin Mercury outboards. I don't know what I expected, but it wasn't this. About halfway to Washington, North Carolina, the Tar River began to mix with the tide of the water basin. The channels were wider and deeper. Teresa opened the Bayliner up for full speed, a practice I heard was frowned upon by boaters at night. There were a couple of times the craft seemed to go airborne, and I clutched the railings at the transom, spray from the engines peppering my face and hair. The whole time, Teresa, the demure, ethereal bookshop owner, steered the boat with a calm serene expression.

In less than 30 minutes we were coming towards the lights of a city.

"Here we are, Handsome—Washington, North Carolina," she announced as she throttled back on the speed. We slowed to a cruise. I felt comfortable, so I eased forward and sat next to her at the controls.

"I don't think I'm drunk anymore," I said nervously. She giggled in a way that made me wish I were recording her. She reached under her seat and handed me a small white towel for my face.

As I dried myself, she rubbed my back. I felt my pants get tight. Three nights ago, this highly sexual effect she had, caught me off guard and made me feel like a raving adolescent. Now I welcomed it like a natural phenomenon and did not question it.

This was a good thing. By focusing, at that moment, on tamping down my libido, I did not over react when I saw Angela Babineaux, of all people, standing with another woman at the docks at downtown Washington, North Carolina.

"There's my buddy—Sara-Helen!" Teresa shouted. She waved, and the woman next to Angela waved back. Angela and I shared the same shocked look on our faces.

As Teresa slowly steered the boat into a slot, I whispered to her.

"How did you know?"

"Know what, Handsome?"

"That my business was with them?"

"Who? The Barklays? Really? What a small world!"

"It was Francina. She called you, didn't she?"

"The sheriff's daughter? Why would that little unfortunate narcotic abuser and I talk about you?"

"You sayin' this is a coincidence, you and I coming to see the same people in Washington on the same night?"

"Tekelius, the term 'coincidence' is used by people with too much faith in man and not enough faith elsewhere," she said as she pulled the boat to a stop. She turned to me, standing between me and Angela and her mother on the dock. She spoke at a volume that only I could hear.

"Sometimes, when your cause is just and you determine to put good into the universe, you get breaks you don't understand, didn't see coming, and are not of your causing. I have learned over the years to accept gifts from the divine like a surprise birthday gift from a rich benefactor."

She kissed me on the cheek and hugged me tight for several seconds, and I was calm, focused, and no longer partially erect from her previous back rub. I turned off the question machine in the back, left corner of my mind and focused on the task at hand.

"Would you do me the honor of introducing me to Sara-Helen, maybe as a friend of yours?" I asked, feeling a surreal sense of contentment.

"Of course," she replied with an equally content smile.

We were all pleasant and polite to each other. Sara Helen Barklay was beautiful in a cultured Southern way. She wore her hair in a sixties bump curl, while dressed in a yellow sleeveless sundress with a dark brown summer sweater that buttoned up in the front. She was soft-spoken and stood with her hands folded across her waist.

What threw me was Angela. The athletic, sexy boat captain by day and leather pants rocker by night was dressed in a pink and red version of what her mother wore. It took everything I had to keep from laughing.

"Teresa, you didn't need to come down here just for sauce," Helen Barklay said as she hugged her friend.

"Girl, it's no problem. I needed to get out of Benoitown for a night; it's been too long since I've seen you. Can I introduce my new friend, Tekelius Manion?" Sarah Helen Barklay extended a small hand, and we shook.

"Mr. Manion, I have heard of you from obvious sources," she said slowly, cutting her eyes over to Angela who stood awkward but looked beautiful. Her face was hard to read.

"All good I hope," I said with my most honest smile.

"Of course," Helen Barklay said. "I assume you are here to see Angela?"

"Um … Helen, Tekelius is working with the police and also working with his company looking for Jolly Benoit's gold," Teresa explained. "He just put two and two together regarding your family connection to Sam Gilley." "Aaaaaahhhhhh," Sarah-Helen and Angela said at the same time.

"If we could go and talk for a few minutes," I asked. "I can get out of your hair."

"How about that gourmet cupcake place?" Teresa said. "I've been thinking about them all the way over here."

It was a slow quiet walk from the dock to the main street downtown. Washington was much larger than Benoitown. Sitting on a wide expanse of the tidewater channel, it was alive with boats, tourists, and music.

Petite Sweets was a small place, most of its seating outside. Teresa and Sarah-Helen ordered cupcakes. I ordered a brownie. Angela had a Pellegrino water. We sat at a table for four in the front of the building where we could people-watch.

"Okay, Tekelius, the floor is yours," Sarah-Helen Barklay said seriously.

"You are a direct descendent of Samuel Gilley?" I asked.

"I am," she said.

"And you never told me," I said to Angela.

"Didn't think it was relevant," she answered, a bit of defiance in her voice.

"Really?" I said.

"Really," she answered.

I was getting riled. She was giving me stank face and attitude. However, she was the one who withheld information that would have been crucial to my investigation. I had to find out by accident.

"Tekelius, I will give you a brief history and maybe you will understand," Sarah-Helen explained in a calm voice.

"Sam Gilley eventually left Gilleyville, Benoitown and Jolly Benoit for New York. He had traveled there many times handling financial matters for their enterprise. While he was there, he became close to the Barklay family, who were second-generation dairy farmers. Sam eventually reconnected with his relatives back in Ireland and brought several of them over to the United States. One of them was his sister. The sister had a daughter, Maria, who eventually married the Barklays' youngest son, Jeremiah. Jeremiah's older brother Algernon became one of the first mayors of Gilleyville after Sam left back in the 1800s. Maria and Jeremiah are my great, great, great grandparents on my father's side."

"Whatever became of Sam's share of the gold?" I asked.

"Aaahhh, well, as best as I know it was totally converted to cash, investments, things like that. Half of Sam's fortune went to Maria. The other half Sam kept for another heir, never heard of a name. Not really sure what happened there. I believe most of that money eventually went to charities, hospitals, and museums when Sam died. You will see the Gilley name on old buildings all over New York. Meanwhile, the Barklay family was split in half. Jeremiah and Maria were millionaires, and there were members of the family who were instantly loyal to them. Jeremiah became the financial leader of the family. However, there were other Barklay family members that remained loyal to the old patriarchs of the family, the dairy farmers. Despite being direct descendants from Jeremiah and Maria, my father and grandfather aligned with the old guard rather than the money."

"Are there any other Barklays down here?" I asked.

"No, the money Barklays are pretty much in New York. The non-money Barklays are still in the dairy business. Neither want anything to do with North Carolina."

"You met Angela's dad down here?" I asked.

"Yep, I came down with my cousins in the late seventies when the city leaders started developing both cities as tourist attractions. I came down here with some of the money Barklays, including some Gilleys from Ireland. I met Cecil Babineaux and fell in love."

"So you don't think there's any gold left in the graves?" I asked. Sarah-Helen Barklay laughed lightly.

"It could be, Tekelius. Anything's possible," she said.

"But you don't think so," I said.

"More importantly, I truly don't care," Sarah-Helen answered, showing some emotions on the edge. "Despite the great Gilley legend, it took its toll on the Barklay family. The money Barklays and the country Barklays fought each other as much as they loved each other. There were even splits within immediate families, like my sister and me. I found my life here with the Babineaux clan to be peaceful."

We sat quiet for a few minutes. Then Teresa and Helen started talking about her sauce order, about recent dreams they had and what the dreams meant. They also talked about gardening and gossiped about mutual friends.

After about an hour, we left the cupcake shop and walked back to Helen's store about two blocks away from the boat docks. It was actually a Washington, North Carolina, version of Teresa's place, books, souvenirs, light food items locally made.

About 30 minutes later, we were walking back to the boat pulling a red wagon with cases of Barklay's Seafood Sauce. In exchange for their hospitality, Teresa and I agreed to deliver sauce orders to Benoit's and a few other locations in town.

"Two more things, please?" I asked of Helen and Angela. "There is no body in Sam Gilley's crypt. Does that surprise you?"

"No," Sarah-Helen said. "There is also a Sam Gilley vault in New York. I suspect he rests somewhere between there, the ocean, or back home in dear old Ireland."

"Secondly, do you know the family name Fisk? Jolly Benoit mentions a Fisk in his journal."

Sarah-Helen thought for a few minutes, but shook her head. "The name means nothing to me, but Teresa's family is more aligned with Jolly Benoit."

"I remember reading that name in Jolly's journal, but the name doesn't show up in any of my family histories," Teresa said.

After loading everything, we said our good-byes.

"Angela, thanks again," I said and reached out to hug her. She just nodded but didn't seem to be as angry as she was earlier. She took my kiss on the cheek.

Teresa took it easy on the boat ride back to Benoitown. That was fine by me. I lay on the backbench and closed my eyes. The motion of the Bayliner rocked me to sleep.

When we idled into Benoitown, my phone was ringing. It was Gerald.

"You ready to roll?" Gerald asked when I answered. I told him where I had just come from and with whom and what was discussed. Gerald also couldn't believe we had a descendant right under our noses.

"Where we going?" I asked.

"Don't talk; just kiss the book lady good night and meet me at the rear of our hotel," he said.

"The rear?" I asked.

"Just do it, Manion," he said and hung up.

I said my goodnights to Teresa and hustled up the street. I saw Deputy Laurie sitting in a patrol car on a side street between me and my hotel. I hung back in the shadows. I wasn't sure why, but because of the secret tone in Gerald's voice, I sensed that I needed to stay off the authority's radar for tonight.

I crossed Main Street between a dry cleaner and a real estate office, slipped between two buildings on the opposite side, and emerged in the alley that ran behind the hotel, which was three blocks down. Gerald was standing outside his car. The big kid from Paladin Security, the one called Bobby Jr., was behind the wheel.

"Get in; I'll explain on the way," Gerald explained. His face was serious. I couldn't tell if this secret was good or bad, involved gold or murder or both. I sat quietly on the backseat half lost in my own thoughts, Glynis and her crazy cousins, Angela Babineaux, and the almost certainty that Fedelito was involved.

We went over the Emancipation Bridge into Gilleyville. In a few minutes, we pulled up at the mayor's house, which also held the historical archives, assorted artifacts, and the bodiless crypt of Samuel Gilley. We pulled onto the drive and, when it ran out, we pulled into the grass leading to the backyard. I leaned forward and tapped Gerald on the shoulder. He held up a finger, asking for a little more patience.

The plot of land for the Gilley mayoral estate went on for some acres, most of it wooded brush. Just in front of the tree line, towards the back of the lot, there was a small structure about 30 feet by 20 feet. It had brown-painted concrete block walls and green shingles. As the headlights shone on the outside of the building, Bobby Jr. flashed the bright light beam three times fast, two slow, then one for several seconds. We parked on the side of the building that would hide it from the front drive but not from anyone looking out of the rear windows of the home.

"Got someone who wants to meet you," Gerald said. Bobby Jr. grinned and just shook his head.

Bobby Jr. gave a rhythmic knock on the building's small entry door. It was from a popular song, but I couldn't get the name in my head at that time. We waited a few seconds, and the door seemed to detach from the latch on its own and eased open just a few inches. Bobby inclined his head, indicating for us to follow him inside.

The room was dark, but I could still make out some shapes of furniture.

"Hey, Man, you still cool?" Bobby Jr. asked out into the room.

"I ... I guess," a disembodied voice came from the dark. I couldn't even tell the direction from which it came.

"Okay, I got some people with me; they are friends. I'm gonna turn on a light now," Bobby explained "Uh-huh," the voice responded.

"Gerald, Tekelius? I want to introduce you to the man of the hour," Bobby started as he flipped a wall light switch so old the click sounded like a finger snap. "I give you Mr. Bo Boulage."

Just when I thought I had no more "Holy bat shit, Batman!" left in me, I did not see this coming and acted as such. Bo Boulage was sitting on the couch, leaning forward on his forearms resting on his thighs. He was wearing a white shirtsleeve undershirt and red warm-up pants. He was barefoot. Most of all, he had that open-mouthed, slightly confused facial expression that told me his mental journeys were uphill battles.

He wasn't mentally challenged. He was a product of a childhood spent having excuses made for his bad behavior or settling things with his fists or applying headlocks and wedgies. Then he graduated and realized life was a much bigger bully. Now he was trying to learn the sandbox lessons of human coexistence most of us learned in grade school. Hard to believe a tough nut like Mimi Boulage would raise such a kid.

I'm sure he started off as the one thing in life she treated with softness, reverence, and compassion. I also imagined her personal brand of pride surrounding him, defending naughty indiscretions as a toddler up to punishable crimes later in life with a mother's protective shield. By the time he was a teenager, she could no longer contain him.

"The number one suspect in two murders is hiding in the mayor's storage building," I said to no one in particular.

"Person of interest," Bo corrected me. "I didn't kill nobody."

"Sorry," I responded. "Where is the mayor?"

"At home," Gerald said and pointed to the farm home three hundred feet away.

"He knows," Bobby Jr. said.

"He knows?" I asked and got nods all around. "What the.... "

"Love for a son," Gerald said. "It appears...."

"It does not appear to be common knowledge," Bobby Jr. said with a sardonic smile on his face. "His Honor the Mayor of Gilleyville is the father of one of the county's most notorious juveniles. Mimi and Managualt set up to hide this unfortunate fella. I was with the group guarding the Sam Gilley tomb for the last 24 hours, and asking some questions. Found out pretty quick that our boy was being hidden here. I checked with Uncle Lem back in St. Louis, and he said to tell his cousin Gerald. Gerald wanted to tell you, Manion."

I stood in the dark room looking at all the players in the room. I felt overwhelmed for a few seconds. The law needed to be involved, but my business was not the law. My business was that of WorldSpan's financial position.

"You didn't kill Lieutenant Perales?" I asked just to get the real conversation started.

"No," Bo Boulage answered in a voice that suggested he had been asked this several times.

"Where were you the night she was killed?" I asked.

"In bed," Bo replied.

"And the night when McLean was killed?" I asked.

"Who is McLean?" Bo asked.

"The soldier face down in the river the other morning," Bobby Jr. said.

"Don't play dumb."

"Oh, yeah, I was in bed then too," Bo replied.

"With whom and where," I asked. Bo just looked at the floor between his feet.

"See, this is a waste of fucking time," I started. "I have had a long day; people in this small friendly community are lying to me left and right. My patience is gone with this Southern gentility bullshit."

The room stayed quiet for a few seconds. I continued.

"You said on both occasions that you were asleep?" I asked. I got on one knee next to the sofa in the face of Bo Boulage. "I want to know where you were 'asleep,' and with whom?"

Bo Boulage sat back on the sofa. He looked scared again. I stood silent and just watched.

"I need to keep this a secret," he said. "It's a little embarrassing."

"Bo, there is a warrant for your arrest for first degree murder," I explained.

"Embarrassment is the last of your problems. Is it a girl?"

"Not exactly," he said.

"A boy?" Bobby Jr. asked.

"Hell, no!" Bo said, sitting up now.

"Hey, Man, no judgments here," Bobby Jr. said, stifling a small laugh.

"I don't care," I said. "I need a name."

"Names," Bo mumbled.

"Excuse me?" I asked.

"Names. I was with two girls both nights," Bo Boulage said with more shame than bravado. Someone in the room let out a low whistle. "It's the Bandy twins, Willow and Winona."

"The twins you boss around with Val Cedars?" I asked just to be clear. "Will they vouch for you?"

"I don't know," Bo said. "They got a mother from hell, probably got more fear of her; than love for me."

"Well, we will cross that bridge at the proper time. What about the pictures on Twitter?"

"I was just blowing off some steam, like the counselors taught me. I was acting out my frustrations instead of going out and pounding on every gold grabbing, out-of-town parasite leeching off my town."

"But the knives?" I said.

"Yeah, there's millions of 'em online sold every day," Bo said, his voice getting louder. "I ain't kill nobody. I don't have a reason."

"Oh, but you do, Kid," Bobby Jr. said. "You suspected Lieutenant Perales and Corporal McLean were searching for the gold for their own benefit. You had enough of the shit, and you killed them."

"That's not true!" Bo yelled. We all shushed him. "Listen, you got to believe me; I got a record. It's a juvenile one, but it's out there. Something like this could put me in prison."

"Okay, okay, I believe you," I said, motioning with my hands for him to settle down. "Bo, we are on your side, but we got a problem. The only way to clear you is to find the real killer. Any ideas?"

"About what? The real killer?" Bo asked. I nodded.

"Not a clue. If I did, I would be out wringing his neck."

"Not much help, Kid," I said. "Who else knows you are here?"

"My mother, my father the mayor, and you guys now."

"What about your boy Cedars?"

"No, I didn't have time before Mom rushed me over here."

"Let's keep it that way; eventually the police are going to figure out where you are, and when they come don't do anything stupid to give them a reason to shoot you."

I stood up and motioned for Gerald to follow me to the door.

"What do you want me to do?" Bobby Jr. asked.

"Keep doing what you are doing; try to keep this one alive. Seems like everyone close to this case ends up dead."

Chapter 27

The next morning Gerald and I were waiting for Sheriff Cormac at his office. The protesters from Reverend Moten's group, Val Cedars' historical preservation minions, and a new group from Gilleyville objecting to everything were in place outside of the City Works Building. When Sheriff Cormac arrived, we called Adam Samuelson and Colonel Sanchez, requesting them to join us. It was time to compare notes.

"Where is Mimi?" I asked but almost sure of the answer.

"On leave, until we get this business over with her son," Sheriff Cormac said. "I know she's hiding the kid, and I found Lieutenant Perales' audio recorder in the boy's room.

That news threw me for a loop. I believed the kid when he said he didn't do it, but this recorder was pretty damaging evidence to leave sitting around in his room, but this was Bo Boulage we were talking about.

"So you sure it was Bo that killed them?" I asked.

"Not totally," Sheriff Cormac said. "He has a pretty bad temper. Got the judge to let me peek at his juvenile record, assault, cruelty to animals, vandalism. Also got a copy of his fingerprints from juvenile records. They match one of the myriad of fingerprints on the knives used in both murders."

"That's pretty damning evidence," Gerald said, giving voice to what I was thinking.

"You would think, but his mother actually reported some of the knives stolen," Sheriff Cormac said wearily. "I took the report myself about six months ago. Mimi was taking them to be sharpened, and they were taken off the seat of her car while she was in the grocery store."

The room was quiet for the next few seconds until Colonel Sanchez arrived with her lead MP. Adam Samuelson arrived a few seconds behind the colonel.

"Let's look at what we got," Sheriff Cormac explained. He repeated his report on what he found in Bo Boulage's room and juvenile file. He also expressed the reasons for his hesitations.

"Sheriff, with all due respect, you may have a blind spot. The suspect is the son of your secretary," Colonel Sanchez said in her intense voice and unblinking brown eyes.

"Colonel, with all due respect, I will follow my investigation based on the facts, the rules of law, and that will lead to a conviction, not just revenge."

"What is that supposed to mean, Sheriff?" Colonel Sanchez asked, her voice going just a little icier.

"I know you want the person who killed Lieutenant Perales...."

"Yes, I do, and it sounds like we have him, as soon as you find him. How long does it take a small town sheriff and his deputies to find one twenty-year-old miscreant?"

"Okay," I stepped in before this went further. "Colonel, what the sheriff is saying is that when we find Bo Boulage, we have to be ready to charge him or we will have to let him go."

I made a gesture to Sheriff Cormac as if to get agreement. He nodded.

"Now we are here to build a case. Part of that is sharing what you have. Did you find out anything by going through Lieutenant Perales' belongings?"

"I did," Colonel Sanchez said, her facial expressions softening into something sad. "She kept a work journal. She talked about the day they found the gold and the wood chest. She wasn't specific, but she wrote about it not feeling right."

"In what way?" Sheriff Cormac asked.

"She wasn't specific," Colonel Sanchez snapped back.

"Okay, okay," I interrupted. "What else, Colonel?"

"I checked her call log on her cell phone. Most of the last calls were to her sister. When I called her, she said Lieutenant Perales asked a lot of questions about a trip they took as children to an old mining camp. They panned for gold dust, and actually found a couple of sizable pieces."

"That makes sense to me," I said. "The lieutenant was in the lab at that odd hour because it was something about the gold that bothered her. She bought Jolly Benoit's journal because she had questions about the gold. She was smart and a trained investigator. She had to know."

"That makes sense, but what did she 'have to know'?" Colonel Sanchez asked.

"What about the other stuff?" I asked.

"First, let me ask you," Colonel Sanchez started and slapped her hand on the top of the desk. "Where is your Spanish friend?"

"Fedelito? Haven't seen him in a couple of days, but he still has a room at the hotel," I explained.

"We ran dust and fiber analysis over Lieutenant Perales clothes and shoes. Among what you would expect —soil and dust, and cotton—we also found a substantial amount of fibers from an exotic material called Jaipur Moroccan linen."

"What is that from?" Sheriff Cormac asked.

"Jaipur is a commonly used material in custom-made European suits and shirts," Colonel Sanchez explained.

"Oh my God, it is Fedelito!" Adam Samuelson said. "This could be an international incident, and we could be totally powerless to prosecute." "Why?" Colonel Sanchez asked.

"Diplomatic immunity," I said, following the chain of thought. "But this means he's likely involved. Fedelito has a penchant for knives and for suffocating people."

"How do you know that? Sheriff Cormac asked.

"I spoke with our naked friend from the other night; she confirmed Fedelito was the one who tried to strangle her," I explained.

"You went to question a crime victim?" Sheriff Cormac asked.

"You said you didn't have time for this one, remember?" I snapped back, fighting to keep my thoughts on track. "There is nothing much to that, but it did confirm Fedelito's character."

"So let's get this right? Mimi's son's knives were used in the murders; he's on the run; he published threats on the internet, and somehow the attaché from Spain is involved?" Colonel Sanchez surmised.

There were nods all around.

"So what's our next move? Do I need to get the State Department involved?" Adam Samuelson asked.

"Yes, wait, no," I said. "Can you put them on notice but tell them not to make a move on it. If we can find Fedelito without letting on we know what he's been doing, maybe he will lead us to the others involved."

"You mean he will lead us to Bo Boulage?" Colonel Sanchez asked. "Maybe," I said. "It's just that Fedelito and Bo make strange bedfellows." "I agree," Adam Samuelson said, rubbing his chin.

"Assuming Fedelito is involved, who is his logical bedfellow?" Colonel Sanchez asked. She pointed from her eyes to Gerald and me. We laughed.

"We have no motive," I replied. "But you are on the right track."

"And if it's Bo Boulage, who is his logical partner?" Colonel Sanchez said, casting a sidelong glance at Sheriff Cormac.

We thought for a few seconds before Deputy Laurie walked into the room. She was carrying a metal stainless steel case. There was a large white sticker on it with the words EVIDENCE in red lettering. She set it on Sheriff Cormac's desk and stepped back to the corner of the room. Sheriff Cormac walked around to the back of his desk. He reached into the bottom side drawer and pulled out a box of latex gloves.

"Let's put these on," he said. We all complied.

Gerald, Colonel Sanchez, Deputy Laurie, Adam Samuelson, Sheriff Cormac, and I stood around the desk looking into the steel case. There were the three gold coins and a wooden chest found by the forensic team. Sheriff Cormac picked up the first coin, looked at it for a few seconds, and passed it to me.

The coin was shiny with irregular edges. On one side was a picture of Charles IV, King of Spain from 1788 to 1808. On the other side was a Royal Greater Coat of Arms of Spain, under the Spanish crown, and surrounded by the royal fleece. There was an inscription around the outer edge around the crest. It was minted in 1801. There was a gritty feel to the coin, but not like soil. The grain was smaller, maybe sand.

During our sessions back in Paris, Rudolph Lemieux told me that most of the world's problems could be solved with patience and silence. Turn the sounds of your mind off so you can hear the problem talking back to you.

I held the coin in my hand, my mind a blank. What was I seeing, hearing, smelling, and touching? There was dirt on and in the creases of the coins, but there was also a greasiness? And a gritty feel on the surface.

"What was done to the coins since they were found?" I asked.

"Nothing," Deputy Laurie said. "This is how they were pulled out of the dirt."

I asked about the oiliness and the unnatural grittiness to the coin. The others noticed but had no conclusions. I looked at the chest, a decayed rough-hewn wood box with hinged lid still intact. I tried to stay quiet and listen to the object, as crazy as that sounded. I got nothing.

After almost thirty minutes, we came up with no clues from the coins. We agreed to tackle some other parts of the case. Sheriff Cormac and Deputy Laurie would continue looking for Bo Boulage. I felt bad not sharing what I knew, but Bo Boulage wasn't going anywhere. If we didn't get a suspect in a day or two, I would let the sheriff know via Bobby Jr. about the whereabouts of Bo Boulage.

Colonel Sanchez said she had to get back to the forensic work, but I suspected at least one of these MPs would be in plainclothes looking for Bo Boulage as well. Adam Samuelson mumbled about working with the State Department to have Fedelito recalled. Gerald and I promised to continue to look for Fedelito as well, but we had one stop to make.

On the way over to Mimi's, I thought about the questions raised in the sheriff's office. Who would be a logical partner for her son Bo

Boulage? Fedelito did not make sense, although the evidence was there. I couldn't sit on the Bo Boulage knowledge for more than another day or two. Also, the forensic teams have been working around the clock and have reinterred most of the remains disturbed by the floodwaters. No more gold had been discovered. The forensic teams themselves came under great scrutiny. They were searched when they came to work and checked every four hours until they left the labs.

The number of strangers walking around Benoitown and Gilleyville had diminished greatly in the last two days—gold enthusiasts, media outliers, and just curious people with nothing else to do. I had not updated Paris in a while, but it looked like this would be a wasted trip. As I thought about all the people, machinery and supplies, I realized there were more fortunes spent and made looking for gold than the actual gold found.

Chapter 28

When I knocked on Mimi Boulage's door, I was not surprised when Val Cedars answered. His fire engine-red sweater vest with buttons down the front appeared to be custom made for him. He wore a white business shirt with button-down collar and of course khaki plain front slacks.

"Mimi can't take visitors now, Manion. She's in crisis," he said, partially blocking the doorway.

"You seem to be visiting?" I said calmly, attempting to look beyond him into the house.

"I'm her friend, here to give her moral support," he said, playing the protective big brother.

"A lot of people looking for your prodigy," I said flatly.

"Don't ask me where he is; I can't tell you. This whole mess has us all so upset. Bo, being hunted like some wild animal."

Something about the way he didn't look me in the eye as he started on this soliloquy made me think he did not know that Bo was under wraps just a few miles away. I tested him.

"The sheriff knows he's out of town. Got it nailed down to three different places—Charlotte, Wilmington or Rock Hill, South Carolina," I lied. His eyes got big, but he recovered quickly.

"Well, good luck with that; I won't tell you," he said haughtily. "Besides you aren't even the police, just another gold grabber."

"And the only thing you want is…." I asked.

"To preserve the historic integrity of this river basin," he said a bit louder as if there was an audience behind me. I wanted to keep him talking, maybe I could get a glimpse of Mimi in the windows.

"Tell me, Cedars, you think the kid killed those two people?"

"Of course not," he said, adding just a quarter turn more indignation.

"What reason would he have?"

"I'm sure you noticed he has a bit of a temper," I said subtly.

"If that's all the police have…."

"Then there's the knives and the recorder," I said.

"I don't believe it," Val Cedars said but with a bit less conviction. "Cormac is desperate for a fall guy; Bo makes a convenient one. I have told that boy many times to be careful in how he carries himself, and with whom he associates. One must always be careful of that, Mr. Manion."

I pantomimed, pointing at myself. He kept talking, and I kept glancing at the windows and doors.

"Yes, you and your Spanish friend. He likes knives, doesn't he? Has great plans for the gold of Jolly Benoit?"

"Yes he does," I said, wondering where Fedelito was myself. My mind was off on a tangent for a few seconds. I don't think Val Cedars noticed I wasn't listening.

The question of two people involved and who made the logical partners. Val Cedars had stopped talking and was standing there, with his standard look of irritation. There was something off here. Mimi was no shrinking violet. I didn't know the lady well, but she didn't seem to be the type to let others fight her battles. I said a hearty goodbye to Val, who never left the door.

I got in my car and drove up one block and around the corner to a side street. Using some new skills from my friend Lemieux, I parked halfway down the side street. The car was just about out of sight from Mimi's front door. I pulled the sun flap down, exposing the mirror on the backside. Then I rotated the flap on its hinge until I could see the front of Mimi's house, watching who may come and go. Then I waited.

I got a text from Bobby Jr. about 30 minutes later.

I paid a visit to the twins; they cracked with little pressure. Confirmed the story Bo told us. They even had video. Brrrr. Scared to death of their parents finding out, but I believe them.

The situation was starting to talk to me, give me a path to follow, or maybe I was tired of my makeshift stakeout. I made two phone calls.

First, I called Deputy Laurie and Gerald. I asked them to trace the source of some information that had come into the sheriff's department. Next, I called Adam Samuelson.

"I need you to call Val Cedars. Ask him to meet you at the Jolly Benoit Wing of the County Museum. Tell him there have been developments associated with the national historic site designation, and you need him immediately."

"Okay, but what do I tell him when he gets there?" he asked.

"Anything, make something up; I only need an hour or so," I explained. Adam Samuelson agreed. I could hear him verbally rehearsing word tracks.

"But I'm with the State Department; why would we get involved in this?" he asked. He was willing to do it, but he wanted to get his lies straight.

"Cedars doesn't know that; explain that you are doing a favor, one agency for another. Save them a trip down here unnecessarily."

"That would just work," he explained.

Adam Samuelson stipulated that I be on the phone when he made his misdirection call. He made a three-way call to Val Cedars with me on the other extension. It worked. Val was excited and promised to be right down. A few minutes later, I saw him leave out the front door of Mimi's home, jump in his blue Thunderbird and speed off, tires screeching just a bit.

I didn't know what would look more suspicious to small-town neighbors, my parking in the driveway and going through the front or walking down the alley that ran behind the houses, hopping the fence and gaining entrance through the back. In the end I opted for the front. I called Bobby Jr. Luckily he was back at the Gilley Vault and near Bo. In about 15 minutes, he drove up with Bo's house keys.

"Want me to go in first?" Bobby Jr. asked as he pulled a small silver automatic from a belt holster hidden beneath his shirt. "I'm licensed to carry concealed in North Carolina."

He had the bravery born of extreme youth. He obviously trained for action. Babysitting a murder suspect and guarding a tomb must have been boring amateur league action for him. But if we were caught, I didn't want to have to explain an unauthorized operative from an unauthorized security firm. I patted his gun hand down.

"Let me take the lead 'Spencer for Hire,'" I joked in a whisper. "It's still my plan."

"Who's Spencer for Hire?" he asked, clearly too young to know the old detective series. I walked past him and stepped inside.

The house was quiet. The foyer led into a small living room with a green sofa and a recliner of multiple colors, none of which were green. Mimi still had a large tube television with the bulging round back and a 30-inch screen.

"Mimi!" I called out. "It's Teke Manion. Your door was open."

No answer.

"Mimi, I want to talk to you about Bo! Where are you?"

No answer. Bobby Jr. pulled his gun out again. This time, I did not pat his hand down. Bobby Jr. took the lead into the kitchen. There were a few dishes in the sink, but no food smells, no food on the stove. We followed the hallway to the one bathroom and three small bedrooms. The first bedroom was a makeshift office with an IKEA desk and chair, and three assemble-yourself bookshelves. The next bedroom was obviously Bo's room, martial arts Fathead wall decals and old-school metal rock posters. Mimi's room was just across the narrow hall.

The door was closed. I tried the knob, and it turned so easy that the door opened slightly. Bobby Jr. silently pulled me back behind him. He slowly opened the door with his free hand while keeping the silver pistol fixed on the doorway.

"Mimi, are you alone?" Bobby Jr. asked as he slowly entered the room, motioning for me to follow.

Mimi Boulage was fully clothed lying on her back atop the bedcovers.

Dreading the worst, I felt for the neck pulse.

"Stop feeling for a pulse, Manion, her chest is moving up and down," Bobby Jr. said after checking the closets and back down the hall. "Just shake her."

I did for almost a minute. Finally, Mimi came fully awake. I kept waiting for the no-nonsense woman to come to and rain embarrassing questions down on us like what were we doing in her home. However, she didn't. She was awake but far from alert.

"Are you okay, Mimi? Can we get you anything?" I asked.

"No, no I'm good. Val just left, and I was just getting off to sleep," she said sitting up rubbing her face and holding her head. She looked at her watch. "My God, it's only been 30 minutes; I feel like I been sleep for a day."

"Manion," Bobby Jr. said. I looked at him. He inclined his head to Mimi's nightstand. There was a glass with a liquid in it that looked like cola. I picked it up and held it up. Bobby Jr. leaned down and took a sniff. He nodded. He left the room and came back with small hand towel from the bathroom. He used it to take the glass from me.

"Who is that?" Mimi finally asked.

"He works for me. I was concerned about you and did not want to come by myself," I explained.

"Concerned? For what, Manion?"

"Well, Val Cedars for one. He's been pretty protective of you."

"He's supposed to be. He's my friend. Val and me go back a long ways."

"I get it," I answered, holding up conciliatory hands. She was sitting up with her back against the light beige padded headboard. I was sitting on the edge of the bed turned to her in a close conciliatory way, like I had secrets to share.

"Tell me, is he close enough of a friend to know the secret about you and Mayor Managualt, and that you're hiding Bo on his property?"

That brought her fully awake.

"Mimi, it's a small town. I'm surprised you been able to hide the kid this long."

"What are you gonna do, Manion?" she asked showing fear and defiance.

"Try to keep him from going to jail," I said. "I talked to Bo recently. He told me his story."

"Those stupid twins," Mimi said, rolling her eyes. "I know their parents. They will do whatever it takes to keep their offspring out of trouble, including lie to the law."

"But that's perjury," I said.

"It is. Unless you live in a small county where your parents golf with the members of the state prosecutors' office. I wish Val had never introduced them to each other. I knew those two mindless troll hoes would be trouble for my boy."

I barely controlled the snicker at the name.

"I'm serious, Manion. My boy has had his share of problems, but he has been good for two years. Then Val got it in his mind to build this group of young people who cared about preservation and historical significance...."

"You don't care about national historic preservation?" I asked.

"I do, as long as it gives Bo something constructive to do. That's Val's thing. He's been on that history thing since high school," she said with a laugh. "He has been submitting applications to the National Historic Preservation Society for the last twenty years on everything old—from minor battlefields to Indian digs to.... "

"To Jolly Benoit artifacts?" I asked, finishing her thought.

"Yes," she said, pointing a finger at me. "That was his ace in the hole. He has been the main one pushing the whole legend. Searching through stacks of old papers and estate sales to gather what we have. He got the Jolly Benoit/Sam Gilley archives and museum pieces chartered with the state."

"Well, that was great," I answered sincerely.

"Good, but not great," Mimi said. "Val has wanted the national declaration. He even has two degrees in history and curator sciences. He could go to the Smithsonian or one of the presidential libraries and do well."

"But...," I asked.

"He wants to be the head curator of a museum in this part of the state. He would rather be the big fish in this pond over being a small fish in the large pond."

They had known each other a long time. When she spoke of him, it was a mixture of pride and affection, like a sister for her brother.

"Manion, a minute?" Bobby Jr. said, beckoning me from the doorway. I excused myself from Mimi, saying I would bring her some water.

In the kitchen, Bobby Jr. stood at the butcher block counter in front of two glasses with small amounts of brown liquid in them. At closer inspection, one was slightly lighter than the other.

"I'm pretty sure our friend, Mimi, has been drugged. I smelled her glass.

Nothing. Took a small taste, it was salty. I went out to the car to get my test kit."

"Test for what?" I asked.

"I separated the liquid into two glasses and poured just a bit on these paper detection coasters. In a few seconds the solution will tell us what we need to know."

"You keep test coasters on you?" I asked.

"Actually that, along with a few other things," he said and pointed to the small bag on the counter. I peeked inside. "Epi pens, snake bite kit, wound clotting solution, and vomit-inducing pills."

"Don't forget the gun," I said sarcastically. Bobby Jr. padded his belt holster. In a few seconds the wet spots on the coasters took on a deep bluish hue.

When Bobby Jr. and I looked at each other, he nodded.

"Does she need a doctor?" I asked.

"I wouldn't think so. It's probably GHB, one of the date rape drugs. She's gonna feel like shit all day with a headache in about eight hours, but no lasting damage," Bobby Jr. explained.

"I'm afraid for her safety, nevertheless. He drugged her for a reason. You gotta tell her about Cedars."

"She wouldn't believe me, and she would run and tell Val the first chance she got," I said. "I'll tell the sheriff to put a car at her house, citing that she may be a flight risk."

"Manion!" Mimi called. I quickly grabbed a clean glass from the cupboard, filled it with tap water, and returned to Mimi's bedroom. She was more coherent now, more her old self.

"You never did explain what you are doing here?" she asked by way of accusation.

"Like I said, we wanted to talk to you about Bo after we found out where he was. To help clear him."

"How?" she asked with a skeptical smirk.

"By finding out who really did it. We believe our man from Spain is tied up in this."

"Really? I never trusted that rat bastard," she said.

"Bo would never have dealings with Fedelito, would he?" I asked.

"Of course not. Bo thought the man was gay and trying to hide it, you know what I mean?"

I nodded and continued. "Mimi, I don't want any harm to come to your son. If I did, I would have turned him in 24 hours ago. I don't think he did it, but I got to find the real killer to help you."

"That's what Val was saying," Mimi said, jumping out of bed now. "If they arrest Bo now, the law will stop looking for any other suspects, but as along as Bo is out of sight we all can find the real killer."

"How long can you keep him on the mayoral estate? Managualt could be prosecuted and at least be removed from office," I explained.

"Look, I trust you Manion, so I'll tell you. Val and I are gonna meet up at midnight at the back of the mayor's property. We gonna get Bo out of town. I got a sister in Wilmington who can keep him on the farm until we all find the killer or get those stupid twins to corroborate Bo's story."

Mimi just spilled her entire plan to me. Her face was vulnerable and her eyes pleading. She was weary from worry, under the influence of a prescription grade sedative, and needing all the allies she could get. I instinctively reached out and put my hand on her left shoulder with a light squeeze. She quickly reached over and put her right hand over mine.

"Why midnight?" I asked.

"Val said everything will be quiet and slow. Everyone will be at the bars in town. Most of the sheriff's patrols will be in town to make sure there is no trouble. Val is going to use his plain white delivery van. We won't attract attention."

"How are you going to meet him?" I asked.

"I'm not," she said. "Cormac will be watching my car. I wrote a note for Bo and gave it to Val to give to him, so he would know the plan was mine to go to my sisters."

"But it wasn't your plan, right?"

"Well, technically Val came up with it, but it's a good plan, Manion. You said yourself if Bo is caught they will probably stop looking for the real killers." I nodded and thought for a minute. The whole idea of the note seemed odd. "There's no way to call Bo, let him hear it from you?"

"We destroyed his phone, and we figured my cell phone and house phone was tapped. I assumed I was being watched, so I couldn't just run out and buy a new track phone. We were thinking this thing up as we went along."

Tears jumped to her eyes for the first time. She wiped them away with a rough swipe, hating to show any frailty.

"Okay, then, I would stick to that plan," I said in my calmest voice. "Mimi, we swear we will not give up Bo's whereabouts. Our plan is to catch Fedelito

Gaspare who will lead us to the other murderer."

"I'll just be glad when all this gold business is done. Sometimes I think the Jolly Benoit Sam Gilley legend is a curse. Sends the wrong kind of people to our town. No offense."

"None taken," I said and patted her arm like a buddy.

In a few minutes Bobby Jr. and I said our good-byes and after thoroughly rinsing the glasses but saving a sample of the cola in a plastic bag. When we got back in the car, I noticed I had several missed calls. The first one was from Gerald.

"Manion, crawl out from under whatever rock you been under and get back to the City Works building," his voicemail said.

"Tekelius, we have not gotten an update from you in some time; there is time sensitive information at stake. And I need my fix as well," Camille said in a voicemail.

Next was Sheriff Cormac.

"I have been listening to this mini-recorder we found in Bo's room. Sounds horrible. She fought to the very end, but can't hear Bo on the recording. Also Bo's prints not on the recorder case. The prints on the case are not in our system, maybe that damn Fedelito. Call me back."

Bobby Jr. headed back to the Gilleyville mayoral estate where Bo Boulage was hiding. I headed into Benoitown. On the way, the plan was forming in my mind. It had a lot of moving parts and only one day to work. That day was today.

When I got to Sheriff Cormac's office, it was a déjà vu experience. All the players from before were there—Sheriff Cormac, Gerald, Colonel Sanchez, Deputy Laurie, and Adam Samuelson. We listened to the small digital recording that had been missing from the crime scene and found in Bo Boulage's bedroom.

It started with Lieutenant Perales discussing what she was doing, how she was moving through the remains. It was a very technical dictation, and I didn't understand much of it. Then we heard a much clearer audio of Lieutenant Perales struggling. We heard her muffled scream, gurgling inside a plastic bag. Colonel Sanchez looked down at nothing in particular, arms folded. The sheriff, his deputy, and Gerald also flinched in the face with each scream and gurgle. We could hear Lieutenant Perales dying. Then we hear her finally breaking free.

We hear her make contact with her attacker. She is coughing and yelling with each kick. Then footsteps running away, the lieutenant's strike of the alarm, and her scream from being stabbed in the back.

"Samuelson, where the hell is that fucking Fedelito? I want his ass in prison," Colonel Sanchez said, stepping forward in Adam Samuelson's comfort space.

The State Department attaché literally cowered away from the colonel.

"I don't know," Adam Samuelson said pleadingly. "I swear that 'State' is doing all they can. We can't find him and Spain says they haven't heard from him."

"Colonel, that's enough," Sheriff Cormac said. "This isn't getting us anywhere."

"I got two dead soldiers and we're sitting here playing *Murder She Wrote,* and I'm sick of it. I want to call my friends in the federal government and declare martial law on this pathetic little country village!"

"Colonel!" I said, loud enough for all to hear and render them quiet. What I said after that was going to be crucial.

"When the redcoats brought martial law to the colonies, when the Nazis imposed martial law in France, why didn't it work?"

"What?" Colonel Sanchez said, thrown off her game for a second.

"You heard me? You were a student of military history. I read it in your background. What happened when martial law was declared by the redcoats and by the Nazis?"

There was a long silence. Everybody wondering where this was going.

"What happened, Colonel?" I repeated a little louder.

"The people banded together—against the authority," Colonel Sanchez said with a deep sigh.

"And further fueled sentiment for resistance," I said.

"Which led to the revolutionary war; in the other case the French resorted to guerilla movements that undermined the German's hold on France."

"Exactly," I said, going on my own. Not even Gerald knew where I was going. "If we come down hard on this community, they will close ranks against us. You will have to feed your own soldiers because no restaurant in this town will feed them. You will need your own water source as well."

The room was quiet for a few seconds to let things cool down.

"So we gonna tell what we found?" Deputy Laurie said.

"What did you find about what?" Sheriff Cormac asked.

"Manion asked Gerald and me to find out where the email tip about Bo Boulage's Twitter photos came from," Deputy Laurie said. "It took some digging but we traced it to an internet café in Kinston. We got lucky. The owner has security cameras. Guess who walked into the café and sent an email at the exact date stamp of the transmission?"

I knew who it was, but I didn't want to rob Deputy Laurie of her moment. "Well who was it, Deputy?" Sheriff Cormac demanded.

"Fedelito Gaspare," Deputy Laurie said and held up a paper copy of the video shot of Fedelito at the Kinston Internet Café. "Of course we can't find him."

That threw me for a loop. I did not expect him to say Fedelito. I thought it would be the other parties working with him. All this time, I had an idea that Fedelito Gaspare was masterminding this whole thing, but he seems more like the puppet than the puppet master.

"So you saying Fedelito did the killing and is setting up the kid?" Sheriff Cormac asked.

"Probably, but it doesn't answer everything," Gerald said. "We said there was more than one person. Fedelito is definitely one of them. Bo and Fedelito don't make sense. They would have no contact with each other. Bo has no interest in gold, not enough to kill for it. Right?"

Sheriff Cormac and Deputy Laurie both nodded.

"Besides, Bo has an alibi for the night of the murders," I said.

"What alibi and how do you know that?" Sheriff Cormac asked, planting a laser gaze on me.

"His mother told me," I said flatly. "He has been spending time with the Bandy Twins."

"Yeah, like they wouldn't lie for the boy?" Deputy Laurie said sardonically.

"Let's not get off track," Sheriff Cormac said. "Now, here's how I see it. Tell me where I missed something."

"McLean and Fedelito enter into an alliance to search for gold at night. They get surprised by Lieutenant Perales; one strangles her, probably Fedelito. The other one stabs her, probably McLean fearing court-martial. Then fearing he would talk when we caught him, Fedelito and McLean agree to meet. So he slips away from the hotel where Nadine has him hidden, and gets killed by Fedelito." "It seems workable to me," Deputy Laurie said.

"Except," I started to speak and the entire room sighed with exasperation. I continued. "First, while it is possible that McLean stabbed Perales, it doesn't seem like him based on what people have said. Second, the night McLean is stabbed, Fedelito has an alibi. He was with the boxer Xanadu Waters. They trained half the night. Then he was having kinky sex with Glynis James, our naked woman running through the streets of Benoitown."

"I have to agree with Manion. McLean was slick and a fast talker, but he was not malicious. He would run and try to lie or bribe his way out of something. He wasn't violent like that. That sounds more like your boy, Bo Boulage," Colonel Sanchez said.

"But they were just trading insults with each other less than a week ago," Gerald said.

"Yeah, but gold makes strange alliances," I explained. I turned to Colonel Sanchez. "Isn't it true that Private Jackson said that Corporal McLean had a buyer set up; someone who could take the gold off their hands?"

"Right," Colonel Sanchez said.

"Who would be better to handle that than Fedelito? He has the backing of the Spanish Government's reward—ten percent."

"So Fedelito is the mastermind. He brought McLean in by the oldest motive in the world. He needed money. How did he bring Bo into it?" Sheriff Cormac asked the group.

"We can get that answer as soon as we find either one of them. We can make them talk," Colonel Sanchez said.

Adam Samuelson cleared his throat.

"Let's hope it's the Boulage boy," he explained. "If and when we catch Fedelito Gaspare, he will have diplomatic protection protocols in place."

"Okay, we'll see about his protocols when we find him," Colonel Sanchez said with a stony resilience.

"Colonel, I warn you against any rash action in this matter," Adam Samuelson warned.

"Well, you tell the State Department and the country of Spain that strange and dangerous things are going on down here in Benoitown, USA."

"That's enough, Colonel," Sheriff Cormac said. "So we keep looking for both of them. Samuelson, no one is going to break protocol, but we do expect—no, we demand—the full cooperation of the US State Department and the Spanish consulate."

"I have a plan," I said, feeling confident enough to put it forward. The pieces coming together but still based on hunches and instinct. "Let's keep a deputy on Mimi's house. At some point Bo is bound to show up."

"I'm already on that, Manion," Deputy Laurie said.

"Yeah, but he knows you. Put someone out there he does not know, maybe borrow a deputy from the next county," I explained, and everyone agreed that would work. "We can set up road blocks out of town. Put Quinten and his water brigade on all vessels moving downstream."

The meeting soon ended. Before I could leave, Adam Samuelson stopped Gerald and me.

"Listen, I'm a little worried about the colonel and her motives. I wonder if I should alert her superiors. This is how small incidents turn into big scandals that end with everyone testifying before Congress. I don't like the little diplomatic scum bag more than anyone, but I'm not about to lose my post because a renegade soldier or cop trampled on his diplomatic immunity...," he prattled on like this for some time, clearly nervous beyond rational thought.

Gerald and I let him vent. Adam Samuelson was a pretty cool customer most times, but it wasn't from nerves of steel. He was the careful type of man who kept his cool by maintaining six degrees of separation from any controversy or danger. After about a minute he took a deep breath, seemingly to regain his calm demeanor. He pulled a sheet of folded paper from his jacket pocket. He looked around as if to check if the three of us were alone.

"I'm not sure what your intent was when you asked me to call Val Cedars to discuss the National Historical Preservation," he said.

"We needed Val to leave so we could get Mimi alone at her house. To try to find out where Bo was hiding," I half lied by way of explanation.

"Okay," Adam Samuelson said. He seemed to run that over in his mind, looked like he wanted to ask a follow-up question, then caught himself. Asking too many questions would get him too close to a place he didn't want to be. He continued.

"Well, I called some distant relatives of mine who actually work at the National Historical Preservation Office in Washington, DC. I wanted to get some talking points before I spoke to Cedars."

He handed the paper to me. I opened it. It appeared to be a report of some kind. It listed articles submitted by the BGNHS, Val Cedars' unofficial historical preservation group. Among the items listed were several gold coins and a wood chest similar to what was found a few weeks ago and sitting in Sheriff Cormac's safe as evidence.

"Looks like Cedars moved fast to get this stuff registered. His whole ambition involves getting a National Historic Registration for this area," Adam Samuelson said.

"Can he do that?" Gerald asked. "Submit items still in police possession? Doesn't someone from the National Historic Preservation have to actually see the items?"

"My contact said that is how it usually works, but Val has been pretty aggressive. I get the impression the procedures on this are fairly tight," Adam Samuelson said. "I'm not sure what all you're doing, Manion, and I don't want to know, but I got this from my contact. Now I have given it to you. I'm out of it."

"I understand," I said.

"That means, if this comes out...."

"I know, Samuelson," I interrupted. "If we are deposed by the authorities or Congress, I will fall on the sword."

Adam Samuelson started to respond to my sarcasm, but realizing he had gotten the assurances he wanted, he prudently waved his hand and walked away.

I read the form again. It had no date associated with it. It appeared to be a screen image of an online form, probably taken by Adam Samuelson's relative/ contact. Looking back on this situation, it was funny that Adam Samuelson, unbeknownst to us at the time, had answered one of the biggest mysteries of this crazy event.

Chapter 29

When Gerald and I got to the street outside the City Works building, I explained what would happen in the next few hours. It was just before five o'clock.

"I think we need to get the word to Fedelito about the location of Bo Boulage."

"Why?" Gerald asked, looking at me as if I had two heads.

"So he will try to kill him," I said.

"What?" Gerald said, his voice almost at a shout.

"Listen, we get the word that after midnight, Bo is skipping town to his aunt's farm outside of Wilmington."

"How do we get the word out without telling the police?" Gerald asked.

"We will have to tell the police but at the right time," I explained. "First, we leave notes for Fedelito where only he will get it."

We jumped in the car heading to the hotel. There was a third car door slam in the backseat area.

"Thanks a lot, Manion, for getting me kicked off the Mimi detail," Deputy Laurie said after jumping in the car. "I know that kid is coming back to his mother's house."

"Sorry, Deputy, but I think my plan is sound," I said, looking back over my right shoulder. "If you will excuse us, we got to make some appointments?" "Do me a favor: drop me off in Gilleyville," she asked.

"Where is your patrol car?" I asked.

"Remember, I have been put on road block duty; thanks to you," she explained, leaning over the front seat. "Now drop me off in Gilleyville so I can get a pickup ride from the state troopers on the road block. We don't have the big budget like you two have."

She made a big deal of looking around the inside of our rental vehicle with mock appreciation. Then she plopped on the backseat waiting for the car to start.

It didn't take long. The ride over to the Gilleyville substation for the police department took less than five minutes. She spent every second telling us how thankful she was for our efforts to bring Bo Boulage in alive. We listened to her in cautious silence.

Gerald and I went to the hotel, gathered some supplies, and left a written note under Fedelito's door. Next we stopped at the gym; we found Fedelito's sparring partner, Xanadu. He denied hearing from the Spaniard, but I assumed he was well paid for his secrecy. I played dumb, explaining that they were looking for Bo Boulage as the only person who could clear Fedelito from prosecution. I also dropped that Bo was hiding at the Gilleyville mayoral estate. The boxer was no poker player. I could see his mind taking the bait by the look in his eyes. Our work was done there. Lastly, we just left a simple message on voicemail to the cell phone number Fedelito gave us but never answered.

Gerald and I got back to the Gilleyville mayoral estate as fast as we could. We got lucky; his honor was home. I requested we meet in the small building where Bo was hiding. Mayor Managualt, his son Bo

Boulage, Bobby Jr., Gerald and I crowded into the sitting room. There we hatched our last trap to catch a killer.

Chapter 30

Captain Bryce Banner of the US Army Military Police was working on the free weights at the Edgewood County YMCA. This assignment was one of the most stressful of his career. Working with the local civilian authorities without military rule was difficult. He had to retrain his men, retrain himself. He also had to constantly remind his immediate commanding officer of the rules.

Colonel Sanchez was a good officer and understood the rules better than anyone. He felt for her on this one. Lieutenant Perales was like her little sister. People had this misconception that military people detached their feelings about death in order to be effective soldiers and officers. The opposite was true. He hated that people died on this assignment, a simple domestic assignment. He felt personally responsible for it as well. One of his guards was part of the problem. One of his Guards was killed, on a non-combat assignment.

The first floor of the YMCA was set up primarily for boxing. There were three boxing rings in the middle of the large room. Around the edge of the space were multiple weightlifting stations and bag workstations. There were doors off the large room leading to the front lobby. Side doors led to locker rooms for men and women; plus, there was one back door.

Looking around, Captain Banner saw the boxer, Xanadu, a fun guy who was kind of a mascot of the YMCA. The guy was always there, looking for people to pay him for working them out. He had his old boxing promotion pictures on the walls, selling sparring bouts with an ex-Golden Glove.

Captain Banner was also a former Golden Glove boxer. Similar in age, the two men knew some of the same fighters, competed at the same tournaments, but in different weight classes. Xanadu was a middleweight. Captain Banner had been a heavyweight. They usually compared notes and reminisced about fighters they remembered. Today was different.

The braggadocios fighter moved tentatively around the gym and spoke to no one. Captain Banner noticed it immediately and decided he would pursue his nagging curiosity.

"What's good, Champ?" he asked as Xanadu walked past the weight stations. Xanadu threw a hand up and mumbled something but quickly kept walking. Captain Banner started after him but thought better. Instead he circled the opposite direction around the center boxing rings. He watched Xanadu move around the gym. He went into a couple of lockers along the wall, removing large bags. Captain Banner noticed they weren't the typical gym bags he normally carried. These were brushed leather backpacks with shiny golden buckles and fasteners. Captain Banner fiddled around at the butterfly press on the universal weight machine with very little weight on it, pretending not to watch Xanadu, who moved around the perimeter of the large room speaking to no one, head down.

In a few seconds he had three of the leather backpacks plus his own satin black Top Rank bag. It was a small duffel-shaped bag. Captain Banner stopped him near the rear door leading to the outside.

"What's all these, Champ?" he asked.

"Oh, hey, uh, nothing. Just some stuff I need to get rid of," the fighter said nervously.

"Let me help you," Captain Banner said and quickly picked up one of the backpacks. It was heavy, maybe 30 pounds and only half-full. "Whooo, what you got in here, Man!"

"Nothing," Xanadu said and tried to snatch it back, but Captain Banner deftly shifted the bag out of Xanadu's reach and slung it over his shoulder.

"I got this one," Captain Banner said. "You get the rest and we can take them out to your car. Come on."

The boxer started to protest, but decided better of it. He clumsily picked up the other two leather backpacks that seemed just as heavy. Then his duffel. Walking single file out the back door, Captain Banner's curiosity became fullblown. It surprised, saddened, then angered him that the boxer would, in the end, be just a common thief stealing from the lockers of others. He would wait until they got outside before he accused him.

The door leading outside was actually two doors with a small space between the two, similar to most commercial buildings. As Captain Banner and Xanadu moved through the small space between the doors, the MP reached up to the backpack on the boxer's shoulders.

"Hey, this one is unzipped," Captain Banner lied reaching out for the bag on Xanadu's shoulder. "I got it."

Captain Banner actually unzipped the bag to get a peek at the contents.

What he saw changed everything.

Chapter 31

"Deputy, what's your twenty?" Sheriff Cormac asked once he got Deputy Laurie on the phone.

"Moving between town and the road blocks," Deputy Laurie answered.

"Did you put the extra deputy on Mimi's house?" he asked.

"Yes, sir," she answered.

"I know you wanted that detail," he said.

"Affirmative, but Manion had the right idea on that."

"You want to make sure we bring Bo in alive."

"Affirmative, sir. That boy is Mimi's world. Mimi is family."

"Affirmative back on that, Deputy," Sheriff Cormac answered with that same stiff military style vernacular.

The line was quiet for a few seconds.

"Anything else, Sir?" Deputy Laurie asked. "I want to follow up on the road blocks."

"No, nothing else," Sheriff Cormac said. Deputy Laurie ended the call without saying good-bye.

He had been sheriff for several years; the rest of the staff were locals who grew up in either Benoitown or Gilleyville. They had accepted him, worked for him, respected him, but there were always going to be times and circumstances when he was reminded that he was not really one of them, not in their innermost circle.

~ ~ ~

Deputy Laurie sat in an unmarked private vehicle belonging to her sister who lived in Gilleyville. She also changed into plainclothes. She didn't like being cryptic to the sheriff. She prided herself on brutal honesty and transparency. This was different.

This gold business dumped greed, betrayal, and death to her town. She was the law, so it was her job to fix it. Mimi was like an aunt to her. Mimi and Laurie's mother were teenagers together. Laurie babysat Bo Boulage when he was a kid. She didn't believe he was guilty of murder, but she would make sure he stayed alive to have his day in court.

But what did Mayor Managualt have to do with all of this? she wondered.

Believing no one was telling the whole truth in this matter, she did some undercover work starting with those closest to Fedelito Gaspare. When she took the ride from Teke Manion and Gerald Phillips, she "accidentally" left a cell phone in the rear seat area. On the floor. Partially hidden under the front seat. That phone had the "phone find" software on and actively pinging. She was able to track that phone and consequently the car in which she left it. The car was now parked on the property of the Gilleyville mayoral estate. She could see from the street that the car was not in the front drive. She had to see what was going on, and it was going to be on foot.

Chapter 32

"Colonel, I'm ready to report my position," Captain Banner explained from the front seat of his vehicle. "I'm at the Tar Road Inn west of town on Highway 64 and Catfish Hunter Drive."

"Is the boxer living there?" Colonel Sanchez asked.

"Not sure. Someone let him in but I could not see who it was. Should we call the sheriff?" Captain Banner asked.

"*No!* Where are you?"

"I'm on the side of a salvage yard, parked amongst some boat carcasses. I can see the front of the rooms from here about a quarter klick away."

"Don't take your eyes off that door, Captain, I am headed to your position."

Colonel Sanchez checked her watch—9:17 PM. She drove to where Captain Banner was staked out watching the rooms at the Tar Road Inn. She climbed into the Humvee with the Captain of the Guard.

She also brought some supplies—food, water, field glasses, infrared night goggles, close range communicators, and two small caliber automatic pistols. They had been in the vehicle on the salvage yard for over two hours. It appeared to be closed as no one associated with the salvage yard approached them. Using the field glasses and goggles, they could see movement behind the curtains but very little else. They didn't say much. Not much to say until the residents of room #3 emerge.

At 9:30 PM, the door opened wide. Two figures walked out carrying luggage. The first one was Xanadu. Captain Banner could tell by his walk and shape of his body. The other figure was smaller, walked more erect, and moved slower and more precise. As Colonel Sanchez watched them in her infrared telescopic field glasses, the two figures began to load the luggage in the trunk of a car, a late model four-door Ford Fusion. Either gray or blue, she couldn't tell. They made several trips to and from the hotel room. When they closed the trunk lid and stood at the rear of the car, Colonel Sanchez got a good look at their faces.

"Bingo! Hello, Fedelito Gaspare," she said. "Captain, let's get ready to roll."

"Yes, Colonel; we following the Spaniard?" Captain Banner asked, fully alert.

"I will follow the Spaniard," she explained, taking her cell phone out and beginning to dial. "You follow the boxer. When they get to a stopping point, we see what the local law does. If they fuck this up, we won't!"

"Yes, ma'am!"

~ ~ ~

"This is Cormac," Sheriff Cormac said, answering the phone.

"Guess who I'm following through Benoitown?"

"Colonel? Is that you?"

"Yeah, how soon can you be in your car and out on the road?"

"Two minutes; you found Fedelito?" Sheriff Cormac asked.

"Behind him with about two cars between us. He's in a grayish blue Ford Fusion. He's also got a trunk full of knives in three backpacks."

"How do you know that?" the sheriff asked.

"Cormac, get your ass in an unmarked car and keep me on the phone so I can keep you abreast of where he's going. We can discuss the habeas corpus and due process later."

Sheriff Cormac grabbed his keys and went to the locker behind Mimi's dispatch desk. The only unmarked vehicle they had was an old supply van they used for that purpose. It would have to do.

In a couple of minutes, he was in the lower level parking garage, starting the old van and pulling onto the street.

"Where are you now, Colonel?" he asked.

"Coming right through town; it appears he is headed for the bridge to Gilleyville."

Sheriff Cormac pulled the van onto Third Street facing Main Street. In a few seconds he saw the Fusion coming down Main. He could see Fedelito behind the wheel. He was wearing shades and a fedora too big for his head. However, he was wearing one of his shiny suits adorned with lapel pins. Cormac could also see the oversized rings on his fingers wrapped around the steering wheel.

About four cars back he saw Colonel Sanchez's Humvee.

"I see you both, Colonel. I'm in a light-blue van off Third Street. Fall back and let me slip in at your position."

"Fine, but you better not lose him," Colonel Sanchez warned.

Before pulling into traffic, Sheriff Cormac called Deputy Laurie on speaker phone. He listened to it ring as he watched Fedelito, as well as the two cars behind him, drive past at Third Street. The sheriff slipped into traffic. He saw Colonel Sanchez's Humvee about two hundred feet behind him. She gave the lights a quick flash and continued to follow.

Deputy Laurie's phone went to voicemail.

"Deputy, I'm following Fedelito Gaspare across the bridge into Gilleyville. I believe he has weapons similar to those used in the murders. Call me back so we can squeeze him in case he's trying to leave town."

Chapter 33

Deputy Laurie was tough, but she was not what you call outdoorsy. Hence, the idea to drive up the road past the Gilleyville mayoral estate and walk up the wooded hill at the back of the property was not her first choice. It was dark as pitch. She used her police-issue flashlight to negotiate through the bramble and brush. She had to climb over three small wire fences used to keep deer and other woodland creatures from reaching the house. She fell over each one, while muddying her favorite cowboy boots.

As she got within sight of the main house, she used her cell phone light to work her way through the thickets, hoping the smaller light would not attract attention. Plus, there were lights on the property near the buildings. Her movements sounded to her like a Brahma bull in a china shop, but she kept moving.

She was 100 feet away, then 75 feet. The trees were much thinner and the ground mostly flat. She could now see her way using the light from the large house. Then she heard voices and hid behind a tree about 50 feet from the small building at the edge of the wooded area. She slowly un-holstered her 38-caliber colt snub-nosed revolver and held it down to her side.

The voices were coming from the small building. She was off the back side of it – no windows. This gave her great cover. Her heart was beating double time in her ears as she ran the rest of the way to the back of the building and listened. She heard voices she knew and some she did not recognize. Then she heard the voice of Bo Boulage. He was giving one-word answers, but she knew his 'okay' and 'uh-huh' when she heard it.

She moved slowly down the rear and then side of the building. As she reached the front corner, she saw all of them standing at the front door. Then her cellphone vibrated.

In the quiet dark, it might as well have been the bells of Notre Dame. They all looked at each other and checked their personal cell phones. She had to make a move.

"Okay, everybody, stop talking and get those hands up," she said in a cracked hollering voice that she hated. The effect was the same. She surprised us all, and we complied.

There was silence for a few seconds save for her vibrating phone.

"Do me one favor?" I asked her with my hands still up. "Don't answer that phone until you hear us out."

"Please, Laurie," Bo Boulage said. "Just hear 'em out. It's important. The shit's going down right now."

Her phone stopped vibrating.

"Okay, I'm listening; you got one minute before I call the Sheriff back."

Chapter 34

"**D**on't lose 'em, Cormac," Colonel Sanchez shouted into the phone. She continued to call Sheriff Cormac's cell phone throughout the ride.

"I'm not gonna lose him!" Sheriff Cormac barked into the phone on speaker.

"But I can't get a hold of my deputies for backup if you keep calling."

"Duh, ever heard of Radio dispatch?" Colonel Sanchez said sarcastically.

"Uh, this is an unmarked supply truck?" he answered back.

"Okay, okay, I'm getting off," she started.

"*Wait!*" Sheriff Cormac shouted into the phone.

"Make up your mind, Cormac," Colonel Sanchez said.

"Don't hang up yet. Fedelito is slowing down; he just put his signal on."

"Left or right?" Colonel Sanchez asked, as if talking to one her troops.

"Right," Sheriff Cormac answered. "There's a small strip plaza center about 500 feet ahead. I'm going to drive past him. You pull over now before getting to the turn."

"Got it," Colonel Sanchez said. "I can find a spot to watch the car and the parking lot."

He watched the Ford Fusion continue to slow and turn right into the shopping plaza. It was an old one. There were a number of empty units, a Subway Sandwich shop, and a shoe repair/alterations shop. He passed the parking lot and glanced repeatedly to see what he could see. Expecting Fedelito to be alone, he nearly swerved onto the curve and blew his cover when he saw the other vehicle on the lot. Sheriff Cormac continued to drive about another half mile. When he saw the side street, it was a perfect place to sit and wait for things to unfold.

"Colonel, you set?" he called into the phone.

"Yeah, I'm on a side street across from the parking lot about 300 feet away.

I'll see him when he comes out."

"Good,   because   we   got   some   interesting   company."

Chapter 35

The small building at the back of the Gilleyville mayoral estate was dark and quiet. Things were set, but we had a new member of the team. Sitting across from Deputy Laurie, I realized that at some point I had to bring the law into this. Without them, this could be a circumstantial mess.

"Damn, Manion, how were you going to execute this thing the way you're shaking?"

She was right. I had been holding the stainless steel pistol belonging to Bobby Jr. I was hoping that Deputy Laurie hadn't seen my hands in the dark. In the end, she ordered all guns holstered except hers.

"Sorry, but I'll be ready. Now we got the law, along with Bobby Jr. and Bo and His Honor the Mayor."

"Yeah, right," Deputy Laurie snorted. "Without me, you all probably would've gotten stabbed."

"Shh shh shh," Bobby Jr. said. "Everybody get ready. Cars pulling into the back of the property."

Everyone did just that. Deputy Laurie and I hid in the back bedroom. We kept the door open but hid behind the door, watching from the space between the back of the door and the doorframe. Deputy Laurie was in the front right up against the door opening. I was behind her.

Then her phone vibrated again.

"Answer that fucking phone, Deputy. He's getting out of the car," Bobby Jr. said with a whispering earnestness.

"Yes, Sheriff," she answered in a strong whisper. I could only hear her side of the call.

"Yes, you're kidding. Both of them? I see. That's just it, Sheriff. I'm already here. In a spot where I can address it. Stay on the perimeter, no lights. Go on my call. If you come now we may not get both of them."

She ended the call just as there was a knock on the door. I peeked through the opening as the front door opened. I checked my watch; it was well before midnight, the time Mimi said that Bo was to be removed to transport to his relatives.

Chapter 36

"**B**o, how are you, my boy?" Val Cedars asked as he entered the small building. He was wearing a tight-fitted black sweater and khaki slacks.

"Where is the light?"

"No, gotta keep the lights off. I'm on the run."

"But I can barely see in here," Val said, his voice sweetly plaintive. Val Cedars stood at the doorway. All he could see was the figure on the sofa wearing a hoodie, sitting still.

"Where is my mother? I assume that's who told you where I was?"

"Uh, yes, she told me. She asked me to help you, Bo." There was silence that lasted a few seconds but seemed like days.

"She gave me a note," Val said, "to prove that I was on your side."

"Why wouldn't you be on my side?"

"Exactly what I told her," Val Cedars said and laughed nervously. He stepped forward.

"Read it," Bo said.

"What?"

"You got a note from my mother. Fine, just read it."

"I can give it to you and you can read it," Val said, showing some exasperation.

"Val, I have to be very careful. The police are after me, and I don't know who to trust."

"You can trust me," Val said. "See the letter will prove.... "

"How did the recorder get in my room?" Bo asked.

"I don't know, Son," Val Cedars said. "Maybe the police planted it."

"What? Why would they do that?" Bo asked, his temper flaring in the rounding of his words. He never moved off the sofa, kept his hood up and the lights off. "Val, what's the plan?"

"It's in the letter, Bo," Val Cedars said and tossed the letter onto the low table in front of the sofa.

Then no one talked for several seconds. Standing behind the door, I could feel the tension in the room. All of a sudden, I felt too far away from the action in the room. If something happened across that table and sofa, I could not get there fast enough. Could Deputy Laurie make the shot from the back of the door and the door frame?

"I've been thinking," Bo said. "I talked to the twins. They said they are going to stand up for me, tell the law I was with them."

"What a minute, Bo," Val said, showing some concern in his speech. "You know how wishy-washy the twins are. You go to the police and they will leave you hanging."

"Maybe you can talk to them; the twins, I mean."

"W ... why would they listen to me? They're two brats protected by their stuck-up parents."

"But you can handle them, Val," Bo continued. "Just like you helped me get the money for the new ceremonial knives by stealing my old ones from

Mom's car."

"Bo, we agreed not to discuss that," Bo said, clearly nervous now.

"My mother would die if she knew she was involved in a fraudulent burglary and insurance claim."

"That's enough, Bo," Val said, getting closer to the table and the sofa. "We need to discuss getting you out of town."

"How come you didn't tell me who my father was?" Bo asked. "I've been talking to the mayor. He's pretty cool."

"Really?" Val Cedars said.

"Really; he has some theories about what's been going on. He says that Spanish ambassador guy had to have acc ... accom ... a partner who was helping him look for gold, a partner who knows about gold."

"I see," Val said, seeming to listen.

"While they think it's me right now. Dad seems to think once I come clean they will realize I don't know anything about gold. I would make a stupid partner for that Gaspare fella."

"But Bo they did have your knives; the recorder," Val Cedars said. "I really think it's time to get the out of town."

"And then what? Live on the run? All they will focus on is finding me as opposed to looking for the real killer. No—I need to stay I think."

"Bo, with all due respect to you and your father, where the hell has he been your whole life?" Val Cedars asked. He was now clearly upset, talking fast and overly smoothing his hair. He continued to ease closer until he was right up against the sofa.

"You may be right," Bo added. "I better read Mom's letter."

Val watched the familiar hooded figure stand and pick up the letter from the cocktail table. Turning away to read the letter by the light coming through the window behind the sofa.

"Where is your father?" Val Cedars asked as he eased closer.

"He's down in Washington tonight. They went to see a play. Be back in the...."

I was watching it but still couldn't believe what I was seeing. Val Cedars was fast. While watching the back of the hooded shirt and listening to Bo's voice, he quickly slipped two of the hunting knives from sheaths from behind his back undershirt.

The first stab hit the shoulder and got snagged on the material in the hoodie.

"Drop the knives, Cedars!" Deputy Laurie shouted, knocking me backwards and coming around from the back of the door. As I got up to one knee, she was running out of the bedroom, her gun out front.

"*Aaaaaarrrrgggggghhhh!*" came a cry of agony. I scrambled to the doorway.

Val Cedars was trying to run for the door, but Bobby Jr. in a Bo Boulage hoodie was holding onto his waist. There was a bloodstained rip in the hoodie and one of his arms was hanging limp. Deputy Laurie was barking orders for Val Cedars to stop.

"Shoot his ass!" Bobby Jr. screamed. He was holding onto Val with his good arm and being dragged along the floor towards the front door.

Val was trudging for the door and stabbing at Bobby Jr. with one of the knives.

"Let him go and I will!" Deputy Laurie screamed back.

Bobby let go hitting the floor hard, and Deputy Laurie put two shots high over the door. The snub nose noise was deafening in the small building and made everyone freeze.

"Val Cedars, you are under arrest! Move and I put the third one in you."

Val put his hands up and started to speak. Then there was the sound of a car starting outside. Everyone stopped for a second or two.

"It's Gaspare!" Deputy Laurie shouted. "He's running."

"I'm on it," I said, running past Val and out the door.

"Noooo!" Val Cedars screamed and made a move for the door. Deputy Laurie raised her gun, and he halted, his face a mask of despair.

The silver 9mm I borrowed from Bobby Jr. was still in the waist holster on my left side. Would I use it? Really shoot someone? I rounded the building, and I saw Fedelito Gaspare in his rental. He was halfway down the drive heading towards the front of the property.

I took off across the yard, yelling for Mayor Managualt to open the back door. He did just as I reached it.

"Front door!" I yelled running into the main house. Mayor Managualt pointed towards the front door while cowering from the pistol that was now in my hand. "Keep Bo out of sight!"

I ran through the public rooms, past colonial furniture and nineteenth century art. I had a laser focus on the front entry wondering how to work the collection of antique and modern door locks. Just then, Gerald appeared from the living room. He went to work on the locks and threw the door open just as I reached it. I never broke stride. He said something about being careful as I ran past him.

My calculation paid off. As I reached the front lawn, Fedelito was coming around the long drive that spanned the immense side yard. He saw me running towards him and sped up.

At the same time, Sheriff Cormac was coming up the drive from the front. He was parking, blocking the drive. He pulled his revolver and shouted for Fedelito Gaspare to stop. Gaspare left the driveway clipping the sheriff's front bumper and sending him diving into the hedges on the outside edge of the drive. His new course sent him over the grass and directly towards me.

By now the front lawn was illuminated by every light on that side of the property. I could see his face and how it lit up with excitement when he saw me taking my stance and pointing the weapon right at him. His expression didn't bother me. I had the same one.

I was sick of this asshole treating everyone and this city like his own personal Kleenex to use and discard. He kept coming, so I positioned myself on the only other way off this property, a piece of lawn that sloped down to the sidewalk and public access road between the estate and some adjacent farmland.

Sheriff Cormac was yelling for me to move when I squeezed off the first two shots; one took out the headlight. The other pinged off the front edge of the roof.

I went down on one knee. He was less than 50 feet away. I pulled the trigger and succeeded to put one in the passenger-side front tire. Fourth shot hit the radiator and sent smoke and liquid over the hood and windshield. He swerved from a lack of control and sight.

Totally automatic, I rolled to the side as his car came past. He had slowed down considerably. Shocked and confused, he drove erratically over the rutted lawn. I took advantage of his confusion, ran alongside and caught up to the side of the car. I could hear police shouting in pursuit. Tires screeched, and sirens blared somewhere in the distance.

I broke the driver-side window with the butt of the gun, showering him with tempered glass. Fedelito Gaspare looked at me as if I was the ghost of Christmas past. Running alongside, I stuck my arm inside the driver-side window trying to open the door and yank his ratchet ass out by the shirt collar.

He recovered, grabbing the steering wheel with his right hand and punching me with his heavily bejeweled left hand. I don't know if it was his technique or the bodacious precious and semiprecious stones on his fingers, but I felt myself going out. It was hard to defend myself and hold on to the car door.

The car began to buck and shimmy like going over uneven ground. I could see the lawn was sloping down to the exit path between the properties. We would be on the street soon. The car wouldn't make it far but then maybe it would. I saw traffic on the public street in the distance, cars going back and forth oblivious to what was about to happen. I knew the Spaniard would not give one ounce of regard for human life.

Fedelito Gaspare was resourceful and cunning. He had managed to elude an entire town for the last three days. People would ask me later what I was thinking that night, holding onto the side of a moving car like Jean-Claude van Damme. All I could think of was not letting him slip away and having some kind of long expensive manhunt. We had him now—*we were keeping him now.*

I could see the road beyond the sidewalk; Fedelito could see it, too. I felt the car lurch again as he sped up. We bumped and banged over the uneven lawn surface, both of us fighting for control of the steering wheel. I defended myself from his punches by holding my head back away from the car. Fedelito had lethal hands but short arms.

"*Bajar mi coche! Te matara!*" he yelled in Spanish.

"Fuck you, Gaspare," I shouted in response to his threat to kill me. "This is the end of your line!"

I could not keep this up for much longer. I was hoping the Ford Fusion would break an axle. Even on three wheels it was rolling along.

At 50 feet, I heard it before I saw it—a large engine roar.

"*Aaaaaiiiiiiiiiiieeeeeehhhhh!*" Fedelito screamed as he looked left over my head. He pounded on my hand that held the steering wheel.

The roar got louder, and someone shouted my name. Peeking over my shoulder, I leaped from the side of the car like an action-movie stuntman, my heart pounding in my ears. I landed hard on the grassy incline of the yard, biting my tongue and banging my head on the ground. I forced myself to roll, not sure how far I jumped. I felt light-headed. I smelled grass and hot metal. Then it came.

The crescendo of metal on metal, there was an engine blow, and the cacophonous sound of airbags. When I stopped rolling, I was 40 feet off to the side of where I left the car, still on the grassy lawn of the Gilleyville mayoral estate. On the street at the bottom were two vehicles. Fedelito Gaspare was unconscious, his head lulled on top of an airbag. The Fusion was destroyed, smashed from the driver's side front corner and down the driver's side by the US Army Government Issue A1 Humvee driven by Captain Banner with Colonel Sanchez riding shotgun.

Chapter 37

The rest of the night and the following morning was a blur for me. Bobby Jr., who played the visual role of Bo in the hoodie, was taken to emergency and released. The knife cut a tendon in his shoulder. Hence, he had trouble using that arm on the night of the attack. I was also urged to get medical attention. They thought I might be having some low-level shock, possibly a slight concussion. Aside from some serious ring bruises to my face, I was cleared.

Everyone was taken into custody: Val Cedars, Gaspare Fedelito, and Bo Boulage. Mimi showed up as planned at the Managualts' house at midnight. She couldn't believe what she found: her best friend in the world, Val, under arrest for murder. She wasn't happy about Bo going into custody, but she was happier that he was alive.

Bo had been in the small building. He did the talking from behind the sofa. We knew we could fool Val in the dark with a hoodie. Bo and Bobby Jr. were very similar in size, but we knew there was no way to fool him on the voice. Gene Managualt and Sheriff Cormac assured her that they would do everything they could for him.

Adam Samuelson hadn't heard from the US State Department, but he warned that when he does—Fedelito Gaspare will probably be turned over to State Department officers via the FBI or US Treasury agents.

They found out that one set of the unidentified trace fingerprints at the crime scenes belonged to Val Cedars. The other unidentified print belonged to Fedelito Gaspare. At the very least, we had Val Cedars on attempted murder of Bobby Jr. Fedelito was guilty of conspiracy to commit murder, fraud, and assault.

The next day and evening were spent taking statements, or refusing to give statements pending legal representation. When Pat Cedars showed up, instead of a lawyer for her husband, she showed up with divorce papers. After some pressure from the sheriff, Mimi, and some private security video around town, the Bandy twins were represented by the amenable law firm of Howell Bunkton. The lawyer submitted affidavits confirming that on the nights in question, the twins were with Bo Boulage. The affidavits did not say what they were doing but did confirm location, dates, and times. The affidavits would not keep them from having to testify in case of a trial, but it would do for now.

No bail was allowed for Val Cedars and Fedelito Gaspare. Bo was released to go home in a couple of days, and the old Mimi came back. We all met in the sheriff's office. The county prosecutor was also there.

Charles Youngblood was television-handsome and serious. I was told he had aspirations for the governor's mansion, so if he took this to trial he wanted to win. I liked the fact that he wanted to challenge the US State Department on the diplomatic immunity presumption for Fedelito Gaspare. Adam Samuelson seemed pretty sure the immunity would hold, but promised us that "State" would work to get him prosecuted in Spain.

"Okay, I got some questions," Charles said. He instructed his assistant to take notes. "At the risk of sounding insensitive, was there any more gold out there?"

"Doesn't appear to be," Colonel Sanchez said. "We have a handful of remains to reinter. No additional gold has been found."

"Are you sure, Colonel?" Charles said, fully intending the effect his question had. "I mean…."

"I know what you mean, Prosecutor," Colonel Sanchez answered calmly and professionally. She had to take it. Two of her soldiers were found involved in gold hunting and theft from graves. Two of her officers were dead. "We established more checks and balances with video and audio backup."

"So what was Cedar's purpose? Was he stealing gold, too?" Charles asked.

The room was silent. I wasn't sure if the reticence was from loyalty to Val Cedars, or because they just weren't sure, or they actually didn't know.

"Recognition and concealment," I finally said.

"You," Charles said, pointing a finger in my direction. "You're Manion the insurance guy who masterminded an unauthorized sting, who also shot at a car with a firearm not registered to you, and who tried to kill himself by jumping onto a moving car driven by one of the suspects?"

I nodded.

He waved his hand signaling me to continue.

"This whole thing actually started with Val Cedars," I stated. "He has had one dream and only one dream—to get a National Historic Preserve Accreditation for Benoitown and Gilleyville. His plan as always was to use the legend of Jolly Benoit and his sidekick Sam Gilley. The problem was that the legend—an exslave, ex-pirate who buried gold amongst the graves of dead slaves—had no evidentiary validity or historical proof.

"Then Hurricane Chester came and the graves were disturbed. The legend had a chance to be proved true. Val couldn't wait; he was going to make it true.

He planted the gold and the chest that was found initially."

"What?" was the collective response around the room.

"How did he get past the Guards?" Charles asked.

"Before the discovery of gold, were there many Guards around the upturned graves?" I asked.

There were head shakes all around the room so I continued.

"I realized it when we examined the actual coins. They had an oily grit on the surface. It didn't feel like dirt. That grit was evidence of the cleaning solution used to clean gold coins found in the ground and the sea. That was also confirmed by the National Historic Preserve. The form they sent to us showed the items as checked in by the NHP. Because the items had been checked in several years ago."

"Was he digging in graves as far back as several years ago?" Charles asked.

"No, those items were purchased from a private collector with federal grant money awarded to the local museum. Val Cedars made the deal to try and drum up credibility for the legend of Jolly Benoit. At some point Val planted the gold among the remains for the forensics team to find, lending credibility to the legend."

"You said Lieutenant Perales had a problem with the coins," Colonel Sanchez said.

"Exactly, something about the coins didn't make sense. That's why she was back at the lab at that time of night," I continued. "Unfortunately, others were there as well, not expecting to be disturbed.

We knew Fedelito was involved, and we assumed his partner was Corporal McLean. Then McLean was murdered the same way as Lieutenant Perales and Fedelito had an alibi. So that's when we realized there was a third person in addition to Fedelito Gaspare and Corporal McLean."

"Then you got the tip about the Twitter post from Bo?" Charles asked the sheriff. "And he went into hiding?"

"Right, but it didn't make sense," Sheriff Cormac continued. "Bo as a possible partner did not make sense. Not enough to kill for it. The Twitter clue was too convenient, as well as finding the recorder in his room in a relatively easy place to find."

"When did you find out where Bo was hiding and fail to tell the police?" Sheriff Cormac continued his question towards me. It was going to be a point of contention between him and me, but nothing I wouldn't do again.

"About 48 hours before the capture," I said as a matter-of-fact. "I know it wasn't kosher, but I felt what we did was the right thing to do. If you had arrested Bo, then the look for the real killer would have all but stopped.

"He told me and my partners about being with the twins. We confirmed it with the twins, so we wanted to make one more attempt to bring Fedelito out of hiding, figuring if we got him, he would lead us to the one person missing in this mix. Instead of Fedelito, we got the third person, Val Cedars. He needed to close the trail leading back to him. Eventually someone would figure out the coins were from a previous find. Eventually when Bo was questioned and investigated, there would be a possibility someone would figure out who was framing him. If Bo died, then the trail stopped there."

"What about Fedelito?" Charles asked.

"He just wanted the gold," I said. "But more so he wanted the recognition back in Spain for recovering ancient gold. He was there that night with McLean and Cedars. He put the bag over Lieutenant Perales, but she fought him off. We believe he ran off, and Cedars stabbed her in the back to keep her quiet."

"We think Fedelito was the moneyman McLean mentioned to his partner Jackson," Sheriff Cormac added. "We also know he was the one who sent a woman into the street naked and half strangled. We don't think his knives were used in any of the murders, but he is adept at the use of knives."

"Then we have him at the scene last night when Cedars tried to kill Bo Boulage. Then trying to flee when Deputy Laurie interceded," I explained.

"So Bo is innocent?" the prosecutor asked.

"Of murder," I explained. "He has an alibi for both times; Cedars and Gaspare were attempting to make him the scapegoat, then kill him so the investigation trail ended."

"Poor Mimi," Sheriff Cormac said. "She really trusted Cedars"

"All right, Samuelson," the prosecutor continued, "what are our chances of putting Gaspare in prison?"

"Not likely," Adam Samuelson said in his careful tone. "My contacts at the State Department tell me that the Spanish consulate will be filing the formal request to extradite him to Spain any day now."

"Even when it's a matter of murder?" Deputy Laurie asked.

"Well, Deputy, he didn't kill anyone. He only conspired to commit murder, and he withheld and tampered with evidence."

"Attempted murder," Sheriff Cormac said. "We matched fingerprints on the bag used to suffocate Lieutenant Perales with the fingerprints found on Glynis when he choked her during sex, with the same fingerprints found in his hotel room."

"All of which will be inadmissible in court during a trial," Adam Samuelson said calmly.

The room was quiet. I understood why. Everyone understood Val Cedars had to go away. Nevertheless, he was local; he was family. He was a murderer, but he was family, and if he had to go to prison, then that slick Fedelito should suffer the same fate.

Over the next few days, Bo Boulage was released and returned to his mother. Mimi had a small party that weekend at her home to celebrate. Gerald and I were not invited, but we understood.

Nadine went back home. She felt like she did her job, but she was a lot less braggadocios about it. Terri Lovejoy and Bobby Farr Jr. went home to St. Louis once he was released from the hospital. Bobby Jr. left a number of video transcriptions of his part in the sting I set up. His boss, Gerald's cousin, Lemon Boy Phillips, was not happy about the sting being set up without his involvement, but they couldn't do anything about it now.

Gerald and I had reports to complete. WorldSpan and the Spanish Treasury were less than pleased about no gold being found. Even I had to admit I was ready to go home. To Paris.

I thought about a quick visit to Florida, maybe find out where my brother and his band were touring, but I decided against it. Bands made me think of Angela Babineaux. I called her every night after meeting her mother, but it always went to voicemail. Yeah, I was ready to go.

The next day we finished our report to home office, covering all things legal, statutory, and civil. Soon everyone detached from the Skype call. I was left on the video meeting with Camille.

"How are you?" she asked tentatively. She was wearing a royal blue flare dress with a choker collar and gold buttons down the middle. I could get a mental scent of the perfume she usually wore. It was good to see her. She felt like home.

"How are you, my Love?" she asked as we watched each other.

"I'm good; just ready to come home," I said with a sigh. "You look good."

"I smell good, too," she smiled and performed that classic long leg cross she does that is so sexy. "I feel even better to the touch, but you can't see that from there."

I wasn't so sure I couldn't. Then she started on me.

"I don't know what to say to you, Tekelius," she said, frowning now. "Do you have a death wish?"

"Of course not," I said. "Mila, it wasn't that bad. I was...."

I stopped talking as the video streamed over the computer. It looked like raw footage from a motion picture shoot. It was a shot of a car speeding through a sloped yard, with a guy hanging on outside the driver's side door. Camille narrated it.

"It's the video from the camera installed on the military vehicle driven by the National Guard. The vehicle that eventually stopped the car and just missed hitting you."

I watched the video as it showed me leaping from the car and bouncing off the ground just missing the wheels of the oncoming

Humvee. I may have felt like a Hollywood stunt man, but visually I looked like a possessed rag doll.

"Is this your understanding of the expeditor job?" she asked, her voice full of venom.

"What did the managing partners say?" I asked.

"Fuck them!" she snapped back. "I am asking the questions here! I am your manager. You answer to me! In more ways than one."

"I'm sorry, Mila. It was a spur-of-the-moment thing. Once I jumped on, I had to stay on."

"Just tell me you are doing all these dangerous things for something more than WorldSpan Secure?"

"Of course, it was probably a matter of life or death," I said.

"Yours or some freckle-faced boatwoman with firm breasts?" she snapped.

"Is this really about our outside interests?" I asked.

"Of course not," she said. "It just seems every time you deal with American women; you select beautiful ones with danger attached to them. Are there no older women who need your help?"

I smiled to myself thinking of Teresa Dorterre'. I laughed, and eventually she laughed. The mood lightened, and I promised to get home in one piece.

"Before you go, Lisette wants a word. She has been more than a usual nuisance," Camille said pleadingly and waving for someone to come into the sight of the Skype camera.

I had forgotten the laundry list of research items I gave to Lisette to work on. I really didn't need it at this point, but she worked so hard. I would make sure it got in my final report.

"Bonjour Monsieur Manion, I have been trying to get a hold of you for some time," she started plaintively but excitedly. "I have some very interesting findings."

"Sorry, Lisette, I've been a little busy," I said with a chuckle. "Please let me hear what you have."

She spent the next 30 minutes explaining minor details about the background of Jolly and Gilley. The most interesting part was not new or original. The new and original information was not particularly interesting or germane to the case. I half listened and smiled as best I could.

I stared at the screen while Lisette read from her notes barely looking up at me. I hoped Camille would come back to the screen. My mind began to wonder about what mood she would be in when I got home, and what would I have to do to get her to bed as soon as possible. Then Lisette said something that brought me back from the champagne sex room of my mind.

"Wait! Say that again!" I said.

"Say what again?" Lisette responded, looking up for the first time in several minutes, pushing her severe black glasses up on a pert little nose. "Sam Gilley refused to be photographed?"

"No, after that," I said excitedly. "About the name with no connection found."

"Oh, you mean the name Fisk," she continued. "You wanted me to find the Fisk connection to Jolly Benoit or Sam Gilley or that area and I found one, but it's not what you think."

"Okay, what is it?" I asked impatiently. Lisette checked her notes and pushed her glasses again. How could she think they look good on her? They were wider than her face.

"Here it is," she started. "There are no connections of anyone named Fisk tied to the area or the two ex- pirates. The most prominent Fisk at the time was a man named Almond Fisk. He was relatively unknown."

"But you just said he was prominent," I said.

"Not him but what he made."

"And what did he make?" I asked impatiently.

"Coffins," she explained.

"Coffins?" I asked.

"Specifically cast-iron coffins," she said. "Almond Fisk invented a cast-iron coffin. He eventually sold the patent to a guy named Forbes who sold it to both sides of the Civil War."

"Okay," I said.

"Fisk died in 1850; Forbes liquidated in the 1880s."

"But I don't see any connection," I said.

"I don't know that there is," she explained. "I brought it up because he made coffins, and all this was about gold in graves. The cast-iron was really needed to preserve the bodies that may have been in the field for months before burial...."

"Oh, shit I got it!" I said before I realized I was talking. I was seeing a connection. It was loose in my mind. So loose I was not sure it was real. I thanked Lisette and abruptly ended the Skype session.

I got back to my hotel room. I grabbed my copy of Jolly Benoit's *Journal* and flopped across the bed. The thought in the back of my head was so incredible that it was hard to focus. If I was right, I had to handle this correctly. I found the passages in the journal referencing the name Fisk. I found part of what I needed, and the picture came into focus just a bit more. I could not believe how simple it was.

I called Gerald, Teresa Dorterre', and Xanadu Waters once he was released from questioning by the police. I made an appointment to meet them the next morning before sunrise. I also asked Xanadu to secure some things for us and keep his mouth shut.

Gerald asked what this was about, but I was so afraid of being right I could not even tell him. I felt sure I was right, but the idea of being right also scared the hell out of me. The anticipation was electric. I couldn't stay still, but it had to wait until morning.

I walked down past the City Works building and Benoit's. I peeked inside the bar and saw Angela Babineaux behind the bar.

"I'll be leaving soon, but I wanted to say I am sorry," I said across the bar when she brought my bourbon to me.

"What you sorry for, Teke?" she asked with a stony expression. "If you knew I was a Gilley would you have tried harder to get in my head through my 'cookies'?" She pointed down to her vagina.

"No," I said stifling a chuckle. "I'm sorry for intruding on your mother and you. It was just me following the case. I guess I was more surprised that you didn't tell me. My surprise came out like asshole."

"True. Ok?" she said her arms folded.

"As for your 'cookies,' they are worth pursuing no matter what your last name is," I said doing my best Matthew McConaughey smirk.

She held her look for a few seconds; then smiled; then smacked my arm with a bar towel.

"So now what?" she asked.

"Now I realize that I may have hurt a very good friend," I explained, my facial expression sorrowful. She turned from me and picked up a shot glass and a bottle of brown liquor off the back bar. She poured herself a shot of bourbon and clicked my glass with hers. I took a sip of mine. She drained her shot and gave me a smile that triggered hazy flashbacks of her looking down at me while her tan, strong, naked legs straddled my hips.

"Forgiven?" I asked. She motioned for me to lean in close. I did so, and she hugged my neck and placed her mouth against my right ear.

"Don't you go thinking this is going to get you a 'leaving town" trip to the cookie store,'" she said jovially. I pulled back looking inquiringly into her playful eyes. I thought they said different, but I had to stay focused.

I looked around the room when she left to wait on another customer. My eyes landed on the two gigantic cousins I tussled with the other day. I realized I had another invite to make. I walked over to them.

"Hey, tell your cousin to meet me with her camera crew at 5:00 AM."

"We're the camera crew," Patcheye said.

"Good for you," I replied and gave them the name of my hotel. "If she makes it, it will be the video she needs to start her show."

They nodded and read my card. I had to get out of there. Tomorrow would be a long day.

Chapter 38

I loved when a plan came together. The next morning Gerald and I came down to the lobby. Teresa Dorterre' was eating jam on crackers and sipping tea with one of the Broyles sons behind the lobby counter. She had her hair wrapped in an orange, green, and red head scarf. She was wearing jeans and a long-sleeved t-shirt with Maxi Priest on the front.

"Did you bring your family journal?" I asked.

"Just like we discussed, Handsome. I have it all up here," she said, tapping the side of her head."

"Sorry, I'm just a little anxious; been a crazy two days," I said.

"So I heard," she answered and took a sip of her tea. "Besides, I didn't sleep much. I still feel an uneasiness in the air."

"You mean like danger?" I asked, having learned to respect the mystical instincts of Teresa Dorterre'.

"Not sure. It's hard to explain, but it's like a huge ball of energy is bouncing around bumping into things."

"Well, if I'm right," I said to her under my breath, "what we'll find is a big ball of happiness."

"Most times sorrow and happiness coexist like a cottonmouth snake cozily wrapped around a box full of gold, two winning lottery tickets, and a cure for cancer," she said.

"Well, you better save some of that charm of yours for the snake," I said and gave her a nervous wink. For a change Teresa Dorterre' looked visibly shocked.

I stepped outside. Xanadu was sitting on a bench for smokers on the front porch. There was also a plain white van parked across the street. They flashed their lights, and I saw Glynis James sitting in the passenger seat. I waved.

"You get what I asked you for?" I asked Xanadu. He reached under the bench on which he sat. He pulled out two beige, long, cotton sacks, filled to capacity. I poked my head back into the hotel and motioned for Teresa to follow me. In another minute, Gerald brought his rental car around. Teresa and Xanadu jumped in the backseat after putting the long sacks in the trunk. I slid into the passenger seat next to Gerald. We continued slowly down Main Street. The white van pulled in behind us. We approached the street that ran parallel to the river. I turned to Teresa in the backseat.

"I want to show you a passage in Jolly's journal. Your family was the closest to him. I believe your family chronicle mirrors his journal in many ways. I need you to show me the exact hill by the river where Jolly Benoit dreamed and schemed with Sam Gilley and met with spies for the Union Army, and transferred gold with the elusive Mr. Fisk."

"You found Fisk?" Gerald asked.

"I believe so," I answered. "Teresa?"

She looked out her window adjacent to the riverbank leading downstream. We were facing north just past the bridge between

Benoitown and Gilleyville. It was dark and still, but looking out over the river and past Gilleyville, I could see dawn's first light.

After a few seconds, Teresa Dorterre' pointed forward toward the upstream part of the river.

"Just ahead a ways. Then we'll need to walk," she said.

We drove on that same street, continuing upriver. We passed the area where the first graves were breached by the flood, the station where the National Guard set up their operations, and the spot where Corporal McLean was found dead.

Less than a mile later, we parked. The river road, on which we continued to ride, gave us a view of the water. However, the land next to the road away from the river rose up to a small hilltop as if the river road were cut into the side of an unremarkable bluff. There were very few buildings at this point on the riverfront. It was still very wooded.

"Most people misinterpret Jolly's journal about where he stood on those mornings," Teresa started. "The river road throws them off. The actual location is just at the crest of this rise next to the river road and over the riverbank."

"So we have to go up this hill from here?" Xanadu asked. "What's on the other side?"

"Wooded acreage full of creatures; it's too narrow and uneven for anything else." Teresa said. Xanadu cursed under his breath.

I got out of the car, walked back to the white van following us. Glynis and her behemoth cousins and video crew didn't like the job any better than Xanadu. When I told them specifically what I thought was at the top of that hill, they started to see their reality television dreams come true. As I walked back to the car, I thought about the power of gold. Maybe it was a mortal power, but power nonetheless. It had all of us out at 5:00 AM with tools and secrecy. All this just on the hint and hunch of gold.

Twenty minutes and countless broken saplings later, we reached the top of the hill. There was a flat area about 200 feet square. It was covered in low brush that made it hard to move. However, my heart leapt when I spotted the twin cedars. Just like in the journal, there were literally two identical cedar trees growing about three feet apart. There were no other cedar trees for miles. I was so excited that I pointed like a small child. Teresa Dorterre' just rubbed my back. It was calming and helped me to think.

I checked the journal again, focusing on every word, and trying to make allowances for the misinterpretation of Jolly Benoit's patois by the Anglo-American publishing industry. I stood in front of the twin trees like Jolly and Sam and others had done 150 years ago. I looked out over the river, which lay southeast of our position.

This hill actually turned away from the river more north and west. However, it gave breathtaking views of both towns. As daylight echoed the coming day, I could see all of Gilleyville. I could see the land that was the Lankin Plantation, where Jolly was a child slave. Turning clockwise from northeast to southeast, I could see the Gilleyville mayoral manor and adjacent museum, the homestead of Sam Gilley. Rotating to west by southwest, I could see the main streets of both cities, Emancipation Bridge, and the Edgewood County Museum and the tomb site of Jolly Benoit. It was sentimental and powerful. I felt I was seeing what they saw 150 years ago, the energy Teresa Dorterre' is always claiming.

"Okay, Insurance Man; we losing the cover of night," Xanadu said.

He was right. I looked around the clearing, but I couldn't decide on one exact spot.

I took the posthole digger and marked three spots within ten feet of the twin trees.

"Xanadu, get a hole started in each of these spots with the hole digger. Then you, Gerald, and I will get busy with the pics. If my hunch is right, we shouldn't have to dig more than a few feet before we know. Teresa, you keep an eye out for any company coming."

"Me? I got to dig?" Gerald asked.

"I'm digging!" I said excitedly.

"Damn!" Gerald said and pulled a pickaxe from the long beige bags Xanadu brought.

We started. Xanadu had the first hole started in a matter of minutes. The posthole digger was the auger style, with a turn handle that drove the auger blades deep into the ground. I started on the first hole. Despite my enthusiasm, I must have made a sorry sight for a real laborer. By the time Gerald started on the second hole, the Glynis' two gigantic cousins – Ben and Fin - couldn't stand it any longer.

"Glynis, put the camera on the tripod. Fin and me are getting in on this dig or we'll be here for a month."

I hated to admit it, but Ben was right. He was the skinny tall one, but he was far from weak.

Ben and Fin shoved Gerald and me out of the way. Watching them and Xanadu go at the three holes was a physical thing of beauty. The three of them found a rhythm, each pickaxe rising high over their heads and striking the holes consecutively.

Every fifteen to twenty strikes, they paused. Then Gerald and I jumped in with shovels to remove the loose soil. Then the three of them would start again.

The whole time Glynis was recording and making audio commentary. The excitement in her voice was genuine but controlled, like a narrator on National Geographic. She was good. She echoed the emotion in all our hearts.

On the second pause, I noticed we were about three feet in as I shoveled. The only light we dare use was one small flashlight and the infrared light on Glynis' camera.

On the third pause, we were about five feet deep. The three pickaxe men were slowing but I wasn't sure if it was from fatigue or doubt. Gerald and I cleared the earth and jumped out of the holes.

Three pickaxe swings later, I was looking around for another place to dig. Then Xanadu struck metal. Everybody stopped but him. He kept picking, several times striking metal each time.

"Xanadu, hold it!" I yelled, and he looked up as if coming out of a trance.

He was smiling.

"Did I find it?" he asked, breathing hard.

Gerald and I motioned for him to move out of the hole. I handed the flashlight to Fin with the patch over his eye. We shoveled the loose earth away and scraped metal as well. The hole was large enough for me to kneel in with room to spare. Gerald jumped from the hole and lay on the ground next to the opening, shining the flashlight down on me.

I brushed and dug loose soil from the metal object until I found the inscription that read, FISK CAST-IRON COFFIN – FORBES CAST-IRON FOUNDRY. I kept scraping soil away. I became aware of a noise, a hoarse laughing cry. It took me a few seconds to recognize that the noise was coming from me.

The Fisk Cast-Iron coffin was more like a body-shaped sarcophagus, with waterproof closures to preserve its contents. Many of the models like this one came with a thick reinforced glass window. Jolly Benoit's coffin treasure was lying horizontally in the ground, the glass panel facing up. Only the top third of it was uncovered.

I stood up in the hole and snatched the flashlight from Gerald. I lowered myself back to my knees. I lay on top of the coffin until my face was right against the glass panel. I could feel sweat and bugs crawling on my cheek, forehead, and down the back of my neck.

I worked the flashlight beam around to find the angle that would illuminate the inside and not just glare off the glass. It took almost a minute, and then I saw it, a cast-iron chest full of gold coins pulled from the stolen lands of ancient civilizations and subsequently stolen from Spanish galleons. I rolled over on my back and lay on top of the casket for a few seconds, looking up at the morning sky, laughing at the anxious faces of my compatriots, and feeling triumphant.

"Is it there, Manion?" Gerald asked, his voice sounding like he had been crying. "Is it gold?"

"Yes, it's the gold. We found it! We fucking found it," I said, my voice full of emotion because I was openly crying.

"Mr. Manion, you da' man!" Xanadu said. "This gold been right under our noses all these years, and we found it!"

"He's right," Gerald said. "Way to go, partner! What's our next move?"

Gerald's question and watching the sunrise sky put my mind into motion. I had things to do and no time to waste. I tossed the flashlight up to the surface. Xanadu caught it. I rose to climb out of the hole. I put one foot on the side of the hole and pushed off on the casket with my other foot. Gerald grabbed my hands to pull me out. As I pushed off, the casket rocked and pain shot through my foot and leg.

I cried out, and Gerald pulled hard on my hands. The pain shot all the way up to my hip. I released Gerald's grip and fell back onto the casket.

"What happened?" Gerald asked excitedly.

"Light!" I screamed. Daylight was starting to make it easier to see, but it was similar to dusk.

Xanadu tossed the flashlight down to me. I turned it on and flashed it frantically around the hole.

There was blood all over one end of the casket and several two-inch-wide blades protruding vertically up from the casket. One of the blades was broken. Further examination found the broken end dissecting my shoe and the foot inside it.

"You triggered a booby trap," Glynis said. She was standing there still commentating and recording. "It's a common thing with finds like this."

"Now, you fucking tell me," I said, more irritated than anything else.

"Be still, Mr. Manion. We'll get you out," Xanadu said.

In a few seconds they had a plan. Ben and Fin held Xanadu by the feet and suspended him into the hole. Gerald, still lying on the ground looking over the hole, used one of the shovels to hold the casket in place, figuring any shift would trigger more blades or something worse.

"On three, we gonna pull you out with one move, Mr. Manion," Xanadu explained, looking down at me as he hung over the hole by his feet. "We gonna pull. Mr. Manion, whatever you do, don't push off on that casket. We will do all the work, just let your body go limp. Mr.

Gerald, you hold that casket." We all counted off, including Glynis and Teresa.

"One, two, three!"

It was like I was flying. I fought the urge to push off to give Xanadu, Ben, and Fin help in my rescue. I focused on Xanadu's face as he grimaced while pulling me out by my forearms, while Ben and Fin pulled him out by his ankles.

The whole thing took less than a second or two. There was another swoosh sound, and I felt and heard my shirt torn from my back. I heard Gerald curse behind me.

I landed in a heap on top of Xanadu, Ben, and Fin. Now my right foot and calf were hurting like hell and bleeding profusely. I was also naked from my shoulders to my waist. We looked back in the hole. The back of my shirt was impaled on several more blades triggered by my weight movement.

There was talk about getting me to a hospital, and I was getting cold and light-headed, but I willed myself to stay focused. Things were about to get real.

"Sit me up," I asked urgently. Ben and Fin propped me against a tree. Teresa Dorterre' was gingerly removing my shoe. It hurt so bad it brought tears to my eyes, but the pain helped me focus.

"We got to stay together on this. If this gets out before we are ready, the authorities will take this from us, but if we follow my lead, we will all get what we want."

"Even me, Mr. Manion?" Xanadu asked. I put a hand on his shoulder and smiled.

"I'm gonna make you famous!" I said. "But first, cover the holes. Fill in the dirt. Second, we need to guard this area. No one should want to come up here.

They haven't for over 150 years but no one can find this. Third, no one says anything to anyone for 48 hours. That goes for you, too, reality show people.

Give me 48 hours. If I can't get it done in two days, we won't be able to do it."

Maybe my confidence was delusionary brought on by the fact that my foot was split open and bleeding profusely. Maybe it was the age-old conspiracy amongst gold discoverers, making us no better and no worse than the gaggle of other treasure hunters that had just come through Benoitown.

I watched Ben, Fin, and Xanadu filling the hole as Gerald and Teresa helped me one-foot hop down the wooded hill to the car. It was full daylight now, but few cars were going along this part of the river road. Glynis was moving her van to a side street so as not to look conspicuous.

"Gerald, make sure they hurry up and fill the hole and get out of here," I cautioned as he dumped me on the passenger seat. He was telling me to shut up talking.

"We don't have time to waste," I said, feeling myself go out. "Gerald, get a meeting set up—WorldSpan, State Department, the governor's office; and someone in authority from the Spanish consulate."

Epilogue

I wasn't out for long. Once I was stitched up, bandaged, and fitted with a walking boot, I got a ride from Glynis and her cousins back to Sheriff Cormac's office. I found Gerald in a conference room on the phone to WorldSpan. He had cleaned up and changed his clothes, wearing his classic business shirt and sports coat.

"Tekelius, you have found the gold of Monsieur Benoit?" Marcel LaRoche asked, the managing partner at WorldSpan Secure and one of the few who spoke English at a level I could understand.

"Oui, Monsieur, but things have gotten complicated. We need to redo our fee with the Spanish."

"That is highly irregular; suppose we secure the assets. Then we can talk about it," Marcel explained.

"Look, Monsieur, in the last 72 hours I have been punched, stabbed, boobytrapped, and dragged by a car. There are at least five other claims to the assets," I explained with a sense of urgency. "If we don't move first, this thing will be tied up in courts for years."

"Marcel, I can independently and conclusively confirm existence of the assets; it will have a market value in excess of $100 million euros," Gerald explained.

"Really? But you don't have possession of it. How do you know its value?"

"By visual confirmation and by weight," Gerald explained his voice dripping with legal eloquence.

He really had no idea of the value, but he knew executives needed numbers. They couldn't make a decision without it. Gerald did what he does best. He estimated numbers about the value of heirloom-grade Spanish gold coins and the weight of the casket subtracting the weight of the cast-iron coffin itself. In the last four hours, prior to our call, we had become experts on the nineteenth century.

There was silence for almost a minute. Then another voice came on the call.

"Okay, Tekelius, what is your plan?" It was Camille on the line now. Marcel had turned it over to her. I stifled the urge to crack a joke or get off script. I gave Gerald a hard, silent handshake off screen.

The next two hours were a type of negotiation with our own company.

On our side, we knew where the gold was and time was of the essence. When the location of the gold became public knowledge it would be harder for everyone to get satisfaction. Including WorldSpan.

On their side, WorldSpan had the leverage and muscle to negotiate terms with the bond holders, the countries of Spain and the United States, and any others claiming rights of ownership. If our small group got anything, it had to be included with guarantees in the terms now.

The final agreement went something like this:

* The contents of the casket representing the gold stolen by the pirate Jolly Benoit sometime between 1830 and 1845 or its monetary value equivalent will be turned over to WorldSpan Secure Underwriters,

and be held in escrow in lieu of interest payments on Spanish government debt.

    * WorldSpan will retain a finder's fee of nine percent for its efforts.

    * The government of Spain will also reimburse the State of North Carolina for their efforts to extract said gold. The reimbursement will be a figure not to exceed 3.5 percent of the total value of the asset.

    * The Edgewood County Museum will retain rights to select treasures to display (on loan from the country of Spain) as a part of the Jolly Benoit/Sam Gilley Historical Collections.

    * The Citizens for the Ethical Treatment of the Ancestry through Reverend Moten was also issued a grant for $750,000 as a consultant fee for the continued upgrade and protection of the sacred graves.

    * In a joint criminal task initiative between both governments, cultural attaché Fedelito B. Gaspare will be tried in US Federal Court for attempted murder, conspiracy to commit murder, evidence tampering, and deadly assault. If he is found guilty, he will serve his sentence in the custody of the Spanish penal system.

    * All charges against Bo Boulage and Nadine Charleston-Phillips will be discharged and their records cleared.

Special addendums for the following parties:

    * Filming and distribution rights for a new gold hunting show, called *Pirate Mysteries* was awarded to British subject Glynis James and her Glyn/Ben/and Fin Production Company.

    * For their assistance in the investigation and recovery of the treasure, WorldSpan Secure in conjunction with the US National Historic Preservation Society will award the following:

* Letters of accommodation to Teresa Dorterre', Michael "Xanadu" Waters, Angela Babineaux, and Dr. Geoffrey "Baliles" Paskiewicz along with a finder's award of $50,000 each or one-tenth of one percent of the value of the assets whichever is larger, in accordance with international laws governing the recovery of historical treasure.

* As a part of the economic revitalization of the Tar River Basin after Hurricane Chester, Angela Babineaux will also receive one of several business grants and loans. She will use hers to purchase shares in TideLand Capital Holdings to build her charter boat business. *(Later Angela will learn that TideLand also holds boat and equipment loans issued to the Clark Fishing Charters. For the next twenty years, she will have a 25 percent proxy ownership on Quinten's family boat business from Washington, NC, through the Pamlico Sound.)*

We got the deal done in about 37 hours. When all agreements were faxed, scanned, emailed and signed, I led the National Guard, Sheriff Cormac, Deputy Laurie, and Adam Samuelson to the hill where Xanadu and Fin were sitting against one of the twin cedar trees. That way they would not be seen from the street below but would be on point if someone came snooping around.

The National Guard used bomb detection and bomb diffusing equipment to dislodge the casket, trigger the rest of the booby traps, and set the casket vertically in the hole.

By the time they lifted it out of the hole, a crowd had started to form on the river road below and in the backyards of the houses adjacent to the wooded hill.

By the time they lifted it up and onto the ground, the press was onsite.

Gerald and I stood off to the side next to Colonel Sanchez, probably the only person not emotionally invested in the "assets." She stood stone-faced, her eyes dead of emotion.

Lieutenant Perales was given a decorated burial. Corporal McLean was issued a posthumous general discharge to save scandal. Private Jackson was also given a "general discharge," less than honorable. It wasn't dishonorable and had no jail time, but someone had to take the fall.

In the end, Gerald's guess was close but short. There were over 496 gold coins of varying sizes; 59 pieces of gold and silver eighteenth and nineteenth-century jewelry encrusted with rubies and sapphires; Total value came to 117 million euros or 150 million US dollars.

Bo and Mimi took over the local preservation efforts with help from Val Cedar's wife. Together, they secured the National Historic Preservation designation from the national archives. They retained a portion of the collection of coins and jewelry items found in the assets. They can be seen every day at the Edgewood County Museum in the Jolly Benoit Wing.

That's where I was about a week later. I had finished all the final paperwork on the deals and side deals I had brokered. I spent way too many evenings sipping tea with Teresa Dorterre'. The mystical ghost love stories she told me will haunt me for years. As I headed out the front door of the museum today, I thought I was seeing a ghost or having a bad trip from the pain meds.

He was in the circle drive of the museum, leaning against an unmarked car but wearing his White Sand Island sheriff uniform and those gold-rimmed Foster Grant sunglasses. He was a vision from my past, and one I was hoping never to repeat.

"Manion, they told me I'd find you here," Sheriff Juan 'JD' Cruz said, walking toward me briskly. The last time that happened, he punched me into the middle of next week for breaking my engagement to his baby sister, Soledad-Marie. This time he just removed his shades and stood in front of me, hands on hips.

"Sheriff, I thought I may have been seeing a ghost. What brings you to North Carolina?"

"You. I need your help, and I ain't asking," he said with a sense of urgency. The last time the sheriff and I were together we ended up in the middle of White Sands Bay, shot, cold, and almost drowning. If there was something amiss in White Sand Island, I wanted no part of it.

"Sheriff, I don't do crime. That's your job. Remember you told me never to return to the island," I said. I was letting anger enter my voice. Old haunts were coming back to mind.

"I know I said that. So I came to you. I need your help…."

"Yeah, yeah, and you ain't askin'," I said. "So who's cuttin' up at home now?"

"Not home—Central America," he said, his face taking on a new look, something softer.

"Central America?" I asked.

"Colombia," he said. "I need you to come with me to Bogota."

"For what?"

"To find Soledad-Marie. She's been kidnapped."

~ The End

Made in the USA
Columbia, SC
27 July 2024

38817474R00176